GETTING TOGETHER

Books by Toby Stein

FICTION

Getting Together   (*1980*)
All the Time There Is   (*1977*)

NONFICTION

How to Appeal to a Man's Appetites   (*1961*)

GETTING TOGETHER

Toby Stein

ATHENEUM   New York
1980

Library of Congress Cataloging in Publication Data

Stein, Toby.
  Getting together.

  I. Title.
PZ4.S8197Ge   [PS3569.T3754]   813'.5'4   79–23724
ISBN 0-689-11027-8

Copyright © 1980 by Toby Stein
All rights reserved
Published simultaneously in Canada by
McClelland & Stewart, Ltd.
Manufactured by
American Book–Stratford Press,
Saddle Brook, New Jersey
Designed by Kathleen Carey
First Edition

To Tom

IN COMMUNION

Acknowledgments

For her keen help, twice over, with drafts of this book, I thank my friend, Nancy Miller Davis. I am grateful, too, to my sister, Patricia Day Stein, for spending a sunny Saturday afternoon on a busman's holiday.

WEDNESDAY

1

Never believe anything anyone promises you at The Four Seasons.

More as a last-minute reminder to myself about the danger of losing one's head during an onslaught of flattery than because it needed fluffing, I punched up the needlepoint pillow on the overstuffed chair in my work room, cased the typewriter I'd come back for, and went out again to the car.

Alec was leaning against the fender on the near side, smiling; that smile as big and complex—and enthralling—as a Russian novel. He reached for the typewriter and placed it carefully in back.

I waited until he had maneuvered the car out of my serpentine driveway before I said, "If I send you a post card from the big city, you want to be able to read it, don't you?"

Alec's glance said he wasn't about to be caught up in that one: if I wanted to haul my typewriter to New York, knowing full well I was unlikely to have any use for it during my four-day stay, that was my business. He passed one car and then another, and I was surprised—for what must have been the hundredth time—at how fast one actually left Hamilton behind. In this late spring clemency and Alec's Porsche 911, the superb condition of which belied its six years, we would make the Syracuse airport in forty-five minutes. To drive me there, to stay with me last night, more than likely to make sure I was as comfortable about the weekend as I purported to be on the phone, he had spent five hours of one day off driving to Hamilton and would spend much of the second driving back to Vermont after my plane left.

But Alec had had something on his mind besides seeing me off lovingly; and even though I had managed to edge out of that conversation last night, I knew it wasn't finished.

"You know," he said now, "you're always trying to work me out, but from a certain distance. Try coming a little closer."

"Can't get any closer." I gestured to the space separating our seats.

"You know I didn't mean the way kids rode around in forties' movies." His tone said he wouldn't so easily be put off this time. "Jessie?"

In the second Alec's eyes left the road for verification and I saw the greyness of them deepen, I gave in. I nodded; but he wasn't looking at me any more, so I had to say it. "What you said last night. Marry you."

"The blood goes out of your voice when you say the words," said Alec.

"Sorry."

We were passing a barn that had burned down a couple of weeks earlier; more people than I had imagined lived within a ten-mile radius were working on it, rebuilding.

"Hey, lady, don't look away, look at me," Alec said. "I weigh at the outside five pounds more than I weighed in college"—he laughed—"and I've got more hair than I had then.

I've got a sweet sinecure of a job and this trusty vehicle, which can do one hundred and twenty without wincing when it strikes your fancy. You laugh at most of my jokes; I can read and write and use a calculator with nimbleness. I play better-than-fair Scarlatti for you on the piano hours at a time and I cook in three or four languages. Besides which, I have your own word for it that I am a loving lover to you—with you, over and under, beside and behind you. Give me one good reason you shouldn't marry me."

Unfortunately, I had one. Yet how I wanted to say yes: how I'd like a thirty-carat emerald ring. And for all its self-awareness, Alec's litany of his attractions omitted the one that seized my imagination and burrowed into my heart. I've met a small horde of self-avowed nonconformists in my time, as alike as the hairs on their exposed chests. I'd never met a man so invincibly, unself-consciously immune to anyone else's ideas about what a man should do with his life.

But I didn't say that, any of it, to Alec; instead, I made a stab at lightness. "The person with all those attributes, none of which I have any intention of denying, has also managed to remain a bachelor lo these forty-four years. What makes you think you know so much about who should and shouldn't be married?"

"I know you," said Alec quietly, "and I know me, and how we are together."

"Yes, you know me, better than anyone since Sam. All right, better in some ways than Sam did." Almost of its own accord, my hand reached out and touched Alec's cheek. "You do know me that way, dear God yes, better not only than Sam did, but better than I did." I didn't feel constrained to admit it, only—again—astonished at how true it was.

"I wouldn't want to press *any* advantage unfairly," said Alec, "but the way it is between us there is not what everybody who hasn't got it all wrong has. I wouldn't dismiss it lightly."

I hadn't, and didn't, and Alec knew that. But I grasped again at lightness. "Who said anything about dismissing it at all? I'm prepared to proclaim it to the world." I opened the sun roof and shouted upward. "Hear ye! Hear—"

Firmly, yet without a trace of violence, Alec placed his hand over my mouth. Only when I had nodded acquiescence did he remove it. He said, "I didn't intend to change the subject, and I won't let you. There's a question on the floor. Marry me, Jessie?"

"And live in Vermont." I sighed.

"You won't even notice you've moved," he said. "Very cold is very cold whether it's in Hamilton or Burlington. Besides, most of the time you're writing seven days a week, and when you're writing you hardly ever leave the house anyway—my source is unimpeachable, remember?" He turned my chin toward him. "Does it really matter that much to you where you live?"

"It matters a helluva lot to me not to make the same mistake twice!" Hearing my vehemence, I forced myself to take several deep breaths before I added evenly, "It's not as though I haven't told you."

Alec didn't say he understood, or even remembered. He remembered—but he didn't understand. His chin said so.

But I had told him, in our first bartering bout of confiding, a lot about my marriage to Sam—and my endurance contest with Hamilton. How, only a month after I'd arrived with my one-year contract—well before the shock of winter's arrival at Thanksgiving—I knew I hated the isolation of that place. So far as I was concerned, a town you had to place as equidistant from Utica and Syracuse simply wasn't near anywhere worth being near. I couldn't wait until June and my return to New York and civilization. Who knew Sam would turn up at a talk I was giving? Who knew that three months later his wife would be dead?

I admit it, I chose to stay on and marry him—even though

I was beginning to suspect by then that it wasn't only teaching at Colgate but teaching itself that wasn't for me. Sam was so much older; when he told me I'd learn to like it there, I thought maybe he was right. Besides, he'd been there most of his working life, he couldn't make a change—I assumed it, he must have assumed it, we never even discussed it. If we were going to be together . . . Besides, I didn't want him to see how scared and lonely—and young—I was. I never dreamed it would take me ten years to stop hating the place— and to notice that, somewhere along the line, the people who mattered in that town had stopped hating me, too. They hadn't come to *like* me, but I didn't give them much incentive. I wasn't about to meet them halfway, not after the way they'd treated me.

Eight years! That's how long Evelyn had been sick. It's a small town in every way—people knew. But you'd have thought, the way Sam's department and their assorted spouses looked at me, that her cancer was somehow connected with me. They couldn't afford to ostracize me—Sam was too entrenched in their little world for that—but though they had me to their homes on requisite occasions, they made sure I knew I'd never belong.

Never say never, right? When Sam died four years ago, they consoled me with acceptance. But by then, I hardly cared. Without really noticing, I had slipped into something very like contentment. It happened, I guess, when I plain got tired of spending most of my energy hating the physical and emotional isolation and learned to make it work for me. I use it now—to write with.

"It's true," I said softly, "I'm in Hamilton because I choose to be, finally. And what happens? You come along— the very same wonderful man you eloquently and, yes, accurately, described a few minutes ago—with this one fatal flaw: you want me to up and move. Alec, I don't have that many spare decades left to learn to live in a place peaceably;

and I have to do my work in peace. What if I can't work in Burlington?''

All lightness flown, I sank low into the car seat, into myself. But Alec, while consistently kind, can also be the most insistently reasonable of men. "Okay," he said, "so let's find out. Come stay for a couple of months. Try it out."

"I have tried," I fought him. "All three visits, didn't I bring my typewriter? But I didn't write, did I?"

Alec nodded. "I thought that fixing up that small room for you to write in—but you barely set foot in it."

Hey, Jessie, he's entitled to know.

"You really did it exactly right, you know," I offered. "Placing the typewriter table so that I was facing a wall instead of the window. How'd you know to do that?"

Adding a smile to my overdue praise, I met unflattered eyes. I looked away, although I knew, even as I did it, that it would take more than that to stop him.

"Jessie," he said.

And waited. When I was good and ready—but far from *ready*—I turned toward him.

Slowly, not flinging it at me, but with a sure aim so I couldn't not catch it, he tossed the truth at me. "It wasn't that you couldn't, Jessie, you didn't try those times. That's right, isn't it?"

I let the ball bounce—once. "I was taking a break. When you work seven days a week, you need an occasional break, right?"

He didn't try to hold it in. He didn't need to; he knew I'd given in: Alec laughed. Nicely, oh yes nicely, no mistaking that. Louder than I did, once I gave in all the way and joined him, but *with* me even before that. With me—invariably, it seemed.

That's what I was thinking about as we rode in silence the rest of the way: no matter where Alec stood on something, he was always, simultaneously, in my corner. It lessened my chagrin some; it didn't lessen my indecision.

When we'd parked in the airport lot, Alec said, "You will think about it, Jess?"

In his voice, want crackled against patience. Nothing less than the truth would do. "I think about it all the time," I said in a low voice.

"Don't you know?" I added, turning toward him, and discovering him halfway to me already. In the end we had to run to make my plane.

2

Halfway to New York it registered with me. Here I was, a person who loves flying, clutching the arm rests on either side of my seat. This was obviously not the time to think about Alec and marriage. Besides, I reminded myself, it was high time I thought myself into the right frame of mind for Margery. I made myself reach into my purse for her letter, to read it yet again—and came up instead with a number ten envelope, my name on it in Alec's hand. At once grateful for the reprieve and wary of what it might contain, I took a deep breath and opened it. Inside, on half a sheet of typing paper (no doubt mine), neatly torn, was printed in pencil:

Dear Jessie,
Try to remember, at the photography sitting, that the camera doesn't take flashbacks.
And have I ever told you, your eyes have a beautiful smile?
Alec

Three times I read those two sentences through. How like Alec to know that just because you know something some days doesn't mean you don't need to hear it other days. I had told him that I wasn't the least bit nervous about giving a speech at Barnard, the main purpose of my trip to the city, and that was true. I hadn't told him what was equally true: that I felt very apprehensive about being photographed for the jacket of my new book, something my editor had arranged when she learned I was coming down. But I hadn't needed to tell him that.

Alec, whose only self-indulgence is fine mechanical equipment and whose only vanity is how he handles it, discovered early on my reluctance to be photographed. I laughed and hid my head behind a pillow; he teased. I stopped laughing and refused in a dignified way; he teased. My chin began to quiver; he put away his camera. Weeks later, when I could bring myself to do it, I showed him a couple of old snapshots of me. He looked at them quietly, the way he does everything (even teases). Then he said that a camera only captures what's there, and that now a camera would see what was in my face now; but when I shook my head, he didn't press me. He held me.

I have what is called an expressive face—by people who have a different kind. Everyone knows a face like mine makes poker playing difficult, but who considers the difficulties inherent in simply walking through life with a wide-open face? People tend to walk right on into it; and yet there's no way to charge them with invasion of privacy, is there? I mean, if you didn't relish their having easy access to your soul, you'd keep your face shut, right?

Wrong. If I could alter the openness of my face, I would. If I could lessen it, I would. But its accessibility is as much a part of my face as is the shape of my lips. It's as though I had an extra feature: two eyes, one nose, one mouth, and one set of feelings. It is this extra feature, so to speak, that makes me hate being photographed.

Take any picture. The one in my Barnard yearbook, for example. Although I haven't looked at it for years, I can see it loudly and clearly. A picture is worth a thousand words? That picture talks much too much. One's college yearbook picture is supposed to be all about commencement. Beginning. And I, by that year, had lost all sense of beginning. Endings were what I knew. They might as well have been my major. The end of my mother. The end of my home. The end of my first love. It was all there in my somber face, looking much older than any face only twenty years old has any business looking. And I minded; I didn't want everyone to know I had caught life by the wrong end.

If that were the only such photograph . . . There was one —it had stood on my mother's dresser—that had been taken by a famous photographer who happened to see me on the beach in Provincetown the summer after my father died, and asked to photograph me. He had, he said to my mother (but I heard him), never seen such a sad child. Time pales wounds; but a picture of the wound when it was fresh and raw reminds you quickly enough. That photograph doesn't stand on my dresser.

Another less-than-happy photograph: the photograph of me on the jacket of my last three novels, a snapshot taken by Sam (while I thought he was photographing a Cambridge swan) two years before I wrote the first of them. It did not, everyone agreed, do me justice. Although I recognized better than anyone that what marred that photograph was the residue of loss it revealed, in my eyes it had one redeeming virtue: it already existed. I let Delia, my editor, think I wanted to keep using it for sentimental reasons. I had never told her about me and cameras: in the beginning, because I didn't know her well enough; after a time, because she knew me well enough to tell me I was being silly. And now it was too late. Delia was bent on having a new photograph of me on the new book's jacket. The sitting was all set for tomorrow. Which was more than I could say for me.

It *was* silly. Had I not, however belatedly, worked my way round to the right end of life? That would show.

Only logical. Only sensible. Only I don't believe it. I believe that if I let someone take my picture now, some sort of reverse time-lapse photography will occur: the photographer will be taking a picture now, but the picture taken will be of me at an earlier time. And I don't want everyone to see, I don't want to see again, how I used to be.

I read it again. "Try to remember, at the photography sitting, that the camera doesn't take flashbacks." Of course; that was easy enough to remember. It was obvious. But was it true?

Jessie. Let it go. Think about how you're going to look on the stage in the Barnard gym: the main speaker, confident of how right you look up there, and of the work.

The work: three published novels, the first one written when I was thirty-four. The work which had been received relatively well from the beginning; the second book, unusually, praised more than the first; the third book, *Esther's House*, receiving both quite fine reviews and my first really substantial paperback sale. I was, albeit in no headline-making way, making it on both fronts as a novelist. That was why I'd been asked to speak at reunion. They'd had their fair share of best-selling alumnae; but if I was in a more modest category financially, I was in a better place critically than some Barnard alumnae-novelists of recent years. Good, and eating. Serious, and surviving. A true Barnard product.

Me.

And why did I accept? Because that's part of being a true Barnard product—remembering that part of what you've become you owe to the college. I had not been, of course, all that representative an undergraduate; I owed more than most to Barnard. If coming down to reunion, at their invitation and expense, to speak about the way I had embarked on a new career in my mid-thirties was something they wanted, I would do it gladly. It had not occurred to me to refuse.

To tell the whole truth, I was rather looking forward to

Saturday. I didn't half mind coming back to Barnard as a minor celebrity.

The admission was enough to make me smile.

Which made me think: my mouth smiles, too, now. A mouth that knows how to smile; eyes that smile without even knowing it.

I glanced again at how Alec had put it: no flashbacks.

All right, then. I would look all right. Suddenly I felt a whole lot better about that photo session.

Seeing Margery was another matter. Seeing her might be enough to set me back some before my sitting. Her beauty had a way of casting a large shadow over anyone nearby. But I wouldn't, I could not, approach seeing her that way. I was not in Margery's shadow; twenty years was surely well past the statute of limitations for shadows.

Still, I wished I had a little more time to get ready to see her again. I hadn't felt ready, automatically, when her letter came. Since it arrived, three days ago, there'd been no readying time. The plane was beginning the descent to LaGuardia; little enough time for it now.

I took out Margery's letter, noticing again, with undiminished surprise, that it was written on paper of undistinguished quality and bore neither Margery's name nor address. I felt slightly embarrassed, as though observing a formerly impeccable friend's smudged neckline. But I lacked the time, I reminded myself, to dawdle over niceties. This was the first communication I'd received from Margery, outside our habitual exchange of cards at Christmas, in years. I tried, quickly, to calculate how many but couldn't. It had been that many. And we hadn't seen each other in longer than that, not since . . . then. It was only natural for me to feel a certain awkwardness.

Jessie.

All right, so I felt a quite immoderate amount. Because, although I occasionally did have to go down to the city, the trips were primarily business, and if I had a spare lunchtime or evening, it was never Margery I thought to call. There was a time, years ago, I'd felt a twinge of guilt on that score once or twice. But not for a long while, until now. Now that, in a brief note which contained little else, Margery insisted that I stay with Leo and her for the weekend.

It hadn't, of course, even occurred to Margery that I might already have somewhere to stay. The college had, in fact, reserved a room for me at the Empire, which, while hardly the Regency, promised creature comfort equivalent at least to my agent's living room couch, where I usually bunked with relative contentment during my trips to the city. But comparing accommodations was beside the point. It was the way she'd invited me.

Margery's letter specified that, with Jon off at Yale (already!), I would have his room. *I would have.* That old inbred certitude of usage. Of course she had tossed in a disclaimer at the end—"If you decide not to, I'll understand." But she wouldn't. Even after all these years, she wouldn't, I felt sure. Margery was obviously still used to people rushing to say yes to her, as used as she must still be to obliging headwaiters and solicitous saleswomen. And, yes, that bothered me. But it wasn't a surprise.

What caught me unawares—and left me rather disconcerted —was that Margery's invitation had arrived too late to refuse by return mail. If it had come even a few days earlier, I could have written my apologies, explained that I was coming down not only for the talk at Barnard, but also for something to do with the publication of my new book—something somewhat time-consuming and even slightly pressured—making me a less than exemplary houseguest. Perhaps another time. I would have managed a *good* note.

Refusing by phone would be more unwieldy, I'd known that instantly. Calling in itself would be awkward; it had been such a long time since Margery and I had spoken that the conversation, especially since I'd be turning down her invitation, would have to include a certain obligatory amount of catching up, an activity, like cocktail-party moving on, I always felt other people timed better than I did. Afraid to linger too long, or to say more than the other person might want to hear, I tended to be brusque in the one case and taciturn in the other. You still haven't learned to *follow*, I chided myself.

Although I hadn't gotten around to giving the meeting itself much thought, I had, in the midst of sorting my clothes for the trip, tried to figure out why Margery might have invited me so tardily. Plain poor manners could not be the reason; Margery's manners were as integral to her as her vivacity. If she had decided to ask me to come stay with them when she'd first seen the notice of my talk in the reunion publicity sent out to all alumnae, the only plausible reason to delay asking me would be a suspicion that I might be inclined to refuse. This could make her reluctant to ask, and thereby lead her to postpone doing it. Or it could make her wait until the last moment because then a refusal would be easier on both of us? Or, conceivably, harder for me because I'd have to do it by phone? Possibilities, certainly, but none fit the Margery I remembered. More likely, I decided, the idea of inviting me had occurred to her belatedly and, pleasing her, yes, she would assume it would please me. Because that's how it had worked for her, always. How clearly I could recall half a dozen occasions when Margery, caught up in a brand-new notion of somewhere to go or something to do, had immediately had company. Because her enthusiasm was contagious, she was never left to indulge her enthusiasms alone. One had to go along. One had truly wanted to. If Margery had the idea that it would always be like that, her friends, me not least among them, had helped instill it in her. Understanding that, I still found it galled me some—her assuming I'd be delighted to come stay. Half our lives had gone by since those days. I'd changed. The whole damn world had changed. Hadn't Margery noticed?

With that thought for stiffening, I'd called her. Still, almost at once, the call went awry. I decided not to mention any business; I didn't want to get near the subject of photos. I took the tack that what probably looked, from the alumnae mailing, like an overnight stay was in fact a four-day visit. I hadn't, I said, been to the city for quite a while. Having completed the final revisions on my new novel only weeks earlier, I had in mind a somewhat gallivanting visit to the city rather than my customary quick business trip. That sounded just about perfect, had been Margery's response. Because, surely, between my outings there would be time, in four days, for us to have a long if discontinuous talk—the kind where you can back up and fill in, the best kind, Margery insisted. There was, in her voice, an irrefrangible enthusiasm—and something else: an unremembered huskiness. As though my visit meant something to her beyond a great good verbal bash between old friends? Nonsense. If she was making a bit too much of my visit, then so was I. Briskly reining in my imagination, I told myself what difference did it really make where I stayed, and I said yes, of course I was coming and, yes, I was looking forward to it, too.

Hardly that. If what I felt about staying at Margery's fell well short of dread, it bore no resemblance to eagerness. Not, the time had come to admit, because of Margery who, if she still assumed people were hers for the asking, was doubtless also still spirited and quick-witted and undeniably agreeable to be around. No, now that the bugs below were recognizable as cars, neither the uncharacteristic pushiness of Margery nor the prospect of seeing her again were what I really minded. Seeing Leo, spending the weekend in Leo's home—there wasn't a doubt in my mind that I could do without both.

I didn't need to think hard to be sure that I hadn't spent a night under the same roof as Leo since I'd spent all the nights of that one long-ago summer in his cramped, militantly untidy apartment on 111th Street off Columbus Avenue, strewn with dog-eared copies of *Hudson Review* and nearly empty bags of Pepperidge Farm cookies. Milano—those had been his favorites: a thin layer of rich chocolate between two thin oblong vanilla wafers; washed down with either beer or orange juice, depending on whether they constituted breakfast or lunch. Dinner was usually a hamburger, late, at the West End; once a week, occasionally twice, we ate dinner at the Shanghai Café on 125th Street, where Leo invariably ordered fish with the head on, a dish guaranteed to limit my appetite. There was, obviously, no need for me to cook; but he didn't let me clean or straighten up, either. Once, in early August, when Leo was making his biweekly excursion to his parents on Tremont Avenue in the Bronx, I secretly washed the sheets on our bed. When Leo didn't notice, I was relieved, but a little disappointed too. There was a big difference.

Funny the things you remember: a particular cookie, doing the laundry behind someone's back—okay to remember. Less all right with me is how shrill in my memory are the keening ambulances of St. Luke's Hospital, punctuating the sounds of our lovemaking. The sounds of our lovemaking: Leo's thick breathing, mostly. He sounded uncomfortable; but since I had nothing with which to compare his exertion, I simply added it to all I had to be grateful for to Leo. How brimming with gratitude I had been; and how graciously Leo had accepted my appreciativeness. Remembering that now, I shivered; wished I remembered less, and less vividly.

Hold on. The summer you first made love would have been memorable no matter who the man was. Granted. Okay. But the man was Leo, and Leo mattered; and that made everything that happened that summer, and just after, matter that much more.

Leo Ezekiel Mellson: the shining light among some rather high-wattage competition his junior year at Columbia. The next year—everyone said it—Leo would win the most prestigious awards, the prizes that counted. No one doubted Leo would go on to Oxford, least of all I who fell in love with his mind even before I found out how his body could leave its mark.

If I had not rented that terrible little room. . . . Grimly small, linoleum on the floor, without a comfortable reading chair, it was a bleak prospect. But it was by the week, and summer rentals were hard to find, so I paid my whiskered landlady twenty-eight dollars, one week's rent plus a week's security lest I deface her plastic furniture, and told myself that it was only for the summer. But June came on like August that year, and my fortitude wilted in the closeness of that room. Luckily, its only window faced on the fire escape, and I took to spending my evenings out there, reading until it got dark and, after that, listening to the sounds of neighbors with sweat-chafed tempers.

One night, a voice from the fire escape one floor above me in the adjacent building offered me a plum. Miraculously, I said yes; marvelously, I caught it. It was underripe; but I wasn't exaggerating when I shouted up that it tasted absolutely delicious. I sucked the pit until I went to sleep that night. I had not realized how lonely I was. Two more plums, a banana, and a tiny bunch of grapes later, the voice invited me to dinner that upcoming Friday at the Shanghai Café.

After fried shrimp and pork lo mein (the whole fish came later), we walked back along Broadway. We were approaching the entrance of Union Theological Seminary when Leo, having asked me many questions in between dazzling me with his wit and erudition during dinner, came up with an answer to everything: I would move out of my room and into his apartment. I don't know whether I was more shocked or surprised; but I stopped short, right there in front of the formidable seminary entrance. Leo must have thought I wanted more courting because, there, he kissed me for the first time.

And several more. Although I had been kissed by a respectable number of males and, on fewer but sufficient occasions, made reciprocal efforts of my own, I had never been kissed like that. "Like that" refers not to what Leo did, but to how he did it. I was, I think, able to hide my astonishment; and I must have responded somewhat appropriately, because Leo did not rescind his proposal as we, eventually, walked southward again, past the long green gate which set Barnard off from Broadway and the world. I was already three-quarters smitten; but not yet so far gone as to go along with Leo's predilection for reordering the process of getting acquainted. Not immediately, anyway. It was nearly two weeks later that I moved in with him.

Much fruit and some more kissing passed between us before then, but Leo obviously felt no need to pressure me with either additional dinners out or advances. He bided his time and left me to decide all on my own. I could have used a friend to talk to, an *informed* friend: my concern was not with right or wrong, but with competence. There was not, in those days, the glut of books which instruct, inspire, and urge on the sexually laggard. With no one else to talk to, I fell back on myself; late into the steamy nights, I worked up my nerve. Finally, I invested eighteen dollars I could ill afford in a creamy floor-length nightgown trimmed with soft ecru lace and told Leo I was ready.

He knew better, I guess. The first night, after I had changed into my new nightgown and brushed my teeth and hair more than was absolutely necessary, he kissed me avuncularly and told me the couch was all mine. I stayed awake all night, waiting. The following two nights I stayed awake again, worrying now. The fourth evening, noticing the shadows beneath my eyes, Leo said he thought I might be more comfortable in his bed than on the couch.

I felt better at once—but only briefly. Leo's bed turned out to be even lumpier than the couch, which didn't keep Leo from falling asleep directly after he hugged me good night. However Leo managed to keep his distance—looking back, I wonder if will power was all he was getting up in the bathroom before coming to bed—it had the desired effect. When, finally, on the morning of the Fourth of July, I woke and turned to him, wide awake and wide-eyed despite the strong light, I was so ready I hardly felt the pain.

The rest of that summer, between Leo's junior and senior years at Columbia and mine at Barnard, was an education for me, and not only a sexual one. During the day, we both worked: I as a salesgirl at Saks Fifth Avenue, selling aqua knitted-silk ties to Texans and navy blue and white polka-dotted foulards to Argentinians, and Leo at his poetry. Sometimes when I came home Leo would still be working. I learned to walk soundlessly through the apartment, not to flush the toilet unless absolutely necessary, and to contain my kiss hello until he was done for the day. He would seldom show me his work; he never showed an unfinished poem to anyone, and his poems were not mere lyrics, they took time. But he would ask about my day: he liked me to describe the customers and what price ties they bought and, sometimes, what each one looked like. In the beginning, I wouldn't always remember which ties and customers departed together; but as the summer progressed, my memory improved. It occurs to me that my knack for remembering the odd visual detail may be attributable to Leo's prodding: part of that summer's education that lasted.

I had only two outfits which met Saks' rigorous standards. On alternate evenings, when I arrived home in my black shantung dress with the V neck, Leo would ask me how many men had wanted me to show them ties from the lowest shelf. I practiced bending down without bending over until I mastered it. Leo said I was silly, but he looked pleased.

Nights we went to the West End, the bar that was as much a part of the Columbia scene as the statue on the steps of Low Library. There, we would always sit at the same table; no matter when we arrived, there was always room for us. And although Leo never *did* anything, in a little while he would become the epicenter of the group. When he decided it was time for us to go home, the table would break up: the party was over for that night.

As late as that might be, we would, when we came home, make love, unless it was Sunday. Sundays, Leo liked to make love in the early afternoon, right after he'd finished the *New York Times Magazine* crossword puzzle.

It did not surprise me that Leo was more knowledgeable about sex than I was; he was more knowledgeable about almost everything. Besides, *I* knew how little I knew, even if I didn't know how much there might be to learn; and Leo found out soon enough. He was so *nice* about it, gentle and patient and understanding. And when I finally got something right, he would smile proudly. I never doubted he had reason to feel proud when I was . . . good. He taught me how to do things, then how to do them better; eventually, I knew how to do them just right. How, then, I rejoiced in Leo's pride in me!

I, too, felt proud, although I didn't let on to Leo. Any more than I let on to him that when I got off the Fifth Avenue bus at 110th Street, and walked northward to his place, I would never fail to read the huge painted sign that said, "The wages of sin is death but the gift of God is eternal life through Jesus Christ our Lord. Romans 6:23." All these years, but I swear that's right: Romans 6:23. I had no faith, and eternal life was something I had never considered, much less coveted; but now I knew what sin was and I was not surprised that one might be called on to pay a stiff price for it. I would shiver, more from excitement than fear and, feeling proud and brave, I would turn down 111th Street.

Leo said once, when we were sitting at our table in the West End—he didn't say it to anyone in particular, but of course everyone was listening—he said: "Some people are innocents. Jessie, for example. She has an innocence forsaking her virginity did nothing to diminish." I had no idea what he meant, and was less than delighted to have him refer to my virginity or loss of it in front of his friends. Still, sayings things right out was in the spirit of the West End, so I didn't mind all that much. Besides, there was in Leo's voice no disapprobation: it was all right to be the way he said I was. And he had singled me out. He didn't do that often when we were with his friends; I learned to cherish the times he chose to acknowledge my special place.

In truth, I *was* innocent. And maybe Leo knew; maybe he was giving me, if not fair warning, a hint. But I heard none, enclosed as I was in the carapace of my belief that with Leo, through Leo, my life had changed for the good, and for the better. I didn't know then what distinguishes first love from the other times. You don't know, that first time, that love can end.

For me, that summer ended rather late, and love far too soon, the second week of October. The summer. Us. Everything. The summer that Margery still didn't know had ever happened.

Back in the spring, when Margery's roommate, Nan Saltonstall, decided to transfer to Radcliffe because proximity to her new Harvard fiancé seemed imperative, Margery had asked me if I would like to take Nan's place in the fall. Most dorm rooms were singles; Margery's spacious room at the top of Brooks Hall was exceptional, not only in size, but because of her fine hi-fi and the huge, vivid Thai silk pillows on the floor and a small illegal refrigerator. And because of Margery, whose generous laughter and keen head and vast portfolio of goodwill helped make her quarters the choice place in the dorms to spend an evening when there weren't any men or much work.

I hadn't been too flattered to say yes. It had been settled well before Margery left for Block Island, and the prospect buoyed me during my search that ended in that awful room I lived in—before Leo.

Now, coming to our room—Margery's and mine—our first day back at school, I was buoyed up even beyond my quotidian happiness by the fact that I had something new and shining to bring to my reunion with Margery: my summer's discovery; my ongoing, growing adventure. My Leo.

I planned to tell Margery *all* about him—I was fairly bursting with accumulated treasures—but I didn't get a chance that first day back. Margery's summer had been difficult: her mother had remarried again that spring, and the new husband had paid too much attention to Margery, and her mother had insisted it was Margery's fault, and the tension was almost as awful as he was; and there were only the same old boys, no gleaming new prospects, nothing to take her mind off the mess at home. It would have been worse than rude, I felt, to interrupt Margery's endless account of her disappointing summer with *my* summer. I had waited this long, I could wait until the right moment to share my joy with Margery.

Before it came, I was walking past Riker's with Margery one afternoon later that same week when we bumped into Leo coming out. I introduced them, of course, and the three of us talked for a few minutes. I could hardly keep from beaming, so pleased was I; now that she'd seen us together, I felt sure Margery would *know*. We were both on our way to class and there was no time then, but when I got back to our room that night I was all geared up for a long talk. I'd even come back to the dorm earlier than usual so we wouldn't be up all night, there was that much to share.

Almost as soon as I came into the room, Margery said, "That Leo friend of yours, he's charming, intense but charming." I nodded. Caressing one long, suntanned leg, she added, "I'm so bored with shaving. I wonder if a depilatory isn't worth the messiness. Ever tried one?"

I shook my head and went to bed.

She hadn't asked anything. And I didn't say, I simply could not say, "That Leo friend of mine? He's my lover, Margery.

I love him, Margery.'' I blamed myself: if only I had told her right off, the first day back. Now, I felt awkward. I would have to wait again for a natural opening.

I waited too long. Two days later, Margery returned from a lengthy phone call in the hall not even attempting to hide her delight. Without any hesitation—she had no reason to hesitate, did she?—she told me it was Leo on the phone. I suppose I could still have said something—cried out. Made a sound. Something. But the pain was too intense: I could not speak. Margery was unafflicted; she spurted on: Leo hadn't asked her out, but they had talked—about everything—and she just knew he'd call again.

I did, too.

He called her every day after that, late in the afternoon. She would wait in our room to be sure not to miss it. I did the same. In the evenings, I continued to accompany Leo to the West End and, later, to his apartment; often, still, we had to run the six blocks back to Barnard in order for me to make curfew. Neither of us mentioned his calls to Margery; neither of us mentioned Margery.

The strain of trying to act as though nothing were wrong, as though I didn't know my days were numbered, was exhausting. One night, I was simply too worn out to make the effort. When I called Leo to tell him, he said that was okay, some other night then. He didn't say tomorrow night. But the next night I did go, and he acted as though that was all right with him, too.

He didn't, in fact, act very differently toward me. He *didn't:* I watched; I listened; I felt his hands on me. But his calls to Margery got longer; he began to call her lunchtimes as well. We were both, Margery and I, spending more time around our room, listening for the phone. Despite her fascination with Leo—augmented by his failure, still, to ask her out—Margery noticed that something was wrong with me. And about that she asked. Why, I ached to say to her, didn't you ask me what was *right,* when all my world was right? But, of course, I didn't say that; I didn't say much of anything; I said nothing was wrong, not really. Why didn't I tell her that the end of the world was imminent? Because in me there was this one slim, emaciated strand of hope that, so long as Leo said nothing to me, so long as I said nothing to Margery, there might yet be a reprieve. That was one reason. The other was that I knew there wouldn't be: like the man in the death cell, I was playing only for time. Every day was another day I'd see Leo . . . have Leo. One more day. Please, God, just until the end of this week . . . just through this weekend . . . tonight? Spirit-draining velleities. In the end, of course, I couldn't stand it any longer. I broke.

And broke it off. Leo, who again had bided his time and gotten what he wanted, was solicitous. I howled; he held me. I whimpered; he held me. His generosity that night was boundless. It was, in fact, bounded only by my one-thirty curfew. Leo was in no hurry; he made that very clear. He wasn't—in any sense—pushing me out the door. We had, he said the words, all the time in the world. A natural mistake; after all, his world wasn't coming to an end that night. Mind you, he did not depreciate my loss: he comforted me—damn him! And I—damn me!—let him. Even now I feel the shame of it rising sourly in my throat, that I allowed him to. I was past *wanting,* understand that, believe that.

If I had, when I got back to the dorm that night, told Margery . . .

Jessie. Twenty years. Long enough to have let go of all that pain, isn't it?

Only, of course, I thought I had. And, perhaps, had—until Margery's invitation to stay with her and Leo had come, bringing old anguish to the surface, slowly, thickly, with reason-defying force. How, after all these years, *could* those ancient wounds feel raw? The old resentments, heavy and ragged, press down on my chest? Not, how clear it was now—even clearer than it had been back then—resentments against Margery. Because I had known, even then, that Margery had taken Leo from me in all innocence, without deliberation, without malice, without *knowing*—just by being her beautiful sweet bright golden self. It had been impossible, always, not to forgive Margery for what she couldn't after all, help: being everything I wasn't.

But not Leo. Leo I had never forgiven. Leo I did not forgive.

Twenty years, Jessie.

So?

Walking through the terminal, I remembered the effort it had taken just to continue going to classes; to eat; to dress. Beside ordinary acts like these, the effort required not to let slip a word to Margery about the previous summer was inconsequential. I said very little about anything at all that fall; what little I did say required conscientious effort. Besides, insofar as I wanted anything anymore, I wanted Margery *not* to know . . . not to find out my shame. I wondered, once or twice, that no one else told her, before I remembered that, except for Leo's loyal West End crew, no one knew. Their silence extended to me: when I would occasionally pass one or another of them on Broadway, he would nod or smile vaguely but never stop to speak. Just as well with me, convinced as I was, most days, that hello-how-are-things was quite beyond me.

No one knew. It was as though I'd been part of someone else's dream—and she'd awakened.

It got better. I have no idea when it started to get better, but I wasn't as surprised as I might have been. More than most people my age, I had reason to know that the worst thing about losing someone you love is that you do live through it. The pace of my limp resurrection was imperceptible, but by the time of Margery's wedding, two weeks after graduation, I was all right.

I was one of eight bridesmaids—the only one, I was certain,

who hadn't gone to Miss Porter's—in a full-scale, full-dress High Episcopalian wedding, which Margery's mother not only suffered but insisted on, as though putting a face on things would help her save face with her friends: if Margery had taken leave of her senses, *her* sense of decorum was intact. The—height—of the wedding having been determined, Mrs. Leigh met with Leo's mother on the deceptively neutral ground of the then most chic restaurant in Manhattan. What was said between them remains forever between them; but on Margery's wedding day, both sides of the aisle were filled by the bride's side.

I thought about that sometime during the ceremony—that Leo and I were probably the only Jews in the church; but I didn't extend that to feeling we had something in common, even for the moment. I suppose if I had been completely myself I would have realized that we did have something in common: we both thought Margery the most spectacular girl in the world. Coming down the aisle in strait white lawn, Margery shone. I followed her glance: Leo looked triumphant and humble and very happy. I looked away; the rose window was commendable.

At the reception, I drank all the toasts indiscriminately but modestly; and I danced with each of the groomsmen, even Margery's fifteen-year-old brother. When Margery went to change, I did my part in helping her pack a few last-minute items. I admit that when she threw her bouquet I did not raise my hand. But if I did not feel that lavishly sporting, I felt self-satisfied. I had carried off my wedding chores, as I had endured Margery's prenuptial activities and the preceding months of courtship, like a lady. I was done.

Slowing as I reached the baggage pickup treadmills, I smiled to myself. Barnard may not have been able to teach me to be a golden girl, but I'd learned—picked it up, somehow— to be a lady.

Whatever that means. It was all a very long time ago. How

a lady did or didn't act in a particular situation hadn't occurred to me in fifteen years. My bag came round, and I grabbed it and headed for the taxi area. The bag wasn't heavy and, despite the weight of the typewriter in my other hand, I was walking at my normal pace when I caught sight of myself in the glass front of the terminal. I did not slow down to examine my image, but I was sure, as I lifted my hand to signal a taxi, that the me reflected in the glass was no more a self-conscious lady than she was a slightly too innocent girl.

A taxi pulled up. "Riverside Drive and 105th Street, please," I told the driver. Adding, just so he'd know where we stood, "Take 110th across."

3

Architecturally, the building was imposing if not particularly interesting. Doubtless, there had once been a doorman; he had been replaced by a buzzer system permitting two-way verbal communication, but the admitting buzzer sounded in response to my ring, and I got the door in time. As I find buzzer systems even more intimidating than I used to find doormen, I considered the foregoing a good omen. The lobby was marble-walled, but entirely bare of the furniture that used to be as ornately obligatory in such places as it had been in, say, the Loew's 175th Street of my *Roman Holiday* period.

Margery answered the doorbell at once, without preliminary footsteps. "Jessie! Welcome!" she greeted me. She held the door wide; the apartment foyer rather than Margery was in my direct view. Only then, incredibly enough, did it occur to me that seeing someone, anyone, after so many years would be seeing someone who *couldn't* look the same; and Margery was getting first look. For that instant, a mirror seemed the one thing in all the world I needed. It passed, of course, as any moment, however disconcerting, does; and I stepped inside the apartment.

"I do hope the traffic wasn't horrendous," Margery was saying, apologetically, as though she were willing to assume responsibility. "Here, let me take your suitcase." She pointed to my typewriter case. "And that."

"It's not heavy, thanks," I said, my first contribution to our meeting.

"Do you take it absolutely everywhere?" she asked, quite as though it were a particularly fine ring which, were it hers, she wouldn't leave at home either.

"A reflex," I said dismissively. Alec, suddenly present, smiled.

"But it's absolutely fine," Margery said. "As it happens, while Jon takes his typewriter up to school, of course, he doesn't take the typewriter table, so you're all set. Come on in and I'll show you."

In my self-consciousness about how I'd look to her, and she to me, I hadn't yet looked directly at Margery. Now, as she walked ahead of me past the living room and down a narrow hall, I verified that she was as slim as ever, maybe even slimmer. Feeling foolish and cowardly, but more curious than either of these, I noted that her posture, even carrying my suitcase, was as superlative as I remembered. I straightened—and smiled, recalling my ancient conviction that wealth was invariably associated with good carriage, good penmanship, and good linens. I hadn't thought of that in years; yet, as I followed Margery into a sizable corner room with three windows, I found that nothing had happened to me in the intervening time to smudge that . . . caricature?

Margery set my suitcase on the bare top of a pine desk. The last time I visited Margery, the only time I visited Margery at "home," it had been her mother's home the weekend of the wedding, and there had been a luggage stand for my bag. I read the absence of one now as a sign that my visit was not one among many: guests didn't wander in and out of this home the way they had at Margery's mother's.

"Your room, Jessie." Margery smiled.

She had done things to make it seem that way. On the bedside table lay the Modern Library Jane Austen, my habitual bedtime reading when we'd shared a room. Beside the book, in the Steuben vase I had given her as a wedding present, slightly too squat for it, stood a single branch of lilac, my favorite flower—as hers, I recalled, was violets. Through the bathroom door, I saw heaps of white towels; back at Barnard, Margery had marveled at my propensity for using all the available towels every time I showered. Stepping over to the bed, Margery turned back the plaid spread.

"Only you would remember!" I exclaimed. "How lovely they still are." I touched a pillow slip. "And soft. Is there anything in all the world softer than cotton sheets that have been laundered over and over?" Margery had made up my bed with sheets, part of her huge trousseau of linens, that I had, even in my then spiritless state, been dazzled by. Ferns of forest green imprinted on sharp white cotton—and my memory. The green was faded to a more muted tone now, differently beautiful.

Margery said, "I felt silly, I almost took them off again, but I can still see you." She looked at me. "You do remember." Pleasure suffused her face. Her face. Faded more than the green of the ferns. Still beautiful? The change was too great for me to decide. Margery's hand went to her too-thin neck. I must be staring.

"Margery, of course!" I said, moving to the window and looking out. Below, trees and water—but I wasn't really looking, only giving her a moment. Then I turned and said brightly, "Do you still have them all? I think you got married with more linens than it would take to run a medium-size hotel."

"It must have seemed that way," she said, laughing lightly. "But, no, I only have a few sets left. They are nice, aren't they?" She was looking at the sheets as though they were not on an actual bed in her own home, but part of a photograph of somewhere she'd been once, long ago. It only lasted a moment. Then: "Well! I'll leave you for a while, I think. I do hate anyone looking over *my* shoulder when I'm settling in. If you need more hangers, shout. I'll be in the living room." A blond, trim woman, close on either side of forty, I'd say of a stranger. More. A *pretty* woman, a little too full in the face, perhaps, for someone otherwise thin. But, still, yes, Margery's face—pleased to have an old friend visiting, the faraway look entirely gone from her eyes.

Probably imagined in the first place, I told myself as I opened my suitcase and started putting my things away.

When, perhaps fifteen minutes later, I came into the living room, Margery was seated on a large sofa parallel to the windows, facing the door, a tea tray in front of her on the glass coffee table. For a second, I had this odd feeling that she was posed . . . poised . . . like an actress waiting for the curtain to go up. But she smiled in greeting and I saw that she was in fact only waiting, as any hostess would, not knowing a guest's pace, slightly concerned lest the tea get cold.

She said: "We'll be waiting dinner for Leo, of course, so it might be rather late. I made you a sandwich. Ham and cream cheese?" Her head was tilted to the side, playfully, as I walked over.

I took the plate from her and sat on the far end of the sofa. "What a memory you do have," I said, then began to laugh. "I *was* amazed at how good it tasted, wasn't I?"

"And when *I* realized," said Margery, "I thought the heavens might open up and we'd both be struck dead."

"I never thought things like that mattered, you know, but I did think it couldn't possibly taste right." I took a bite out of the sandwich. "It's good," I said. "Still."

"Milk? Sugar?" said Margery.

Not a lapse of memory; we didn't drink tea in those days. "Black, thanks."

Margery poured my tea, and then hers, attentively. I noticed a slight tremor in her hands and then, when she handed me my cup, in mine, too. This sign of my own apprehension did not increase it; and Margery's, which was unexpected, unexpectedly settled me some. It put us on a more equal footing.

Around the room, which was furnished mostly in academic modern, were a few fine old pieces and a Sargent drawing I recognized from Margery's mother's house. The old pieces fitted in with the old-fashioned molding on the walls, vestiges of an antique construction era, better than the leathers and tweeds of the rest of the furnishings. The overall effect was less than successfully eclectic; more haphazard, really. Still, there was no way to obliterate the elegance of the few good pieces.

"Those inlaid end tables, didn't they flank one of the sofas in your mother's living room?" I asked.

Margery nodded. "I suppose she started to relent before then, but didn't know how to let me know. You know Mother would never say anything right out. Anyway, when she moved to Hawaii she gave me a few pieces."

"She's still alive?"

"*And* married again," said Margery. "Only four years ago."

"Which is this one?"

"Number five," Margery said. "I think, if this one dies or she divorces him, she won't do it again, though. I suspect Mother would think more than five husbands tacky." Margery's grin was less than empathetic.

"Do you ever see her?" I asked.

"Once. She sent me a ticket to come visit her—two, three years ago. It seemed such a huge gesture for her to make that I went. She looked pale—and quite beautiful. She never goes out during the day, to avoid the sun, and she'd put on some weight—to stave off wrinkles, I guess. The new husband was extremely pleasant, and Mother *tried,* and God knows I tried." She looked past me a moment, then shrugged lightly. "After three days, I gave it up and flew home." A pause. "I'm sure she was as disappointed as I was."

Then, with a distinct lift: "She keeps in touch, before you ask, in her own way. She sends Jon unseemly large checks each Christmas."

"His birthday, too, I bet."

Margery shook her head, a glint in her eye. "I'm not sure you're going to believe this, Jess. See, when Jon was born, we weren't in touch at all. And . . ." Margery was trying to contain this funny little smile, unsuccessfully. "Actually, Mother doesn't know when Jon's birthday is. Naturally, she won't ask, and I suppose I plain dug in my heels about it— all right, a tiny stroke of vengeance. I could, of course, have mentioned it in passing on several occasions these last years. I guess I never found it in me to let *Grandmama* off that easy. Anyway, take my word, the Christmas check more than covers it. And I suspect that since, aside from this nice enough husband of hers who happens to have a modest few million of his own, and her favorite dog charity, she has no logical beneficiaries, one day my son will be a rich man."

"Do you mind?"

"No, I don't think it'd mess Jon up."

"I meant, that she never changed her mind about disinheriting you?"

Margery looked surprised; then she chuckled. "I'm not as stable as Jon," she said. Then, checking her thoughts as she spoke: "I won't, you know, know for sure until she dies, but I've always assumed she wouldn't change her mind about that. She was very angry. And hurt."

I pointed to the lovely Venetian end tables. "She gave you those."

"Oh, Jessie, she has a thousand things. It's her standards

that are precious to her. A chest, a painting—they aren't money. She can't ever trust me. Jessie, don't you see? I betrayed her. In her eyes, by marrying Leo, I chose not to be her daughter."

"But after all these years . . ." I protested.

She nodded. "But Mother has convictions. I suppose, if ever her anger threatened to die down sufficiently, she'd apply a reserve conviction, like another log to a dying fire. At least I think that's how she operates, Jess." Margery smiled. "You always were intrigued by Mother."

"Guilty," I admitted. "She wore her prejudices with such panache. She was so polite to me." I literally shook myself, to be rid of an unexpected residue of awe.

"I'm sure she was afraid of you. She was terrified of Leo. But superficial rudeness would have been impossible for Mother. Hers is on another level entirely." On the surface, Margery's voice was explicatory; but underneath, there was a denseness.

"I would have thought," I said cautiously, "that when *your* child grew up, you might be inclined to view your mother more . . . sympathetically?"

"I love my child."

There it was. "Do you still think that, Margery? That she never loved you?" I was surprised that we were already into a subject so acutely personal, yet I was as disinclined as Margery apparently was to pretend we knew less about each other than we did. The years may have brought a certain discomfort; they did not effect amnesia.

"I knew that," Margery was saying, "before I was old enough to know I knew it." She shrugged. "I think, when I was very young, she tried. But, you see, I started off on the wrong foot—with the wrong face, looking like my father as I did. Things must already have been going bad between them. And, later, I must have been a constant reminder of him. Still, if I had . . . made a suitable match—she would have relished a handsome sportsman of a son—if I had brought her such a son-in-law, that might have made up considerably for my initial failing."

"And all Leo's brilliance!"

"Jessica. What do *you* think?"

"I guess not," I said. I did not want to stay on Leo, I thought it time to leave Mrs. Whatever-her-name-was-now, too. "Tell me about Jon," I said.

"That's easy," said his mother. "Jon is handsome. He's got Leo's coloring, but otherwise he's very like my father. You know, he was the only one who left Mother. She saw to it that she left all the others. Why are other people so much more obvious to us than we ourselves?"

"Nature's way of keeping the suicide rate down, I guess," I said.

Margery, in a near whisper, solemnly: "You mustn't joke about suicide, Jessie." In a more normal tone, she said, "In Judaism, you must know, it's the most serious sin there is."

I shook my head. "No, I didn't," I said.

"Yes."

She laughed then. "But let's not get bogged down in theological trivia. I was telling you about my son. Jon is—Jessie, smart isn't a strong enough word. He's every bit as brilliant as Leo was when he was in college, but in a quieter way. Let's see." She lifted a hand, ticked his virtues off on her fingers. "Jon is kind. Jon is good. Jon is sensitive. He's solid, too. He even has common sense—Lord knows where from, certainly not from his mother *or* his father. Jon is quite marvelous, really. I'm sorry you won't be meeting him—this visit, anyway. When I told him you were coming in to give the talk, and that you might be staying with us, he said he'd like to be here. But exams are coming up—he takes exams seriously, the way we did, not the way most kids do today. But he really meant it, wanting to meet you."

"But why should he?"

"He knows all about you, of course."

"Margery, whatever could you have told him that would intrigue an eighteen-year-old?"

"He's read your books, Jessie, for one thing. Besides, he's not any old eighteen-year-old."

I laughed. "Forgive me. I really do grasp that he's not. And I'm flattered he's read me. I don't expect my books are required reading yet," I said lightly.

As lightly, Margery said, "But they are—in this house."

I pulled back inwardly, but kept my tone matching hers. "So you've made your son read my books. Dear me, I'm just as glad we won't be meeting then. This whole thing makes me feel a maiden aunt whose pets one is obliged to inquire after."

"You've got it wrong, Jess," explained Margery. "Of course, Leo and I read everything you publish as a matter of course. Jon, being voracious, picked one up, then sought out the rest on his own. He especially liked *Esther's House*, I remember. He said it was less clever than the others."

"I see," I said. Perhaps he was as smart as his mother thought; *Esther's House* was less clever than my earlier books. I had worked for that.

"And I've told him," Margery was going on, "about school, and us meeting in metaphysical poetry—how I always looked up to you—how you had everything. . . ."

"*I* had everything?"

"That mattered." Matter-of-factly; *obviously*.

"Such as?" I was more than surprised; I was utterly astonished at how Margery had turned things around.

"You were smarter than I was, smarter than anyone I knew until Leo."

Ignoring that last, I said, "Margery, you were *magna*. I didn't even make *cum*."

"*I* had to work very hard for every good grade I got," she said.

"Margery, don't overrate facility. It took me years to learn how to curb my runaway writing. I still write a book through the first time quickly—but only to find out what my story is. *Writing* that story is rewriting that rough draft, however many times it takes to get to the truth of your characters —what *they'd* do, what *they'd* say. Until I learned to rewrite, to make revision after revision, I wasn't a writer."

"Not of real books." Margery smiled. "That's what Freddie would have said."

"Did, how many times." I sighed.

"I thought of you when I saw her obituary in the paper. Did you feel very sad?"

"Yes."

"It happened quite a while back, before your first book came out, wasn't it? It's a shame. She would have been very proud of you."

"Not then, I don't think, not all that pleased. Maybe with *Esther's House*. I dedicated that to her, did you notice?"

"Of course. Jon asked me who she was."

"What did you say?"

"Who she was," said Margery. "A teacher of ours, a stunningly brilliant teacher, who gave the best of herself and demanded the best of us. And that she died young."

"It's hard, looking back, to think she was only eleven years older than we were." I remembered something, pushed it aside—changed my mind.

"A few years ago," I said, "I was down here on business and I met Lois Spain on Fifth Avenue. We had tea at the Plaza and, while the waiter was getting our pastries, she casually said that she'd been sure, back in school, that Freddie and I were lovers. I was dumbfounded, I didn't know what to say."

"A simple no would have sufficed."

"There was nothing simple about the fact that it wasn't true."

"So Freddie loved you. She never made any . . . demands on you," said Margery.

"Except that I break my ass working."

"She didn't ask all that much more of you than she did the rest of us—and only because she knew you had it in you. She wasn't the only one, Jess, you know. I never doubted that you'd one day write seriously—write novels, and good ones. Don't look like that, I just always knew." She was grinning at me.

"I don't believe this!" I said. "This is Jessie, remember me? I was going to be a great historian, another James Anthony Froude—only more scrupulous. Remember? *Your* short stories were always finer, more subtle. Mine were obvious little tales heavily overladen with alliteration."

"Yes, your stories were simple. Yes, you were smitten with the sheer sound of words. But under that, once you got past the lovely language, inside those plain little plots of yours were real people. You saw inside people, Jessie, and it came through. And as for my perspicacity, I'm afraid you'll simply have to reconcile yourself to the fact that I knew you'd—well, do what you've done. Are you in town now because there's a new book coming out?"

"Not coming out, just finished," I said, my voice dulled by surprise at all Margery said she'd seen in me back then.

"Is it even better than *Esther's House*?"

I laughed. "There are some questions one doesn't ask," I said. "Don't you know that?"

"Certainly I do. Is it?" said Margery.

"Yes."

Now she laughed. "That's terrific," she said. "And between now and when you get proofs, you're a lady of leisure?"

"I was planning to take a real chunk of time off, but there're these two people taking up more and more space in my head."

"I do know better than to ask you to tell me about them," said Margery. "But it is up to you, whether you start on it now or take time off?"

"Me—and those people in my head, yes."

"It must be nice to be your own boss, to set your own schedule. No one to tell you you have to do something."

"Except that this boss is tough," I said. "All those years I wasn't writing to make up for. Besides, there are still people telling you what you ought to do—even what you have to do."

Be photographed. Tomorrow.

"Tell me," I said, reaching for a safer topic, "now that you've reminded me, your stories were really promising. You never write now?"

"Letters," she said self-deprecatingly.

"Once a year, on a Christmas card," I said.

The expression on Margery's face, that innate gentility surfacing visibly. If only I could have retracted my words.

"I'm sorry," she was saying. "I do write letters. I correspond quite regularly with three or four people." She seemed to look past me then; but not behind me. After a moment, she said, "I haven't, actually, been keeping up my end of that for a while now."

"This is silly," I said. "Why should you apologize? After all, I haven't exactly been a conscientious correspondent all these years. People—even friends as close as we were—drift apart." She was still looking as if she didn't feel quite right about it. Why not say it? "In fact, I was really quite surprised when you asked me to stay after all this time."

Slowly, she brought her eyes back to me; and all uneasiness was gone from her face. "It's a reunion!" she said. "Barnard reunion, your coming in to speak at it, gave me the idea." She seemed suddenly quite pleased with herself. *"This* sort of reunion is fun, I think, don't you? I'm no expert, I must admit. I haven't ever gone to the regular kind. Have you?"

"No," I said. "This will be my first. But I would have thought you'd have been, living so close by. Weren't you ever curious to see anyone . . . see how they've come out?"

"No." Decisively. Then, after a moment, in an upbeat voice:

"Are you excited? Being asked back like this, I mean? It's an honor, isn't it?"

"Not exactly in the same league as being awarded an honorary degree by Columbia," I set her straight. "But, you know, when they asked me, months and months ago, I was still working on this last book. I felt I should say yes, and I did. Then I more or less put it aside, the way pretty much everything gets put aside when I'm working. It was a date on my calendar. But now . . . well, yes, I'm not excited exactly, but I'm certainly pleased. Very pleased. Will you be coming?"

I asked it only in the spirit of that moment. It didn't matter to me, one way or the other, if she came, but I suppose I had assumed she would.

"I hadn't really thought," said Margery, obviously ill at ease again.

Quickly I said, "There's absolutely no reason, actually, why you should. After all, it's not even one of our reunions."

"Of course I should go," said Margery. "To hear you." All, it seemed, was in hand again.

But, to me, her offer seemed too . . . personal. "Oh, I think you'll have your surfeit of me here. Tell me," I added, moving hastily if randomly into a potentially more comfortable area, "do you ever see Nan? Or Minnie Hitchcock?"

"Only mentioned in a column occasionally," Margery said. "Very occasionally. I don't really have time for that sort of thing."

I wasn't sure whether she meant seeing old friends who lived in the city or reading social items in the paper; and was again struck by how much I did know about Margery—and how much I didn't. I had by now, in snap exposures, gotten a pretty good look at her. Her slimness was exaggerated, as it hadn't been in school, by the fullness of her face, so I couldn't be sure that she was thinner now. The one sure change was a dimming, especially of her eyes. And while there was no clearly discernible grey in her hair, its goldenness had faded, like the silken arm of a chair placed too close to a southern window.

"Do you?" Margery was asking. "See anyone?"

"Diane Witt occasionally, and Shelley," I said. They both lived in New York, which made my statement something of an admission, but Margery didn't look taken aback. Maybe she didn't read the class news column in the alumnae magazine either.

"Shelley?" she repeated, obviously trying to locate a face in her mind. "Oh, Rochelle Levy."

"Levin," I said.

"Levin, yes. What's her name now?"

"Levin."

"She never married him, that boy she was living with, the dirty poet with those terrible teeth?"

It was as accurate a critical and physical description of Sanford Baum as I'd ever heard, and I nodded. "They went out west together for a few years, but after a time she came back."

"Good move, I'd say," said Margery. "What's she do? She was so witty."

"She's a free-lance writer."

"Sounds unsettled, a free-lancer."

"It suits Shelley. I think I agree with you, though. I'd find it unsettling to live that way. If my income isn't steady, the work's as steady as I want it to be."

"Yes," said Margery, "knowing what you're going to do each day when you get up in the morning, that's very important. It puts order in one's life. Don't you think?"

Yes, but it takes a certain internal order to. . . . I let it go. "As a matter of fact, I do," I said. "That's one reason I start work the same time each day. And I try to stop at a set hour, too, although living alone, I sometimes forget and go on way past what could plausibly be called the dinner hour."

"Speaking of dinner—and order—" Margery said, nearly all the intensity gone from her voice, "I think next in order on your agenda might be a little private time? How does that strike you? I do have a few things to do in the kitchen."

"Can I help?"

"Heavens no. There're only a couple of things. Besides, I like it—Jessie, you should see the look on your face!"

"I guess I just never imagined you cooking. And do not tell me your mother taught you how."

Margery laughed. "Hardly. But I was, as you've kindly pointed out, a pretty fair English student, and most cookbooks are written at least partly in English. I learned. In a little while, you can judge for yourself how well. Now," she said, standing, reaching for the tea tray, "can I get you anything?"

"I'm set, thanks." I stood, too, and started out of the room. "On second thought," I turned, "I noticed a phone in my room. I'd like to check in with my agent and my editor."

"I thought this trip was a vacation," said Margery, but her eyes were twinkling.

I was embarrassed. At some point I'd have to mention there was something besides the talk I had to do—but not just yet. "They're very maternal," I said, "I'll just tell them I've arrived safe and sound."

"Of course, Jessie. Call whomever you like. I was only teasing. Feel free, please." Earnestly: "I want you to feel at home."

"Thanks," I said. I thought of adding, I do; but lies should be saved, I think, for when they're truly necessary.

Liz Mondavi, Angela's secretary-assistant-first-reader-buffer, told me she was on another line and asked if I wanted to hold. I said sure and kicked off my shoes, raised my legs, and leaned against the headboard. But Angela came on almost immediately. "David Susskind I can talk to any day! You're here. You are here?"

"Mmm," I muttered, giving in to temptation.

"Don't tell me you've got a cold—runny eyes—a red nose. Christ, Jessica, your sense of timing—"

"Hey! I'm fine. I say, 'Mmm,' and you concoct an entire terminal scenario."

"You're fine," repeated Angela dully—for her.

"I am, you might say, the picture of good health."

"Save your wit for the Barn-*ard* girls," said Angela.

"Funny," I said, managing not to laugh, "I always thought you thought Convent Station wasn't a bad place to have graduated from."

"At least in my day the nuns dressed decently." Angela chuckled. "Just this noon, I passed two nuns on Fifth Avenue. Neither of them was even wearing a cross, but I'd give you odds they were sisters. I mean, if there were a Coty for dowdiness . . ."

Angela herself dressed expensively, stylishly—and invariably in red. As she had red hair, that lent a certain discordant quality to her appearance. I thought she looked great. But once, after too many glasses of white wine, she admitted to a certain trepidation that she would end up fat and frowzy like her mother, who, according to Angela, had cornered the market on royal blue bugle beads years ago.

"I won't look dowdy, I promise. I've been practicing applying false eyelashes for weeks."

"To your runny eyes, right?" said Angela.

"Exactly," I admitted. "I did remember to bring my eyelash curler, though."

"Good. Your eyes are your best part," said Angela.

"I beg your pardon?"

"Don't be smutty," said Angela.

"*I* didn't say it."

"I *didn't* say it."

"Right," I said. "At Convent Station, they wouldn't have—"

"Wrong. But I was a slow starter."

We both laughed, because Angela had long since made up

for any time she'd lost back then and thoroughly enjoyed talking about it.

She said, "A bit of business, if you can tear yourself away from my sex life."

"Speak."

"The sitting's at three, according to my calendar. Do you want me there?"

"Good God, no!"

"Thanks."

"Thanks, no," I corrected myself.

"You going to call Delia to make sure the time's still the same?"

"Soon's we hang up," I said. "Anything else?"

"One small item. Charlie Tedlum called me late yesterday. Seems word of how good the new book is is getting around."

"How, I wonder?" I teased. Only Angela and Delia had copies.

"He made an offer," said Angela, ignoring my crack, "for the next one. Seventy-five thousand for the hardcover rights, sight unseen."

"No, thanks."

"Just like that? No discussion of the pros and cons? Tedlum's had two novels on the best-seller list in the past year."

"How nice for Tedlum."

"And his authors," said Angela.

"Okay, and his authors. I'm Delia's author."

"Look, he might even go higher. He wants to have lunch and talk about it."

"No."

"That's it?" said Angela sharply. "You know, you were practically unknown the other time, after the first book, and you didn't know all that much about the business, need I remind you? Besides, you didn't have me," added Angela.

"Right on every count. No lunch."

"Think about it a couple of days," said Angela.

"I don't need to," I said. "Ange, I will say it once more. Maybe this time I can manage to say it clearly enough. When Delia took me back, after the gorgeous deal I fell for at The Four Seasons turned out to have a neat hole in it, I swore—not to her, to me—that it'd never happen again. I like Delia. And not so incidentally, she's a first-rate editor. She does all right by me. No lunch with Tedlum."

"Seventy-five grand ain't hay," said Angela.

"It ain't the world, either," I said.

"You're sure?" said Angela. "No?"

"No."

"That's what I told Tedlum."

"You—witch!"

"It's my job to tell you about offers."

"Which you blithely turn down without even asking me!"

"Why can't all my clients be as easy to get along with as you are," said Angela.

I laughed first.

Angela spoke first: "Look, in case I haven't mentioned it this month, I think you're one sensational writer and if you're slightly idiosyncratic—"

"*I'm* idiosyncratic!"

"Any . . . individualism of mine is part of my professional credentials," said Angela.

I gave in. "You're probably right," I said.

"As usual," said Angela, "and therefore an appropriate note on which to end this conversation."

" 'Bye," I said.

"Jessie."

"Yes, agent mine."

"Tedlum sounded genuinely disappointed," she said.

"Thanks," I said.

"For what in particular?"

"Oh, for my needlework pillow. For the whole bit."

"You, being sentimental?" scoffed Angela.

WEDNESDAY 47

"Yeah," I said. "Charge it up to this camp reunion I'm going to."

"Barnard was no summer camp," said Angela, unable to keep the respect out of her voice.

"No, it wasn't," I said, meaning something else entirely.

Delia confirmed that the sitting was still at three o'clock.

"In your office?"

"In Bagditch's office, in the corner. Better light there. Where would you like to have lunch?"

"Anywhere nearby would be fine," I said.

"We're in no hurry, we can go anywhere," said Delia. "You choose."

"The Four Seasons, the big room," I said.

Delia laughed, her quiet, Baltimore society laugh.

"Called your bluff, huh? Okay, tell me what price range we're in," I said.

"Price has nothing to do with it. Don't underestimate yourself around here. I could hand in a chit for the Palace and they wouldn't balk. I just thought you might like to go somewhere off the beaten path."

Delia's genteel Baltimore upbringing was as ineradicable as Angela's Bayonne Irishness. Besides, we'd worked out my Four Seasons escapade between us four years back. "All right with me," I said, "just so long as they serve something that'll give me a look of utter contentedness in the photograph."

"Utter contentedness, eh? I think I know just the thing. The chocolate mousse cake at Café des Artistes."

I remembered it. I savored it mentally. "That ought to do the trick. What time?"

"How about twelve thirty? One wants to eat mousse cake slowly, I should think."

* * *

Turning off the shower above the veined old tub, a relic of the days before apartment bathtubs had been shrunk to fit the cubicles presently called bath*rooms,* I reached for one of the towels Margery had set out for me. Its original whiteness dimmed, its thickness eroded by years of use, it retained a quality that proclaimed it had never been purchased two-for-anything. Spreading it along the shower rail to dry, I noticed that the deep blue embroidered monogram was intact, no threads torn: small M, slightly larger M, small A: Margery Addison Mellson. I slipped into my thin cotton kimono, brushed my hair perfunctorily, and went to lie down.

I folded the deep plaid spread over the back of Jon's desk chair and lowered the blinds. Easing onto the bed, I found the mattress satisfyingly hard. The pillows, entirely expectedly, were soft as the down of which they were doubtless made. . . .

As soft as the piece of old velveteen I had found on the top shelf of the linen closet when I was getting out of the apartment after Mama died. A piece too small to be called a remnant, really, too small ever to have been put to use. For some reason, she had never thrown it away, though. I recognized it at once.

My new dress. Dark, dark red and soft as a cat when you touched it. It was a secret dress, Mama had said. The dress was for me, for my birthday, but the surprise was for Papa.

Everyone around the table was singing a song to me. The mothers standing around behind the table were singing, too. I looked over my shoulder, and Mama was smiling as she sang the happy birthday words. She wasn't looking down at me, though. I followed her eyes and Papa was standing there, in the doorway. *He* was looking at me. But he wasn't smiling, he looked very serious.

I got up from my place and ran to him, but he didn't grab me and hug me the way he always did. Instead, he put his hands on my shoulders and held me away from him and moved my shoulders to make me turn around. I thought it might have something to do with my being three now. But then he did pick me up, like always, holding me even tighter than usual. I felt something wet on my cheek, but when I looked up at Papa, he was smiling. Could you cry and smile at the same time? I would have asked him—Papa always answered all my questions, he never said "just because"—but right then Mama began to laugh and then Papa began to laugh and I did, too. Secrets like my dress made people happy, I decided. It was so wonderful. It wasn't even nighttime yet and Papa was home from work and it was as if all the other children and their mamas had gone home, as if there were no one in the whole world but the three of us. Laughing.

Years later, holding the piece of dark red velveteen fabric in my hand, I stood in the linen closet, neither laughing nor crying, but clutching that piece of material as though it were the fabric of my life.

Now, burrowing into the softness of Margery's pillows, I thought how, finally, I had found a way to use that velveteen. It backed a slightly enlarged snapshot of Mama, Papa, and me in the park—the only picture ever taken of all three of us together; taken, marvelously, only a few weeks before Papa died. *Still*, I thought, brushing a vagrant tear away, how much happier my childhood had been than Margery's. They would, my parents, have given me, if they could, the world. But their intended largesse was continually thwarted by my father's invincible knack for making deals in which he ended up being dealt out; and complicated by his equally invincible optimism about his ship's long overdue arrival. My childhood wasn't rich in toys or dolls or edible treats or expensive outings to the circus or the ice show; but it abounded in stories and walks in the park and listening to the Philharmonic on the radio on Sunday afternoons and trips to the then-free zoos and museums—and attention. And so much love it could have been the air. It was almost as if they knew from the beginning that they wouldn't have all the time in the world to love me.

I closed my eyes. There was a long time when, remembering, I would have cried. And, before that, a time when I would not yet have been able to cry. But now I could just remember them, as softly, as caressingly as the cotton of the pillow slip against my cheek, in its prime after nearly two decades of laundering. The incomparable luxury of old cotton—*that* we'd had at home. Even though it hadn't been, as Margery's home was, laden with thick toweling robes or feather quilts or heavy linen tablecloths or smooth silverware heavy in the hand. . . .

In my hand I held a silver spoon, less heavy, but also handsomely marked. I laid it on the cloth before me and raised the wine glass and drank again, and tried to keep a sober, listening face. It was an effort not to smile: *they* were smiling, the man and woman sitting to either side of me, pleased with my pregnancy, the baby I was carrying whom they would think of, they said, as as much theirs as mine. Smiling they were, and saying glowing things about my baby-to-be, speaking of its shining future. So certain were they that I would birth a fine baby, they said, that they were giving me their baby present now, even though it was six months before my due date. And, ceremoniously, they handed me this large, handsomely wrapped box. And I said, Oh thank you; but they demurred, saying a baby like mine deserved the world from its godparents; and then we all three toasted my baby once more, and I went home.

I could hardly wait to open the present. But I forced myself to unknot the ribbon and carefully undo the paper without tearing it. Then, flushed with excitement, I raised the lid of the box. And there it was! Properly round, the continents in place, and the oceans: the world. Delighted at its perfection, I scrupulously lifted it out of the box, expecting it of course to be heavy. But it felt surprisingly light. It was then that I noticed, in its top, a narrow opening: the result, my first thought was, of a minor, tidy earthquake—no catastrophe. To make absolutely certain, I looked closer. Closer still. The slit in my world was . . . large enough to take a quarter.

Why had they played such a terribly cruel joke on me? *Why?*

—Awake. Awakened by my own cries. Sitting up. Sweating. Realizing. And, then, listening. Margery must not have heard me. Relieved, I wiped my forehead and tried to smile because it had been only a dream. This time.

My lips stuck together. I lay back, breathing deeply.

Jessie, stop. A, it *was* only a dream this time. B, when it did happen, it was as much your fault as theirs. Of course, they promised you the world—they never thought you'd take them literally. If, when you got down to the contract, it turned out they were offering you somewhat less than the world, that the clause-by-clause world had faults aplenty—well, that's what distinguishes contracts from lunches. I punched the pillows full and sat up and, remembering my pillow back home, I managed a smile. Angela had, the first Christmas after she became my agent, done the needlepoint for me. *Never believe anything anyone promises you at The Four Seasons.*

Not pithy enough for needlepoint, but the real point, I reminded myself: it's all right to want the world, practically everyone does. What's not all right is really thinking someone may give it to you.

Life, lady, contains a lot of small print. Theme for another pillow, maybe? It was eight months to Christmas; I'd drop a hint to Angela.

It was also nearly seven o'clock. I hadn't heard anyone arrive, nor any voices, but the apartment was large. I decided against going out in my kimono to check, and slipped on jeans and a shirt. A minimum of make-up. I was ready.

Yet, at the door, I paused, and went back to the closet door to inspect myself in its full-length mirror. The face the camera would see tomorrow? No. Because Margery looked so different, I felt the need to check out my own face.

But, also, I did not try to pretend to myself that I had forgotten that Leo would be seeing me now. I did need to verify what he would see.

Starting at the bottom because the top was better: long, skinny feet; longish legs; flat but bone-wide hips; a waist slim enough to be a vanity; a narrow midriff; rather full breasts; narrow shoulders. A body a good sight better, despite its edging into softness, than my twenty-year-old, candy-bar-comforted version, I decided.

And moved upward with increased confidence. My hair, whose natural curl I had tugged at for years to no avail, seemed acceptable to me now. The eyes, yellow-green and large, were almost beautiful. The nose, hooked, the bane of my teen-age years, would by the time I was eighty, I told myself, resemble the proud prow of a handsome ship: only forty years to go. The mouth . . . spreading into a smile, more at me than with me. A good enough mouth: the lower lip slightly too full.

Jessie, Jessie, to glance is human, to dissect is vain—in both senses. No, you haven't changed as much as Margery has. And, yes, you've changed for the better. You look like you are now. Go.

4

As I came into the living room, Margery was standing beside the long bookcase, head bent over an outsize book. Even as she quickly closed it and replaced it on a low shelf, I recognized our Barnard yearbook. She, too, had been checking out the differences the years had made. Instantly, I knew that neither of us would refer to it. I walked to one of the windows at the far end of the room, facing uptown. In the distance, the George Washington Bridge looked gracefully utilitarian. Nearer, to the left out the window, people just home from work walked their dogs. The clusters of old people were breaking up for the day; in pairs and threes, they cautiously crossed Riverside Drive and slowly ascended the steep flight of steps leading up to 106th Street. I imagined that dusk, my favorite time of day, must be unwelcome to them, forerunner as it is of night. Behind me, Margery switched on a lamp. I turned.

"Leo called," she said. "Oh, the phone in your room is

turned off. You're on vacation, remember? He'll be home very soon, he said." She glanced at her watch. "It's only a quarter past seven. Would you like a drink now or do you want to wait?" Margery switched on another lamp.

"Nothing now, thanks. That's one downright gorgeous view you have laid out there," I said, coming away from the window.

Margery was moving around the room. Stopping at a table, she adjusted an ashtray and aligned a small pile of magazines. "It's not as pretty as it looks from up here," she said. "Not any more. You sure about not wanting a drink now?"

"No, but go ahead," I said.

"I think I'll wait too," said Margery, sitting down on a spare, ungraceful chair upholstered in a tweed so dim it was impossible to say for sure whether it was green or grey. I sat down on the sofa, and looked around the room for a topic of conversation. On one of the inlaid end tables stood a framed picture I guessed to be Jon. I hadn't noticed it earlier and said so.

"Yes," said Margery, "I know. Talking about him made me bring it in from the bedroom. I wanted you to see him."

She got the picture and brought it to me, waiting in front of me for my reaction, making me study it longer than necessary. Luckily, I found his face appealing. "He's every bit as handsome as you said." I handed her the picture. "He looks young for a high school senior," I added, having assumed it to be a graduation photo.

Replacing the picture, Margery laughed. "He's smart but not all that precocious. It was taken for his . . . thirteenth birthday." She sat again, looking hesitant, then said, "He was going to be bar mitzvahed, he completed the classes, but—at the last moment, we changed our minds."

"Oh?" I said, to all of it. But when Margery only nodded and did not go on to something else, I dredged up, "He decided it wasn't for him?"

Again, she looked hesitant. Why, then, didn't she change the subject; why had she brought it up? Annoyed, I decided to wait her out. "No," she said, finally, "Jon's like me, he rather likes ceremonies. He was actually looking forward to it, but Leo decided we shouldn't go ahead."

I continued to wait. Let Margery drop it there, it was fine with me. But she continued, her hands clasped tightly in her lap. "He felt it would be . . . inauthentic. You see, since I'm not Jewish, strictly speaking neither is Jon. Although he thinks of himself, I know, as more Jewish than Episcopalian, certainly. Leo felt that was inadequate, that the rabbi was excessively permissive, that more was involved than a question of Hebrew classes or Jon's *feeling* Jewish."

"And you? How did you feel?" I asked, my curiosity piqued. Margery's mother's grandson in a yarmulke?

Margery was looking past me, vaguely out the window, apparently taking my question under serious consideration, as if she'd never thought about it before, how she felt about Jon's bent toward Jewishness. When she looked at me, the tentativeness was gone from her expression.

"Well, you know, I've *been* something like Jewish. Years ago, but still . . . . Being rich, I mean. I remember what it felt like. People pretending they don't care, that they don't even notice, but they never forget it for a moment, that you're rich. Or Jewish?" She smiled. For the first time since I'd arrived, a smile took over her face and I could, looking at her, see that earlier Margery smiling.

My response to what she said was delayed by the forcibleness with which her insight struck me and, also, by a series of flash-card memories. Before I could express what I was thinking, Margery said, "I only said it was *something* like being Jewish—not enough like it, of course." A tinge of ruefulness in there somewhere—but I wanted to get back to her initial idea. It was so true.

"Do you remember about the cookies?" I asked.

Margery laughed; almost, it struck me, with relief. "You mean the cookies I used to bring from home for Eaton Cartwright's seminar? God, how you used to hound me for yet another and then another, until I was sure there wouldn't be enough left to go around the table Monday afternoon. You were impossible!"

Quietly I said, "They tasted very different from the candy bars I got out of the machine by the elevator."

"Yes, I guess they *were* good," said Margery.

"The idea of them—packed so neatly in a pretty tin, covered with waxed paper, smelling of butter and chocolate and a large white kitchen."

"Jessie, they were just cookies," said Margery. "And I only had so many."

"Of course," I said, and I did smile.

"Only," I added, just as glad to be able to get away from the smell of them—still, after all these years, enough to make my mouth curl in anticipation—"that wasn't the cookie story I had in mind.

"You told me once that when you were seven or eight, on Block Island, you went to visit this little girl whose family lived on the Island year round—"

"Mary," said Margery. "Mary Curry. Her mother did our laundry."

"Yes, her. And you went there without telling anyone—"

"Oh, I told Greta. I only made her promise not to mention it to my mother."

"And your friend and you had milk and cookies—"

Margery winced. "And I said, 'Your cook bakes wonderful cookies.' And she, Mary, said, 'My mother made them, we don't have a cook.' And I gulped down the rest of my milk and I made some excuse and I got out of there as fast as I could—I was so ashamed. I'd hurt Mary terribly." Margery shrugged helplessly. "I didn't know everyone didn't have a cook." She paused. "I never played with her again."

WEDNESDAY 57

"She must have wondered what she'd done, why you disappeared from her life like that."

"But she must have known why. God, I was mortified. I think until I told you, I'd never told anyone that story."

"Margery, why should she have known? Aren't you assuming not having a cook mattered to her? Didn't her mother bake perfectly good cookies?"

Very slowly, Margery nodded. "Chocolate with pecans, and a slight taste of orange. They were delicious." Her chin was trembling but she was smiling.

"You were right, you see, but it works from both ends. What you felt that afternoon, that baroque self-consciousness, that's *very* Jewish. The funny thing is, until you said that about having been something like Jewish, I never saw it in you. To me, you seemed never to have to think about yourself —how you looked, how you were coming off. I thought you were so lucky, never to have to think about what impression you were making. I saw that fantastic nonchalance as . . . an Episcopalian virtue, an Episcopalian gift—the way Jews seem to have a gift for the violin." I listened to myself; how clear it all was. "When it came to living, you were born with perfect pitch. If you only knew how that fascinated me!"

I was thinking back, and seeing. "Yet, of course," I said after a moment or two, "*I* wanted to be thought of as *not* different. I didn't want to be regarded as an object of fascination any more than I wanted to be snubbed. How I yearned for social anonymity—at least until"—I laughed—"I was invited to tea at Cynthia Martell's house, and her grandmother was there, and after, Cynthia called me, *called* me, to tell me that when I left, her grandmother, who had failed to catch my last name, asked what it was, and when Cynthia told her, her grandmother said, 'My, I couldn't tell she was Jewish.'"

"And Cynthia, poor dumb Cynthia, thought to make a special call to pass the . . . compliment on to you. Unbelievable." Margery was shaking her head; stopped.

"But why do I say that?" she said. "It's absolutely believable. Damn! How hurt you must have been."

"Hurt? Hell no, I was furious. Swore, then and there, that no one would ever make that particular mistake again. You might say that incident marked the beginning of my day-glo Jewish period."

Margery laughed too, but I got the impression her heart wasn't in it. I could understand that; I could also understand Cynthia a little now. "You know," I said, "Cynthia wasn't mean, she just wasn't very bright. She was trying to make me feel better about something she assumed I must feel bad about.

"Actually, she made attempts to brighten my other . . . distinctive situation, too. For graduation, she lent me that lovely yellow linen dress she'd worn the year before to hers. I had to lose more than twenty pounds to squeeze into it, but it *was* worth it. And she had given me a beautiful sweater—she'd bought it at Jane Engel and it was too big for her and instead of going downtown again to exchange it, she gave it to me. It was ten times nicer than anything I owned, and I used to wear it all the time. It was grey cashmere, with small grey pearl buttons, and a big pussycat bow. Cynthia did try." I paused, remembering. "She was delighted at how often I wore that hand-me-down sweater of hers. Almost invariably, she'd comment on it, how glad she was that I was getting so much use out of it."

"What you're saying is, she never let you forget she'd given it to you," said Margery.

"I don't think that was her intention," I said. "But it was certainly different from the way you were about the bathrobe."

"The bathrobe?"

"Oh, Margery, after all these years, isn't it all right to mention it now?"

"It's all right to mention anything," said Margery.

She didn't remember; no, it wasn't possible. "The bathrobe you sent me from Lord & Taylor without a card? I

WEDNESDAY *59*

thought you were absolutely wonderful, to notice. No, I assumed everyone noticed—but you cared. I did feel awful, having to go to the shower in my clothes. I don't suppose, since we never talked about it, that you ever did know why? My bathrobe was at the cleaners when my mother died and, would you believe, that old man we'd gone to for years claimed he didn't have it? Of course I had no receipt—we didn't need one there. Anyway, he kept it. Obviously, I wasn't in any position to go out and buy a new one, and I was terribly embarrassed and self-conscious about it. And I've always been grateful to you. I didn't say anything only because it was so obvious you didn't want me to—you were shy about it. I could understand that, we weren't good friends yet when you did it. I mean, you did send it anonymously, and I respected that. It took me nearly a week to find out that it was you who'd been to Lord & Taylor.'' I smiled.

Margery tried to. It didn't materialize. "Yes, I see," she said, "that was clever of you." She looked as though, even after all this time, she'd rather I hadn't mentioned it.

"I was beginning to wonder if you'd really forgotten," I said, beginning to feel uncomfortable myself.

"No, I remember the bathrobe," said Margery. Then, brightening, "Not nearly as vividly as I remember that sweater Cynthia gave you though. You lived in that sweater!"

I wore her bathrobe every day, to the shower, around the halls. But if talking about it any more was only going to make Margery uncomfortable . . .

I said, "Wearing one thing day in day out was, I rush to point out, a characteristic I shared with some of our classmates who could have sported *far* more extensive wardrobes. Don't tell me you never noticed that Annabel Wainwright wore the same skirt every single day for all of our junior and senior years? I used to wonder when she ever managed to have it cleaned."

"Doubtless, she didn't," said Margery. "Annabel had a

rather unusual system." For a second, Margery looked as if she were about to stop; then she shrugged and said, "I happen to know for a fact that Annabel used to wear the same bra and panties—always Saks' finest—for weeks and weeks and weeks, until they were really *filthy*. Then she'd throw them out, buy another set."

"Why didn't she wash them out? They'd dry overnight."

"I don't think she knew that trick," said Margery, deadpan.

"Come *on*," I protested.

Margery laughed. "You're shocked," she said.

"I think you just invented that story about Annabel to go with mine. I never heard that about her."

"That was no accident. Annabel's . . . idiosyncrasy was something we Episcopalians were just as happy not to have get around."

"I believe you!" I burst out, beginning to laugh as I remembered. "On my first job, there was this girl who hated *Marjorie Morningstar*. I mean she *hated* that book. If she could, she'd have had it removed from every public library. She said, '*We* know what we're like, but why let the *goyim* know!'"

"I think," said Margery, "it's called washing your dirty linen in public?"

We were laughing loudly as a key turned in the lock. Stopped, oddly still together, as Leo came into the living room. For a second only, he paused; then, before I had brought myself to look fully his way, he was striding across the room toward me. Without a break, he extended his arms, took my hands, and lifted me from the sofa. Trepidation fled; I disengaged my hands. "Hello, Leo," I said, sitting down again.

Leo lost his advantage but not his presence. "And to you," he said, "hello and welcome." He moved away slowly, his eyes tolerant of my distance. Bending to Margery, he kissed her cheek. I couldn't be sure, of course, but it did seem to me that Margery didn't lift her cheek toward him; the kiss was uncustomary, was my hasty guess. "I smell marvelous scents emanating from the kitchen. Something special for our illustrious guest?" He was talking to Margery but looking at me.

"It's *your* favorite, darling," said Margery.

"A double treat, then. A visit from the long-lost Jessica and coq au vin all in one evening. What a lucky man am I."

If he had delivered the line straight, I would have been less embarrassed. I glanced at Margery, who did not look embarrassed but, rather, impatient. As if attention had been too long elsewhere? No, I decided, that couldn't be it. If Margery had held people's attention, it was not because she demanded it.

"What can I get you to drink, Jessie?" Leo was asking.

I squinted at the bar across the room. "Dubonnet?" I said. "With lots of rocks, please."

"Margery?"

"That sounds refreshing," she said, looking at me. "I think I'll have the same thing." She smiled at Leo then, waiting until, realizing she *was* waiting, he smiled back. He looks as though she'd asked for some terribly complicated drink instead of a simple Dubonnet, I thought—foolishly, because he hadn't looked that way over my request for one. But how Leo looked interested me more than his expression. He looked young; really, at first glance, quite young. He was fit, with no hint of a paunch; and the cut of his clothes emphasized the shape he was in. He wore his hair campus-stylishly long and it held no trace of grey. But he did, I noticed, comb it straight across the top of his head to camouflage a bald area. His face was free of wrinkles; but wore, now that his entrance was past, a . . . disappointed look. On second thought, I decided, Leo didn't actually look young; he looked like a man working at looking young.

When he'd brought us our drinks and got himself something Scotch-colored on the rocks, Leo eased himself into the requisite Eames chair, cast his feet up on the hassock, and sighed. "Why does the spring semester seem so much longer than the fall?" he lamented. "I *crave* summer."

"Do you go away?" I asked Margery.

"Some years we rent a house in the Berkshires," she said, enthusiasm brightening her voice as she glanced toward Leo.

"I think we'll be staying put this summer," he said, to me. "I've been working up isolated chapters for a book for too many summers. I think this summer it's put-up-or-shut-up time."

For a moment, Margery paled noticeably. Then she said, "Well, then, if you finish it, next summer we can take the whole summer off. Maybe go to Europe again."

"Maybe," said Leo. "One summer at a time, dear, all right?"

He said it kindly, which seemed an odd turn of tone. But, then, maybe I misread the way he said it, because Margery looked really quite put off.

I plunged in. "What sort of book is it you're writing?" I asked Leo. It worked, too. Margery didn't seem to resent my evasive action, and Leo looked relieved. From that moment until dessert was served, Leo talked with wit and depth and, increasingly, enthusiasm about his study of unconsummated incestuous relationships in American fiction. I was, I must admit, fascinated by both the substance and Leo's grand style and, had he himself not interrupted his account from time to time to praise Margery's cooking, I would, I'm afraid, have forgotten my manners entirely.

The food *was* good; it was just that Leo's ideas were even more delicious than Margery's cream of spinach soup or her properly robust coq au vin. With the chicken, we drank the remainder of the bottle of Beaujolais that had gone into the sauce. Another bottle sat on the sideboard, but we never got to it, as Margery and I drank only a single glass apiece. Dessert was a simple—although, I happened to know, torturous-to-make—chocolate roll, over which my compliments flowed easily. Leo said, "It is delectable, almost like a memory of itself. Have we ever had it before?" And Margery said, yes, they had; to which Leo replied he was surprised he could have forgotten.

I listened to this rather formal exchange with encroaching uneasiness, as if it were, instead, quite inappropriately personal. As I had earlier reacted with a twinge of discomfort when, in praising the coq au vin, Leo had said, "It's delicious, Margery; I'd forgotten how well you make it."

Now I dispersed my disquieting thoughts firmly and said, "Your book-learning served you well, Margery. A *magna cum laude* meal, no question about it."

Margery, flushed with obvious pleasure, lowered her head to hide her smile, as Leo said, "Well put, Jessie. Now, I must, reluctantly, leave you two. I'm afraid I have several students who expect their preceptorial even on such a special night as this."

Margery's head remained down an instant too long; still, when she raised it, her smile seemed genuine enough. She said, "Of course they do. You'll be home at eleven, then?"

"Give or take a persistent questioner," he answered lightly. Then, almost as lightly, "Don't bother waiting up for me," adding, "either of you."

Was that last meant to be funny? Or, perhaps, a smoothing over? More likely nothing more than an empty courtesy. Coming at the tag end of too many for me for one evening. I felt tired: the rich meal, Leo's lavish theories, the excessive politeness of their give-and-take.

But, mostly, I guessed, I was tired from expecting the evening to be difficult. It had had its odd moments, certainly, and a couple of uncomfortable ones; but it hadn't been hard, not really. Still, my weariness must have been real enough to show: Margery turned down my offer to help with the dishes, and when I said in that case I thought I'd turn in, she didn't protest even perfunctorily.

Lying in bed, a few minutes later, I decided that to the extent that I had felt discomfort, it wasn't from seeing Leo again so much as from witnessing the exceedingly careful way he and Margery seemed to handle one another. Their speech lacked intimacy, and seemed, therefore, far more revealing than the ordinary give-and-take between a long-married couple. I would call it strained, their way with one another; but then my upbringing did not prepare me for any degree of formality whatsoever between family members. Maybe, it occurred to me, they didn't feel the strain. Either way, I did.

Especially as I'd prepared myself for the wrong one. It was seeing Leo I'd girded myself for.

Not the first time in my life I'd done that: written a scenario in my head which, when the time came, played itself quite differently.

Margery and I had been friends for two years before I met her mother, who was, at that time, called Mrs. Leigh, being temporarily wed to one Mr. Leigh. Actually, I suddenly recalled, I'd *almost* met her once before.

Usually, Mrs. Leigh sent the car for Margery around four on Friday afternoons, so that at least on the weekends her daughter would not be subjected to the questionable influences swirling around Barnard. On this particular Friday afternoon, I was coming into the dorm and spotted Margery standing in Brooks' living room, waiting—I assumed for the chauffeur. I'd just gotten a paper back from Freddie with a surprise A on it—my first ever from her; and I went over to Margery, to tell her. As we were marveling over my breakthrough, Margery, who was facing the door, said, "Here's my mother now." Something—discretion? timidity?—made me not turn, giving Margery the chance not to introduce me to her mother.

I heard them talk a moment and then walk out together—just as though I weren't there. To this day, I have no idea why it was her mother who came to pick Margery up that particular Friday. Nor do I know why Margery grabbed the chance not to introduce us—I'd not meant her to, obviously. The subject never came up between us. Although, for me, it stayed between us, like a tiny, possibly lethal air bubble, for the whole following year.

When I did, finally, meet Mrs. Leigh, it was at Margery's shower. I had heard through someone else (Cynthia, yes; who else would repeat a thing like that to the person involved?) that Mrs. Leigh at first put her foot down about my being in the wedding party, but that Margery had her way. Maybe Mrs. Leigh gave in because it was hardly worth having a knock-down drag-out fight about a bridesmaid when the groom's background already, decisively, spoiled the wedding party.

For days before Margery's shower, knowing how her mother hated Jews, I prepared myself for the iciness of the rebuff she would mete out. But when, at the party, I was brought over to her, she took my hand in her delicate one and said, exceedingly politely, that she was glad to meet me at last. As I mumbled a reply, I saw, in her eyes, not the hatred I had anticipated, but fear. Mrs. Leigh was afraid of me. Of me? *Of all Jews?* Instantly, my terror of her dissipated; and I felt, as I excused myself, a surge of pity for the woman.

How about me, tonight? Had my feelings about having to see Leo been pitiably irrational? No, I hadn't been terrified of seeing him. But I had certainly been apprehensive about what I might feel.

I felt—about me—all right. Quite all right. And about him? Yes, pity; not a surge, certainly—a small spurt, perhaps? Leo was not the man I had thought he had to be; even after a couple of hours I was sure of that much. No, he wasn't the man, I added, drifting off, we'd all of us thought he'd be. Including Leo. Especially Leo. . . .

I had no idea what time it was when the sounds awakened me, nor where they were coming from. From outside, down in the street? Closer. Someone in a neighboring apartment playing a middle-of-the-night movie too loudly? Closer. Outside the door of my room. Now, isolated phrases stood out in harsh relief from the generalized angry sounds I'd first heard: Leo and Margery, quarreling.

A pillow barrier. I tried to separate myself from the sounds, but they were too loud, too strong; I could not obliterate them.

"You can't stay up all night," Leo was saying.

"There's no reason to go in there when I can't sleep anyway!"

"If you don't sleep, you'll never be able to carry off . . ." Leo's voice faded.

Margery screamed: "Don't say that!"

"All right, I'm sorry. But you have to get some sleep."

"I can't. You know I can't!"

"Then do something so you *can* sleep!" Leo was nearly shouting now. "Do what you always do!"

"No! Just leave me alone!"

"I can't go off to bed and leave you like this," said Leo.

"Why not!" shrieked Margery. "Ignoring me is your specialty, isn't it?"

I pressed the pillow against my ears. I could no longer hear them—except in my head.

Eventually, I slept.

THURSDAY

1

I awoke early, the pillow still clutched to my head. What I experienced immediately was not remembering, but knowing; and lay still, listening to the silence.

Choosing it.

In a while, I got up, made the bed, washed, dressed, and left my room, resolved to hide, by lying if necessary, that my sleep had been interrupted in any way.

But there was no one to pretend for. The door to Leo and Margery's bedroom was closed. In the living room, I considered the recuperative powers of inanimate objects: the lethal phrases of the previous night had not pockmarked the walls or frayed the upholstery. After I had looked out the window for a while, and there was still no movement from the master bedroom, I decided that making myself breakfast would not be presumptuous.

Taped to the fridge were a set of keys and a note, signed by Leo, saying that Margery might be sleeping in, and telling me where the breakfast things were. And that he'd see me later.

I put up coffee and, while it dripped, I drank some juice and poked around Margery's culinary accouterments—far more intriguing to me than probing the contents of someone's medicine cabinet. When the coffee was ready, I had two cups and a slice of toast without butter but with marmalade, and decided to take a walk. My head needed airing. I added a P.S. to Leo's note, addressed to Margery, saying I would be back directly after my walk. Allowing myself leeway, I deliberately neglected to mention the time I was leaving.

Downstairs, instead of heading straight for the Drive, I turned uphill, toward Broadway. Most of the buildings along the street were considerably smaller than the ones, like the Mellsons', which bordered the Drive. Renovated brownstones stood wall-by-wall with houses whose shabbiness was unameliorated.

Walking the two blocks to Broadway, I passed several people. Only one, a dog walker in his early thirties, even glanced in my direction. I was back in New York all right; and, remembering myself, I didn't nod or say hello to passersby either. Near Broadway, on a vividly unswept stoop, sat a woman of indeterminate age. Despite the near-warmth of the morning, she wore heavy outer clothing; she did not, however, wear stockings. Her legs were maimed by open sores. She was talking rather loudly, not so much to no one in particular as to everyone within earshot. I looked away and passed her quickly, afraid she might try to stop me. To talk? To beg? To accost? To threaten? To abuse?

Fiercely annoyed suddenly, I proclaimed myself a fraud. All these years I'd been posing as a New Yorker who just happened to be living upstate. The difference, Jessie, between New Yorkers and visitors from Hamilton or Hoboken or Borough Hall or Forest Hills is that the honest-to-God New Yorker takes the city's realities in stride: the movie star on

57th Street, the lady on the stoop without a calendar to tell the seasons by.

Catching sight of my frown in the window of a Spanish religious goods store, I stopped and regarded my angry reflection. Hardly called for, Jessie. The city is different; things have changed since you went away. These days, only the insane are not even a little afraid. Even the citizens bearing switchblades carry fear in their other hip pocket.

I walked on, the anger seeping out, sadness infiltrating. The lady on the stoop had relatives of varying ages. The world's last holdout on marijuana, I could still tell that that group of three, there, were on something less sweet. And the sidewalk was strewn with refuse of the inanimate variety, too. The hardness of that thought, its cold judgmental tone, stopped me in my tracks—and magnified my sadness. Because, in my time, the realities of the city had been less . . . real; and prejudices surfaced less abruptly.

In my time. My time . . .

I had, once, walked with Leo all the way from the Shanghai Café on 125th Street to 96th Street, stopping along the way at every place that looked as though it might offer a passable egg cream. We had six egg creams; one passable, two totally unpotable, three pathetic, good-natured attempts. Even then, more than miles separated upper Broadway from Lower Broadway.

Another time, Leo and I embarked on a neighborhood fried dumpling contest. We went, one Saturday afternoon, to five Chinese restaurants in a row (we would not have been so foolhardy as to try this on a Sunday afternoon, when Chinese restaurants were packed as full as wontons in a bag). In each place, we ordered fried dumplings: one order between us. Aside from making us somewhat unpopular and beggars after gall bladder trouble, the afternoon made us, we figured, fried dumpling cognoscenti.

Chinese restaurants still lined Broadway. Not the ones I remembered, though; even if some of them looked sufficiently aged to be. Some bore signs announcing that they were Chinese-Spanish, others Spanish-Chinese. Was the difference in emphasis, I wondered, due to any culinary distinction or, more likely, to ethnic pride or, most likely, the caprices of sign painters? Mostly, though, what I passed were outcrops from provinces only a student of Far Eastern geography, and not merely a Chinese food aficionado, would have heard of in the fifties. I wondered if these new restaurants, boasting their Hunanese or Szechuan origins, could possibly be as good of their kind as the more modest Cantonese and Mandarin establishments had been. I was not about to sample dumplings, however.

If the faces of the restaurants had changed, so also had the faces of the passersby. That there would be more Hispanic countenances I knew enough to expect; the many black faces failed to surprise me. What did catch me unawares was the poverty of nearly everyone's dress. And the pace of people: most of the people I passed walked more slowly than the West Siders I remembered; an unusually large number of them weren't actually walking at all, but rather just moving around. They were gathered in clusters, often not at the curb or storefront edges of the sidewalk, but casually straddling its middle. Some were there out of arrogance, I felt, others from obliviousness. Some were standing together, some were simply juxtaposed.

In my day—that phrase again, aging me each time I thought it—the interesting thing about the Columbia neighborhood (bordered, in my mind, by the Shanghai to the north and the Tip Toe Inn—that incomparable cole slaw!—at 86th Street to the south) was that it was so blatantly diverse not only ethnically but economically. There'd been plenty of upper-middle-class people living on the Drive and along West End Avenue in those days. For all I knew, they were all still there, entering and leaving their houses by stealth—and taxicab. They were not walking along Broadway this morning—except, just possibly, for that thirtyish woman who, a moment ago, came from behind me and was already half a block ahead. That outfit she was wearing could be a Loehmann's Anne Klein.

I stopped, wondering how far I'd come. I used, of course, to know at any point along this part of Broadway what two streets I was between. But too many familiar places had been replaced by strange ones. The street sign up ahead said 88th Street. Squinting hard, I could—just—read the clock above the bank at the corner of 86th Street. For some reason, I was unsurprised to find *it* functioning still. I was, however, slightly taken aback to discover that it was past eleven—11:11 the bulbs recounted prettily. I had better head back.

Turning right toward the Drive, I walked briskly. At the corner of Riverside Drive I turned north, acknowledging the Soldiers and Sailors Monument across the street. The pace I set I kept: what looking about I did, I did without slowing down.

The buildings along here were at the very least sturdy; several were little short of elegant. No longer immaculate, chipped here and there, sullied by graffiti, still they were not unimposing. Across the street, mothers sat on benches, paired for company, one ear cocked toward their adventuresome young, the other toward survival rations of conversation. Old people—there seemed to be so many in the old neighborhood—sat also in twos and threes. And svelte young men on their own, stopping occasionally to inveigle another dog walker to alter his direction. No social wasteland this, I decided. Broadway seemed more than two blocks away.

At the apartment door I hesitated, key in hand. If Margery was up and about, would my using the key impose on her the need to say something about having been asleep earlier? But if she was up, she'd have seen the note on the refrigerator and know I had a key and, if I didn't use it, that I was uncomfortable about something. Hell, I'd been asked to make myself at home, and here I was standing in the hallway subjecting myself to a syllogistic interrogation.

Before I closed the door behind me, Margery was there: dressed and made up, a cucumber in one hand, a vegetable peeler in the other. "I'm fixing lunch for us," she said brightly. "Just a gargantuan salad with Gorgonzola dressing. No bread, no dessert. A no-guilt meal." She grinned. "And then I thought you might like to go someplace? I'm free as a bird all afternoon," she added, turning back toward the kitchen.

I followed. Except for some slivers of red pepper which would keep, the salad fixings were not yet washed, torn, or sliced. "What fresh produce!" I said. "And I am sorry, I should have mentioned this to you yesterday, but I'm afraid I'm not free this afternoon." I felt unprepared still to mention the sitting to Margery—unprepared and dumb.

Dumb was worse. "I've an appointment to be photographed for the jacket of my new book this afternoon, and a luncheon engagement first with my editor, and dinner after."

Margery started, at once, to put the salad things away; but her disappointment was palpable. Braving it out, I said, "I've got a little time before I have to get dressed. How about a cup of coffee?"

When, after ten minutes, Margery hadn't even once referred to the photography session, I was so relieved that I did. "I don't much like being photographed," I said.

"Can't say I blame you, I never liked it either," said Margery. Who looked as lovely as any model? Who, always, in her photographs was smiling?

"Your face is so animated," Margery was saying, "you must make a wonderful subject."

"Margery, I haven't been photographed in years." I paused; said it. "I dread this session today."

"Someone as beautiful as you? The ways we concoct to torture ourselves," said Margery. "When did it start, this silliness of yours?"

When I knew you. While I knew you. "A while back," I said, managing a smile. And then I did see the humor in it: "There's this small gap in our ongoing conversation, isn't there?"

Margery nodded. "A small gap." She smiled too. "I was thinking this morning how little I know about your life now. When Sam was alive, even though I never met him, the fact of his presence in your life helped give me a picture—what life for a writer married to a professor in a small college town must be like."

"A pretty picture, yes? If not a fenced-in cottage, a small pretty house, modest but not too modest, on a nice, tree-lined street. Contented little teas with other faculty wives. Lots of solid intellectual conversation during social evenings with Sam's colleagues—"

"Whoa!" interrupted Margery. "Guilty, possibly, on the first two counts; but, darling Jessie, remember I've spent too many years married to a college professor myself to overrate the quality of conversation available during professorial dinner parties. How I've learned to despise the small-mindedness of academic specialists: their minds are so cluttered with the trivia of their expertise that there's no room for an adult amount of knowledgeability about fiction, or film, or who's got a chance at the presidency—unless, of course, it's the presidency of the college. Jessie, the boredom of it!"

"I have a feeling," I said, "we've been to some of the same dinner parties."

"I don't go anymore, actually," said Margery.

"Nor I. See, we do have things in common still." I smiled.

Margery looked about to say something . . . personal; but her expression retracted and she said, instead, "But up there, you could escape to the slopes. I used to love to ski. When I was at Miss Porter's, I used to go to Switzerland during Christmas break—it couldn't sound more frivolous to you than it does to me." But her eyes belied her deprecating tone.

"You were good," I said.

A moment. "Yes I was. But how did you know?"

"Oh, the gleam in your eye, I guess."

"Are you?" she asked, caught up.

"I *don't*. You know me, Margery, once I got walking right, I figured to quit while I was ahead."

"You give up too easily," she said intently, old enthusiasms lightening her face.

"Only on some things. Look, you're here in the city where there are ten thousand things to do—that *I* would do."

Slowly, she nodded. "Okay," she said.

But I was sorry I'd said it; something had switched off in her face. I prattled: "I don't mean to disclaim the prettiness of the snow, mind you—I like to look out at it, really. But once I'm out *in* it, I always seem to end up with wet feet."

"Don't you wear boots, ninny?"

"Of course. They just never manage to stand between the snow and my feet."

Margery laughed. "Thank you," she said.

I raised an eyebrow.

"For your wet feet. For not being—quite—perfect."

"Margery, what *are* you talking about?"

"Never mind," she said. "Tell me more about Hamilton."

I considered Hamilton for her. "It is lovely. And my house is pretty. It's a town of pretty houses. Not unlike a picture post card." I remembered. "Who in hell, I used to shout at my kitchen window, wants to live inside a picture post card? In some ways, Hamilton simply isn't real. A few years back, a black geologist joined the faculty. He stayed one year; his wife said there was no way she would allow her children to grow up in a town where black children were cute and quaint. I knew what she meant: I could have worn white leather gloves to the Grand Union my first years in town and not have passed for white." Remembering, I stopped. A shudder passed through me. In some ways, Hamilton was real enough to inflict pain.

"Say more," said Margery.

"I was different," I said. "I was just different from the other faculty wives. And differentness in a faculty wife was neither cute nor quaint. It was unacceptable."

"How were you different?"

"I was . . . opinionated: I had opinions, I expressed them. Unless your husband's tenure preceded the Korean War or thereabouts, you were not expected to express your opinions. Unless they were domestic. Concerning the stuff about which commercials are made. I've always read during commercials. But I had opinions—about things I knew about. I didn't know about dishwasher detergents or how to cut velvet; I knew something about national politics." I sighed. "Don't get me started. I have a long afternoon ahead of me in which I'm going to be expected to look on top of the world. A little peace with my world seems a prerequisite.

"Besides, Hamilton's not all bad. Not having people you want to talk to—to be with—does away with the temptation to do something other than work and recuperate and work some more. I don't work especially long hours but when I'm done, I take nearly as long to unwind as I spend writing. And what I really want to do when I'm working on a book but done work for the day is *nothing*. You know, people always talk about how lonely an occupation writing is. Nonsense!

Who but a writer gets to choose the company he keeps all day long? It is a quiet life. I must say it suits me . . . now."

"Before . . . before your husband died—I feel odd calling him Sam, since we never even met—anyway, then you weren't so alone?"

"Sure I was, or nearly. Sam was an old-fashioned kind of teacher. He *prepared:* even when he was teaching a course he'd been teaching for fifteen years, he prepared. And he kept up. He gave me what time he . . . deemed appropriate." I took a breath. "I don't blame him—I didn't. I married him largely because he was so paternal to me."

"He was much older, wasn't he?"

"Twenty-two years. It didn't seem like so much when I was twenty-five; seven or eight years later, it seemed . . . more."

"Did he pamper you?"

"Yes."

"That can't have felt all bad."

"No," I admitted. "But paternalism has its underbelly, as every minority finds out sooner or later, right?" From out of nowhere, it came to me, the smell of baking—and the anticipation of unpleasantness.

"I'll tell you a little story," I said. "We didn't have a decent bakery in town, so I would try, every so often, to bake a cake for dessert. I'd never baked before. I didn't like it, but I felt I should try. It's so mechanical—exact: so different from cooking. But I did try. Once, I got a few bits of eggshell in some white icing. Never, not once, after that, did I ever bake a cake with white icing but that Sam would ask, 'Is this with or without eggshells, darling?' If we were alone or if we had company. . . . And then he'd laugh, oh so nicely. And I'd want to break a box of eggs over his head."

Margery said, "You should have."

"Yes, you're right. If I had, he'd have stopped saying it. I let him go on saying it, didn't I? I conspired with him in that little joke of his." I sat there, thinking about how Sam had always made fun of me, too, because I never felt confident about changing the vacuum cleaner bag and he'd have to show me . . . again. "Being on my own now has its advantages. I never have mastered certain domestic arts, like changing the vacuum cleaner bag, but the lady who comes in to clean knows how. And she never says much of anything except, 'It's cold out today, good day to stay indoors.' Which it nearly always is —and I nearly always do, so I'm in her good graces."

"What about being alone so much of the time?"

"Well, it's not really all that different from when Sam was locked in his study every evening from right after the news until bedtime. I don't mind it, I guess."

"Lots of being alone, I don't like that," said Margery.

"You get used to it." Unthinkingly.

"I haven't."

She had, of course, been married to a professor a lot longer than I had; and she didn't have a profession of her own. But Margery seemed oblivious to my ineptitude. "I once met a nun," she said, "who came from a family that considered the Episcopal Church the only respectable one to which to belong. When she'd converted to Catholicism, they'd simply ostracized her. Maybe if they hadn't, she wouldn't have entered the convent. Who knows? Anyway, this friend of mine at Miss Porter's was her niece, and used to go visit her aunt in secret, and once I went with her. Making conversation, I asked about their routine. I was horrified to find out they got up at five twenty every morning—black of night in midwinter. Her eyes crinkled at my obvious dismay. She was so contented-looking, it made me ask her how long it had taken her to get used to getting up that early. I'll never forget the way she laughed; it didn't match the severity of her habit at all. 'Margery, my dear,' she said, 'I've been in for thirty-two years, and I haven't yet got used to it.' "

"Sounds like a lady who accepted the realities of her life," I said—and wished it unsaid.

"Maybe her faith made the difference," said Margery.

THURSDAY *81*

"Maybe having something—Someone—to believe in helped her get up all those mornings all those years."

"More likely it was a loud alarm clock," I said, because Margery was looking too discomposed for comfort.

"Right," said Margery. Exactly the right response in the correct tone.

Trapping me—because now she sat there, waiting for my next lame-brained remark. All right; who says you get off easy? I said, "Leo must be very involved with his students if he's teaching preceptorials. He probably doesn't even get paid for that. But, then, I expect he's the kind of teacher whose office hours are honored more in the breach than in the observance." I paused; Margery continued to wait, as patient as a wall. Finally, feeling coerced, I said, "That's hard for you, Leo being so caught up with his students?"

"They're the air he breathes," she said, resigned.

I'll bet they are, I thought. Leo, who had found inordinate satisfaction in the devotion of his coterie of peers twenty years ago at the West End must, these days, be mainlining student attention. Such attachment was not, in the unnatural course of events, implicit any longer in the teacher-student relationship. Whatever turns you on, I thought, although not without disdain.

Margery, whose intensity made her apparent psychic powers seem almost expected, said, "You can't blame him for being popular. It's not his fault he's an academic chameleon. As each student generation comes along, Leo seems, with no discernible effort, to learn their language. I don't mean merely their jargon. I mean he speaks to them as though he's from the same country they're coming from. It's a gift! And I don't blame him, I truly don't," Margery was rushing on, "for not hanging around here more. I mean it would take such an extraordinary *intention* for him to be here instead of there. And it's not exciting here, or interesting even . . . with Jon away."

I was convinced the remark about Jon was an afterthought, a covering over. Margery was looking at her hands; her fingers were forming a small figure from a piece of dampened rye bread. She worked attentively for a minute; she finished it: a nun in old-fashioned garb. The paragon, whose faith was sufficient—who, like me, had everything that counted?

"I really have to get ready," I said, "or I'll be later than someone who isn't famous yet can afford to be."

Margery looked up at me. "Thanks," she said, "for talking."

She said it as though I'd *given* her something. I waved my hand dismissively, and feeling slightly ashamed of how glad I was to be getting away, I left Margery studying the rye-bread nun.

I got myself together in triple time, not forgetting to use the eyelash curler. Just before leaving, I took a minute to ring up Shelley. "Hi," I said. "Look, forgive the shorthand but I'm running late. I wanted to check if we're still on for tonight."

"I'm counting on it," said Shelley.

"Me too," I said. "After that bloody sitting, I may need a friend."

"Need me or not, you got me."

"Where're we meeting?"

"Chez Levin. Peter insists on meeting you. Besides, I haven't cooked for you in a while."

"Sounds lovely. Can I come straight on over when I'm done?—not sure when that'll be, mind you."

"Sure," said Shelley.

"You are not only agreeable and efficient, but very pleasant to do business with, you know? See you."

"Jessie?"

"I've got to go. We'll have all evening to talk."

"All right, go. It'll be all right . . . probably."

"What will?"

"You're in a hurry."

"*Shelley!*"

"It's just that I—I thought I should mention—we've invited someone else, too. That's okay?"

"Why not?"

"You're not bad to do business with yourself. I know how you hate anyone butting into your pri—"

"This someone else is a *match?*"

"Maybe yes, maybe no, you're a free agent, right? Jessie, he's special. His name's—"

"Shelley, you invited him, you invited him. I *have* to go. See you later."

"You are coming?"

"I'm *coming.* I may not be staying."

I wasn't mad at Shelley, I was mad at me. All right, I was mad at her, too. But one reason she felt free to ask a man for me to meet was that she didn't know about Alec. Although Shelley and I talked on the phone at least once a month and I saw her practically every time I got down to the city, I had not even mentioned Alec to her. In more than a year? I'd better deal with *that* sometime.

But even if Shelley knew, so long as I didn't tell her it was battened down, that we were getting married, she'd be matchmaking. Having never been married, Shelley is an enthusiast for the institution and wants to commit everyone she knows to it except herself. For herself, she long ago decided that outpatient therapy, in the form of a string of short-term live-in lovers, was the preferred method of treatment.

2

There are some restaurants, like certain lighting arrangements, designed to flatter. Café des Artistes is not among these. None the less, it is among my favorite eating places. Its baldly hierarchical layout, working from the light, elegant front room, past the somewhat dim, definitely squeezed-in tables of the middle room, to the utilitarian three-booth bar at the back (to which those without reservations whom the maitre d' deigns to admit are relegated), immediately puts you in your place. As immutably as in prewar Poland. The waiters manage to convey that, if there were indeed justice in the world, you would be serving them instead of the reverse. Still, the women in the famous, slightly raunchy Howard Chandler Christy oils are as plump and sensuous as the desserts displayed in the front room. And the food almost never disappoints, rare in even the finest restaurants given the unionization of the kitchen class. As always, I entered with a sliver of anticipation.

I spotted Delia at once. Her dark suit was as unchanging

as her grey Dutch bob, and as unflattering to her thinness. She was sipping her customary martini. As I walked toward her, she signaled the waiter in a manner reestablishing the diner-waiter relationship nicely; virtually as I slid onto the banquette beside her, a cassis was placed before me.

"Hello," I said, and raised my glass. "What are we drinking to?"

"The new book, of course."

I shook my head. "Too late and too soon. We drank to it when I turned it in; next legitimate time is pub date, I think."

"I think not. There're going to be the book club sale, and paper rights, and maybe a movie sale," said Delia matter-of-factly, as though ticking off an errand list.

"You sound like Angela," I said, laughing.

"I very much doubt that," said Delia. "But it's time, I think, for all that. The manuscript's very good."

"Don't leave out your own fine hand," I said.

"It isn't my custom to minimize my contribution, but you're enough to make an editor entertain the possibility of the easy life."

"Thank you," I said. "To the easy life?" I raised my glass. Delia looked slightly skeptical, but then she nodded and we drank.

"I wasn't flattering you, I assume you know that," said Delia. "Your manuscripts, from the first, were clean—no scenes displaced, no major changes required. But the stories have gotten richer."

"Are you sure you haven't been here waiting for quite a while, Delia? You sound positively hyper."

She blushed; Delia Underwood blushed.

After a minute, I said, "Delia? What is it?"

"Whatever do you mean?" Sternly.

I almost stopped there. Delia, unlike Angela, never inquired into my private life; and she, so far as I knew, had none. But my intuition gave me a big shove. "I just have this feeling . . . there's something different about you."

"A little praise goes a long way toward overfeeding your imagination. My goodness, I must have been stingy with compliments these past years," said Delia.

"All right," I said, "you win. Don't tell me. I realize it isn't exactly my business—but, Delia, I wasn't just being nosy, I am very fond of you. Anyway, whatever it is, it agrees with you; and I'm awfully glad."

A single tear slipped down Delia's averted cheek into her martini. I'd been wrong, obviously, all wrong; and I'd hurt her. Instinctively, I touched her hand with mine, then pulled it back; one didn't go about patting Delia Underwood. But she grabbed my hand and held on, and said, "There's no way to escape the foolishness of it; it follows me everywhere."

I waited.

Delia returned my hand to me carefully and wiped her eyes with a handkerchief. Who besides Delia, I thought, carries an honest-to-God handkerchief in this day and age? Who besides Delia exposes her eyes to the world without rimming them with mascara and can, therefore, dab at them with impunity? I was, again, waiting.

But what Delia said was, "Let's order, shall we?" The subject was, apparently, closed. Delia ordered pâté and the sole. I ordered a shrimp cocktail.

"That's all?" Delia was up to sternness again.

"I'm saving myself for the mousse cake," I said.

"You eat like a bird," said Delia.

"You, my dear editor, blithe possessor of thin genes, know nothing about the price exacted for slimness from the rest of us."

She smiled, was all right. "You don't want me there this afternoon, I trust?" she asked.

"I wouldn't put it that way." I smiled, remembering Angela's predilection for taking any such wish personally.

"Of course not, but *I* may," said Delia. "I'll be in my office. If the photographer molests you, scream. Someone not totally absorbed is bound to hear you and summon me."

Our food came. Delia picked at her pâté and watched me reproachfully as I ate the shrimp I'd ordered. "All this merely to ensure your looking wan and glamorous for your jacket photo," she said.

"Glamorous? Yes, Delia, my expectation exactly."

"You'd be more glamorous with five pounds more on you," said Delia.

"Delia, has anyone ever told you you have the makings of a Jewish mother?"

She regarded me severely, then nodded. "My secretaries do, invariably. Is it a calumny?"

"Not in my book. In Philip Roth's, maybe."

The waiter removed our plates and brought Delia's sole. She ate one forkful, put down her fork. "I can't eat," she said.

I gave in. "All right, I'll order an omelet."

She shook her head. "It's got nothing to do with you. I'm just too nervous to eat."

The very idea of Delia Underwood nervous was untenable. She was serenity defined.

But not today. "You're sure you don't want to tell me?" I asked, turning on the seat toward her.

She looked at me for a full minute, then she sighed. "Yes," she said, "I'm afraid I do want to. You're sane and—you *won't* laugh at me?"

I could not imagine it, shook my head decisively.

"I'm getting married," she whispered. Gingerly, she raised her left hand. On her engagement finger, she wore an old-fashioned ring of rose diamonds. I hadn't noticed because it looked . . . like Delia.

"It was his mother's," she said shyly.

"It's beautiful," I said.

She looked at her hand. "A woman my age with an engagement ring." She shivered. "But he insisted."

It occurred to me that I didn't know how old Delia was. Fifty? Fifty-five? More? *Under* fifty? It was possible. In any case: "Oh, Delia, I'm so happy for you. I don't even know his name, but I just know he's marvelous."

"Yes," she admitted, "he is wonderful." She sighed "That's what makes it so hard to comprehend." She paused, then continued, trying to present the facts devoid of emotional coloration. "Jessie, he owns the bean store near my house. I've gone in there to buy fresh-ground coffee every Saturday for years. He and his wife ran it together. She was as nice as he was, a lovely-looking woman. So lively—friendly to everyone." Delia caught her breath. "She died last year. A month ago, Lawrence, that's Mr. Peters' first name, asked me to have dinner with him. I said no, of course. I mean, I couldn't see why. The next Saturday, he asked me again. It seemed rude to say no again, so I had dinner with him. And then again. Two weeks ago, he asked me to marry him."

I looked at her.

The tinge of suspicion in her eyes dissipated. Her chin began to quiver, but she gained control of herself. "I was married once, you know," she said.

I didn't, of course. I was sure no one who knew Delia professionally did—and I'd never considered that there might be people who knew her another way.

She nodded. "In a way I've had a . . . romantic life. It was during the war. He died in the Pacific. I hardly knew him. I have one snapshot of the two of us. I remember thinking him handsome." She sighed. "*Lawrence* is nice-looking—no, he's got a wonderful face."

"And he's a good person?"

"Oh yes!"

"That's marvelous!" Delia was twisting the ring. "Why on earth are you nervous, Delia? To think you wanted to drink to the book!"

"But what will people say, Jessie? He *is* terribly nice-looking. And he's six years younger than I am—and looks fifteen."

I made her look at me directly. "I should think," I said,

"that the fools will say, how lucky for you to have grabbed him up; and the wise ones will say, how lucky for Mr. Peters to have grabbed you up."

Her chin trembled again. "He wants to take me to Florence for our wedding trip. He says his daughter-in-law will take care of the store. If not, he says he'll *close* the store."

"My, he does sound sane," I said. "It's simply marvelous."

"You keep saying that," said Delia.

"Only because it is," I said.

A moment. "Oh!" said Delia. "Yes, it *is,* isn't it?"

3

He grinned with self-satisfaction. I felt my face close. He shook his head ruefully.

"Sorry," he said. "I know how you feel."

"Do you?"

"I don't like a lens aimed at my face," he said. "I get all self-conscious. I don't know what to do with my hands. Without a camera in my hands, they're . . . surplus. Don't you know? Everyone feels funny in front of a camera. Omit the egomaniacs and who's left—everyone!"

"You know, you're a nice man," I said.

"Yeah, I'm pretty nice, but it happens to be true. Actually, your face is extremely mobile."

He kept taking pictures.

"Like then—almost too mobile. I see something and before I can catch it, it's gone, and there's something else there."

"Sorry."

"Don't be." Dismissively.

"But don't you want to get a good picture?"

"I will." He stopped working the camera for a moment.

"How do you know?"

"Is your book good?"

I nodded.

"That's how I know. I take good pictures."

He was working again. His matter-of-factness was so different from what I'd anticipated. What? Solemnity, I guess. Bossiness, certainly; a certain amount of artistic pretentiousness. No solemnity, no bossiness, no pretensions. He approached the job, and me, directly, in a friendly way. But he didn't assault me with friendliness. This was business.

The first surprise occurred almost as soon as Delia introduced us and excused herself. He didn't begin by placing me. He started by talking about himself; where he lived, that one of his kids showed promise of being an Olympic-class swimmer, that he used to teach math in junior high school. Without thinking, I had sat down on the sofa; and, at some indefinable point, he had begun snapping pictures, while we went on talking.

"I never learned long division," I said. "I skipped 5A."

"Have you ever missed it—long division?"

"No." I laughed.

"So you didn't miss anything. In the town I grew up, there wasn't any skipping. By the time I got out of high school, I was ready to skip the whole town." He climbed up on Bagditch's desk.

I looked up at him. "Did you?"

"Good. No, my father taught at the local college and I got free tuition, so I decided to get myself a degree. But I left the week after graduation. I hated that town."

"Whereabouts was it?"

"A place called Clinton. Upstate. No reason you should have heard of it," he said, jumping down off the desk. He kept taking pictures.

"I live less than half an hour away," I said, smiling. "Hamilton. So you're a Hamilton graduate."

"Strangers never get that right, do they?" he said. "That Colgate's in Hamilton and Hamilton's in Clinton. You a teacher?"

"Not any more."

"World's nicer since I quit teaching," he said. "Yours?"

"Amen. Am I all right where I am?"

"Unless you're uncomfortable. You want to stand a while?"

"Would that work for you?"

"Why not?" Gerald said. His name was Gerald Van Vleck, and I knew him well enough now to believe him.

I walked around a minute or two, then settled down on the ledge of the bookshelves lining one wall. "This okay?"

"If it is with you, it is with me," he said.

I shook my head. "You sure there's film in that camera?"

Gerald lowered the camera again. "You feel better if I told you to tilt your head to the left a little?"

"Probably," I said.

"Okay then. Tilt your head to the left a little."

I didn't.

"Okay?" he said.

"Okay."

After a while I said, "I can see where permissiveness could be very hard on a child."

"With my kids I'm not permissive. I'm a tough father." He grinned. "But you're not a kid, right?"

I moved over to a chair and sat down. Five, ten minutes had passed, I suppose, when Gerald said, "Got it! Where *were* you? I know it's none of my business and if you don't feel like . . ." He shrugged.

"Riverside Park," I said. "About twenty years ago. This boy was taking my picture and then I took his. It was the Fourth of July. The national holiday I picked to lose my virginity. This was after. The pictures were commemorative snapshots." Gerald was taking pictures. "Won't my mouth be open in every one?" I asked.

"In some," he said. "We won't use them," he added mock reassuringly.

"Thanks."

Then, after a moment, "*That* smile was different. Still thinking about going to bed with that guy?"

"Of how shocked I was when I found out he never wore underwear." I laughed. "Sorry."

"Don't apologize for laughing, for Christ's sake," he said.

"Sorry. Oops, not sorry." I started to laugh again.

"Hey, Jessica, you want your picture taken?"

"Ask me that again," I said.

"Do you or don't you want your picture taken?" he said. "Moderation in all things, right?"

"Right. And I . . . want my picture taken, yes . . . moderately."

"So control yourself—but tell me what you were laughing at. *I'm* allowed to keep laughing."

"I was just wondering," I said, "if he still goes without underwear."

"Well, you'll never know," said Gerald. "You didn't marry the guy, did you?"

"You're right, I'll never know."

Was it possible that Leo, in his attempt to keep up with his students, still went without underwear? It wasn't likely, but it was possible. And it did not matter that I wouldn't ever know, did it?

"That's a new one," said Gerald, after a time. "You got more faces."

"What?" I said, coming back a distance.

"Expressions, you have a slew of them."

Don't keep telling me that, Gerald, huh? Please?

"Hey," he said, "that was a compliment."

"Yah," I said.

"That one just then? You were looking . . . sweet," he said.

"Was I? I was thinking about my mother, a photograph of her when she was eighteen, with a sailor collar and long thick braids. She was still in Russia. My mother was a stunning woman," I said.

"Not surprising," said Gerald. "Look, wait until you see these before you frown like that—and you won't."

He started taking down his lights. "You that mad?" I said.

He turned to me, hands on hips. "Not mad, done," he said.

"You're all finished?" I said.

"That's right."

"I'm done?"

"Not so terrible, was it?" he asked, very nicely.

He *was* a nice man. "No," I admitted, "not so terrible."

"Good. Come, I'll buy you a drink to celebrate."

I didn't answer.

But my face had its say. "A friendly offer for a friendly drink, nothing more. You in a rush, you don't want to, that's okay, too."

"You really think you got a good picture?" I asked.

"I'll tell you what. If you don't like the pictures, I'll teach you long division. For free. Fair enough?"

I laughed. "Suddenly I feel like celebrating," I said. "Got time for a drink?"

Shelley lived in what had been the parlor of a dilapidated brownstone on a block of largely unrenovated houses much like it. But inside her one huge, high-ceilinged room all was soft and lush, of an entirely personal opulence. There was, besides the one room, only a bathroom; along the wall abutting that a compact kitchen, open to the rest of the room, made no attempt to appear other than flagrantly functional. The long wall opposite, facing on the street, was broken by three tall windows, whose shutters were polished to a fare-thee-well. On the remaining walls hung several small rugs, quite worn, two of them silk, one particularly fine. The floor was bare of rugs, the parquet kept highly waxed. Set with its head against one of the rug-adorned walls was a huge brass bed of extraordinary grace and obvious antiquity. It was covered with a crocheted spread of creamy color and piled with lacy pillows. There was no sofa, no chairs; huge pillows of apricot velvet and Persian-printed melon cotton served for both. Against one wall stood Shelley's typewriter, as utilitarian as the sink. Above all, four plump cherubs smiled down, one from each corner of the room. I liked visiting it—and Shelley.

When I knocked on the door, it was opened by—presumably—Peter. Of over-ample girth, his round face encircled by masses of orange curls, he was clothed in a bright pink towel. He hugged me damply, said, "I'm Peter and I'll be right back," and disappeared into the bathroom.

"Come here!" commanded Shelley from her position at the sink. I went, as summoned; Shelley hugged me lavishly with garlicky hands, in one of which she held a cleaver.

"You," she exclaimed, stepping back a single step to regard me head-to-toe, "look like a Claire McCardell resurrection—or retrospective—or whatever Diana Vreeland would call it. Glorious! I love it! Turn for me." Obediently, I pirouetted in my grape-colored jersey dress. "One classy lady is my friend."

"And you," I said, "look, as always, ravishing." Shelley wore her fine light-brown hair long and kind of frizzy, a combination that I'd hate on anyone else. On Shelley it looked pre-Raphaelite. Over charmeuse pants of an eggplant shade she wore a thin cotton crocheted top with long wide sleeves. How she managed to cook in those sleeves. . . . But Shelley could. Around her neck hung a huge carnelian pendant on a heavy gold chain.

"Beside you, I feel dressed for a board meeting," I lamented.

"My work clothes," said Shelley dismissively; and, knowing Shelley, it was not necessarily a fib. "Now tell all! The photographer is building his next one-man show around pictures of you, right?"

"Not quite," I said. "But, you know, it did go all right, I think."

"*I* think," said Shelley, to whom I had confided my fears when Delia first announced that I would be photographed.

"Do you?"

"Uh huh." She kissed me.

"I'm still glad it's over," I said.

"That's not the *question*," said Shelley, and waited.

"All right," I admitted. "I'm glad I didn't chicken out."

"Me too," said Shelley, "because I want a copy."

"Why on earth?"

"Because, old friend, I do forget between times how beautiful you've grown."

"You're ridiculous, you know?" But I hugged her. "You smell like a sexy almond. What is it?"

"Amaretto." Throwaway.

"Shelley, even you wouldn't wear a liqueur."

"It's alcohol, isn't it? And it smells good. *Much* cheaper than perfume."

"And if Peter kisses your neck, he doesn't feel his tongue wandered into a medicine cabinet, right?"

"You've got potential, I keep telling you," said Shelley as Peter emerged from the bathroom wearing corduroys, silky fuzz curling on his chest. He had taken awhile, I thought, to put not much on. He looked as though he might be a cousin, once removed, of the cherubs on the ceiling; he did not look sexy. I gave it a focused thirty seconds; no, I could not imagine Peter as a lover. But then, Shelley's men never looked like lovers to me. More like . . . cuddly toys. A thought, there.

Interrupted, without regret on my part, by the arrival of the man who was to round out, or square off, our evening. Dario, Shelley whispered to me as Peter went to the door, was an Italian poet-banker. I wondered, for a moment, if that was anything like an Italian city-state. But only until after we were introduced. There was nothing archaic about Dario. If he wore dark pinstripes, he lowered himself unfretfully onto Shelley's pillows. Dario was not tall and his hair was thinner than the rest of him, but he wasn't cuddly. Dario was definitely not cuddly. That much I concluded before the soup.

Shelley's wonton soup was egregiously rich, more like Jewish chicken soup than Chinese; but her homemade wonton were not ersatz *knaidlach*. They were properly plump with pork and very flavorful; they commanded attentiveness.

So did Dario. He used his eyes like hands; but not flagrantly and not offensively, certainly. He let me know that he approved of me; he did not move in for the kill.

After dinner, in which cucumber played a major role in the first dish and bean curd in the second and third—but which was good anyway—Peter suggested a Scrabble tournament. It seemed a relaxed alternative to discussing banking or the publishing trade. Peter and Shelley each having brought a Scrabble game to their ménage, we paired off. The men played each other while Shelley and I played. Peter won against Dario and Shelley beat me by sixty points. Then Shelley and Peter played each other while Dario and I watched.

It was something to watch: the transformation of two apparently loving persons into feral combatants. They played excruciatingly slowly and with lethal attentiveness. They didn't speak; nor did we, which seemed other than natural to me. Still, in the silence, Dario and I were drawn together in circumstantial intimacy, like two strangers who are witnesses to the same accident. By the end of the game, we had shared discomfort, dismay, and embarrassment. When at long last it was over, Peter vanquishing a livid Shelley by fifteen points, a brief glance between us established a mutual intention to get the hell out of there before the post-game frivolities could begin. I said I felt tired suddenly, it must be all the fresh city air, and that I'd call Shelley soon. Dario apparently didn't feel obliged to offer any excuse.

In the street, having determined that I was headed uptown and he crosstown, Dario assumed he would drop me off anyway. But first, he asked, did I feel like a cup of coffee to counteract the pale tea we'd been inundated with all evening? When I said, I sure would, he did not seek out a stylish coffee house, of which there were surely some in the area, but led me into the first clean place we came upon.

Over a formica table and matching mugs of black coffee, Dario said, "Whew!"

"Shelley *said* you were a poet as well as a banker."

"Do they often lock in mortal combat like that?" asked Dario.

"I generally see Shelley alone," I said. "Peter is rather new. I must say, over the phone she extolled him. I assumed you were the family friend."

Dario shook his head. He held the mug with both hands; his fingers were long and slim. "I barely know either of them. I work in the bank Shelley uses. I'm her banker—at least that's how comprehensively she views our professional relationship. Shelley, being Shelley, couldn't turn in a roll of pennies without establishing a relationship with the teller."

"For someone who claims hardly to know her, you're doing all right." I laughed, but I added, "We've been friends for twenty years," to warn him off criticizing her too much.

"I hope she and I will be. I like her enormously," said Dario undefensively. "I was simply making clear that as of now we are far from old friends. I'd never been to their place before. I did meet Peter once. She brought him into the bank to introduce him to me—I mean, that's literally why she came into the bank that day. She didn't even pretend to need two fives for a ten. And, of course, I knew all about their relationship before that."

I shook my head, smiling. "Neither of us knew all about that," I said.

Dario's eyes were potent: the deepest brown, bright as enamel without its hardness. "If things are like that between them, why do you think they invited us?"

"Maybe their relationship's to the point where they need an audience."

"Not a very flattering reason to be asked," said Dario. His teeth, against his dark complexion, didn't look real; but I was willing to bet they were.

"It wasn't the only reason you were asked," I said.

Dario frowned. The frown eased, and he smiled, slowly. "That's flattering."

"Thank you," I said. "You've *been* married, I gather?"

"It shows?" said Dario.

"Of course," I said. "No, but Shelley would have ascertained your present marital status. The rest was an educated guess."

"Educate me some more about Shelley and marriage. If tonight was her idea of mar—"

"Don't think so. She's terribly pro-marriage; terribly idealistic about it. She wants all the nice unmarried people who enter her line of vision to be paired off nuptially."

"She once had a happy marriage?"

"No."

"Tell me what I'm missing," said Dario.

"Shelley," I said, "thinks of marriage as something eminently sensible for other people—like a lease. Shelley won't live in an apartment where a lease is required, although she's lived in the same apartment for eight years now at least. She claims she needs to be able to move on, if the spirit should move her—"

"So to speak," said Dario.

"So to speak." I smiled. "Without being imprisoned by a piece of paper."

"So she's never been married?"

"Exactly."

"You have," said Dario.

"I have, yes," I said.

"I'm divorced, too," he said, "but you guessed that." Smiling, he added, "I have a sensational little girl, Andrea." He gave it the Italian pronunciation.

"How old is she?"

"Eight, going on seventeen. She's going to have to be watched," said Dario. "Do you have children?"

"No."

"That's a shame," said Dario. Then: "I'm sorry. But they are the beginning."

I raised an eyebrow.

"You require precision," said Dario. "All right, Andrea was the beginning of me. I was, before her birth, a most unserious person."

"Are you very serious now?"

"Only when it's appropriate," Dario said.

"I thought as much. Tell me, why did you decide to leave her?"

"You mean Andrea."

"Of course."

"What an extraordinary way to put it. But of course that was what it felt like. My wife and I had . . . left each other long before we separated." He paused, signaled the waitress for two more coffees.

"None for me, thanks," I said.

He signaled the waitress again, canceling. "I don't want more, either," he said. "It was a way to stay a little longer, talking."

"I'm in no hurry," I said.

"Good." He paused; thinking again. "I left Andrea—you still want to know?"

"Of course."

"I left because she was beginning to think of me as an unhappy man. It made her sad. Now she isn't. Julie—my former wife—she's a very good mother. And I *am* around. I'm not just a Sunday-go-to-the-zoo father."

"I'm sure you're not," I said sincerely to this very nice, undeniably sexy man sitting across the formica tabletop from me.

"How long have you been divorced?" he asked.

I set him straight. "He died four years ago," I concluded. "It was sudden—which was wonderful for him. He was never dying: he was alive and then he was dead. For me, that made it take a little time. But in four years . . ."

"Yes." Dario nodded. "I can see you're no longer in mourning." Those enamel eyes were, incredibly, shot with gold now. I never knew gold was a magnet. "And your life is . . . satisfying?"

"Yes." I smiled. "Although most people might not find it so. But you write yourself, so you know."

"Yes, but it's more than your writing. The rest of your life is . . ."

I nodded. "It's fine," I said, thinking, I should say something about Alec; this is the moment. But what? Besides, it seemed . . . presumptuous.

"I thought so," Dario said. The moment was gone. He paid the check and we went out onto Broadway. He hailed a cab, relaying the Mellsons' address. In the taxi, we were quiet. For me it is a habit left over from the pre-partition days; I could never see talking as though the driver, a person with two ears, simply weren't there. I didn't know Dario's reasons.

When the driver pulled up in front of the Mellsons', Dario gave him enough to cover the meter and asked him to leave it running, he'd be right back. In the hallway, in the elevator, we didn't speak. I was beginning to feel uncomfortable. At the door to the apartment, I said, "What makes you think the cabbie will wait?"

"I didn't give him a tip," said Dario.

"That's ingenious," I said. "Did the poet or the banker figure that out?"

"Take your choice," he said lightly.

Which made me feel uncomfortable again. I was floundering for something to say, when Dario said, "I want to say something to you. No—wait. Listen to me. If I was invited tonight especially to meet you, I'm glad. I am glad I met you. You're a lovely, lively woman; and I would very much like to see you again. But I'm not going to ask how long you're going to be in town, or give you my number for when you get in again. Your—our—friend Shelley has incomplete dossiers on her friends; even, apparently, ones of twenty years' standing. Because you're obviously a lady who's taken." He didn't wait for an answer; he had no question. He bent, kissed me softly, without haste, on the lips, and got back into the elevator.

Quietly, my hands the least bit shaky, I let myself into the apartment. In the living room, by the light of a small TV set recessed in the bookcased wall, I saw Margery. I didn't really feel like seeing Margery just then, but I couldn't just walk on past her without a word.

Pausing in the door of the room, I said, "Hi."

Her head turned slightly toward me; her eyes stopped at the edge of the set, clinging there, as she said, "Hello, Jessie." In her hand, a fragrant cup of coffee tipped, spilling a few drops on her skirt. I moved toward her. "It's nothing," she said, eternally rejecting help. I stepped back. She said: "Forgive me, I'm awfully tired but I just can't bear to turn this off. It's Preston Sturges. Your day went well?"

"Yes, fine."

"Good. Tomorrow, you'll have to tell me all about it." There was, between us, a brand new wall.

"Yes," I said. "Good night."

I had started down the hall when she said, "You had a

call." I backed up three steps to the door of the living room. "A man." Margery said, still not looking at me.

Her voice was formal, or angry. "Was there a message?"

"Just to tell you Alec called."

It *was* too late to telephone a strange house; that must be it. "Did he just call?"

"No, much earlier." Her attention was fully on the TV screen again. I couldn't, in the reflected light, read her expression. Did I, now, think I could read Margery's face at will, anyway? Unlike mine, it didn't speak to strangers . . . or long-out-of-touch friends. Just as well, probably; the woman deserved some privacy in her own house.

"Thank you," I said. "Good night."

Margery nodded. I walked back to my room. Passing their bedroom on the way, I saw through the partially open door that Leo was lying atop the bed, reading. I tiptoed past, gratefully closing the door to my room, and undressed.

I sat on the bed for some minutes before I dialed the operator and, charging it to my home number, put a call through to Alec.

He answered promptly. The only phone in his house was in the big main room, on the floor near his easy chair. "You weren't asleep," I said. "Good."

"Hi," he said.

"High enough."

"It went well."

"Somehow, yes," I said.

"Lucky guy, that photographer."

"Luck had nothing to do with it," I said. "The man has a real gift."

"I certainly hope so, if he earns his living that way."

"I meant for getting you to relax. He was relentlessly matter-of-fact. You can't fight that."

"Even you?"

"Even me," I said.

"You fought off my compliment."

"Me? Never. I must have missed it. Do I get another shot?"

"Why not?" said Alec. "Lucky photographer."

"Oh. Thanks, flatterer."

"For a writer," Alec said, "you ought to check into the difference between a compliment and flattery sometime soon. But not tonight. Get some sleep. I only wanted to say hello."

"Me too. I'm glad you called."

"I'm glad *you* called," Alec said.

"Good night—wait!"

"I'm here."

"I got your note. I . . . read it once or twice. Thanks."

"Okay." The sheer primary niceness of him.

"I *like* you," I said.

"Sleep," said Alec.

But I didn't sleep, not right away. Alec hadn't asked me about the rest of my day, I hadn't asked about his. That wasn't the sort of question we asked each other; although, if something interesting had happened, we'd usually report it. There was no sense that we should account for our time. And I didn't feel that I had to account to Alec for this evening, for Dario. What had happened, what Dario had said at the door, was interesting. Yet I couldn't tell him that, it wouldn't make sense, without telling Alec about the entire evening—which included how attractive I found Dario. I wanted to think about whether to tell Alec about that; but I already knew that, without that fact, the story wasn't *whole*. And I felt that, if I told Alec, it should be when we were together. When he would be able to read in my face that I wasn't so much telling as sharing, and why.

Why was what I had learned tonight. Dario had caught me unawares, but he had been right. If he had asked to see me again, I would have said no. And that surprised me. In the year I'd been seeing Alec, I hadn't considered that question. I hadn't had any reason to: I hadn't met a man I found particularly attractive, and to consider the question abstractly had never occurred to me. I'm not good at abstract questions;

frankly, they don't interest me very much. But Dario wasn't abstract, or theoretical: he was real, and I found him enormously appealing. Yet he knew, before I did, that I wouldn't go out with him. He sensed that I was . . . what? Taken, he'd said. An expression. He meant committed. An even less comfortable expression.

But true?

True. Without any discussion with Alec or even with myself, certainly without any promises asked or given, I had, somewhere along the way, made some sort of, okay, commitment, to Alec. As a word, exclusivity sounded heavy to me; as an attitude, it came naturally. And I suppose having arrived at it, however unconsciously, it made *me* natural and easy with Dario. That, my easiness with him, must have been his clue. Uneasy first encounters, dozens and dozens of them, waved like flags of affirmation in my mind.

Which drifted, then, to a first meeting I'd come close, because of uneasiness, to not letting happen. It was during a business trip to the city, a little over a year ago, a year ago March. I was in an audio store, torn between the tape deck I'd come in to buy and another one the salesman was pitching. When the salesman went to take a phone call, I headed for the door, unwilling to succumb to his pressure, unable to resist it and insist on the deck my modest research had indicated was the one I needed.

"You don't have to get it somewhere else," a voice said.

Not used to having my mind read, I stopped in my tracks.

"I wasn't reading your mind," he said, doing it again.

"No?" I said.

"No. It's only human nature, what you're doing. Incidentally, from what I've read, you're right about which deck to get. And even if that guy is coming on to you strong, their price is right, too. So why not buy what you want and let him hassle someone else without denying yourself the benefit of their good price?"

He smiled this dynamite smile and then *he* walked out of the store, leaving me with my mouth ajar and, ten minutes later, the tape deck I'd come in for going out UPS to my home.

A little while later, estimating that I had nearly three hours to kill before dinner at Angela's, I decided to reward myself for sticking up for my consumer rights (with a little help from an anonymous browser that was already receding in my mind) by seeing the latest Louis Malle film before the after-work deluge.

Even now, though, ten minutes before the five o'clock showing, there was a line. I'd given up waiting in line to see a film about the time Radio City Music Hall stopped playing Greer Garson movies, but I figured ten minutes wouldn't be long enough to make a hunchback of that particular principle, and joined the line.

"Hello again," he said, a minute or two later.

He was standing directly in front of me in line.

"You following me?" I said, and I suppose I have said something baldly stupider in my life.

"Afraid not," he said, smiling.

I raised my left eyebrow.

He smiled again. I did wish he wouldn't keep doing that. It was like a boxer hitting an ordinary person and calling it a fair fight: that smile constituted a lethal weapon. He said, "If I were, I'd have prepared something terribly clever to say by now."

I had to admit it. "I think you said it already, back at the audio store. You left without my thanking you."

"You bought the JVC," he said.

"Of course," I said, not smiling. "It was what I knew I wanted, wasn't it?"

"Not everyone has that head start," he said. "It's a big help, isn't it?"

He didn't try to pay for my ticket.

He didn't talk during the movie, or edge close.

Afterward, we had coffee at a counter place. I paid for mine.

Then I called Angela, who said leftover pot roast was used to being turned down when something better turned up.

We had dinner; somewhere.

I didn't try to pay for my dinner.

By then, he knew that I came to the city only about three times a year; and I knew that he came down only about once a year; and we were beginning to feel more than a little lucky. But by then we also knew that we lived more than a five-hour trip from where we were—and from each other.

"That sounds like a triangle," I said.

"Easier than some to solve," he said, telling me there wasn't anyone else in his life.

I nodded. I knew it already; my gut had told me so, but the confirmation was welcome.

After dinner, we walked around, like kids with no place to go. I couldn't take him back to Angela's. He didn't suggest taking me back to his hotel.

Finally, I did. "It'll be all right, I think."

"Are you sure?" he asked.

"No, but we can't keep walking around all night."

I was wrong. It wasn't all right. It was firecrackers emblazoning a velvet sky. The Fourth of July all over again.

Only better.

The next morning, when we said good-bye, there was no question that that would be all there would be. Because there was no question, it didn't need to be said. He put me in a cab for the airport and kissed my nose through the lowered window. I didn't cry until he was out of sight, and then only from the blissful exhaustion of having so much joy flung at me. My arms ached from stretching.

I slept on the plane; and, when I got home, I took a nap. When Alec telephoned, waking me, to say he was home, too, and hello!, I felt immediately more thoroughly awake than I'd ever thought possible.

Yet it wasn't all that different, the feeling, from what I felt now: tired, warm, and good in myself, unashamedly fond of Dario whom I'd never see again, and close in to Alec whom I'd be seeing soon, and again, and again. I slept.

This time, when the sounds awakened me, there was no confusion about their source. Directly outside my door, Leo and Margery were quarreling.

"I want to talk to her! Let go of me, I want to talk to her!" Margery was protesting.

"She's asleep." Leo was whispering, trying to lower *her* voice. "You told me she had a long day."

"Only for a few minutes. I only need to talk for a few minutes!"

"Talk to me," said Leo. "Come into the bedroom and talk to me."

"Why do you always ask the impossible of me?" Margery cried out. "You hardly ever ask me for anything—and then only if it's impossible." Her pain cut through the wood of the door like a karate chop.

"I'm sorry," Leo was saying. "Can't you try to talk to me?"

"You're sorry!" scoffed Margery. "For how many years now have you been sorry?"

"For a long time, Margery. For a lot, and for a long time. You know that."

"But she doesn't!" Margery's voice held a shrill note of triumph now. "She doesn't know what you've got to be sorry for, does she? That's why we've got to talk. Don't you see?" She was sinking, not her voice, but her tone. *"How* can I talk to you—when it's about you I have to talk? Don't you know that's what I have to tell Jessie—about you!"

THURSDAY

Leo said, "Tell her tomorrow. Whatever you want to tell Jessie about me, whatever it is you think she should know, will still be there to tell tomorrow. Margery, please, come to bed. I promise, I'll stay up with you as long as you want. I'll read to you."

"In that voice generations of students have crammed classrooms to hear?" How she despised him.

"Yes, Margery, in that voice," Leo was saying, seeming to accept the spittle without wiping his face. "But just for you. Let me read to you, Margery."

"And hold me?" The *scorn* in her tone. I cringed.

But Leo's voice contained no cringing. "If you want me to," he said plainly.

"Don't you dare condescend to me!"

"I'm sorry," said Leo. "Can I, may I, read to you?"

"All right."

"Come," said Leo. "Come, let's go to our room."

"You'll doze off!"

"You know I won't."

"Yes, that's right, you won't. Even if you have to dig your nails into your palms, you'll stay awake, won't you? Such a *perfect* husband."

"Margery, what would you like me to read from?" I could hear shifting around, as though Leo were positioning her better in order to help her down the hall.

"Anything I want, right?"

"Whatever you want."

"I think," said Margery, beginning to move with him, "I'd like to hear . . . something dirty. Something really dirty."

"All right." Leo sighed. "Come lean on me. Get into bed and I'll find what you want. That's it, Margery, come, dear. I know what book you want."

Shuffling sounds, fading. And a door closed.

FRIDAY

1

Leo was mixing eggs when I came into the kitchen. "Onions or cheese in your omelet?" he asked.

I was taken aback: to find him home, in the kitchen preparing food, acting normal. Each part of that, all of it, surprised me. The actual question he had asked was lost on me.

"I'm making one anyway," he said. That much was plain to see. "All right," he continued, "you don't like to make crucial decisions this early in the day, I'll choose. Onions. All right?"

There was such a transparent wish to *go on* in his face that I said, "I love onion omelets—and I'm famished."

A few minutes later, we were seated across from each other at the dining room table. Buttering toast, Leo said, "On my one weekday morning home, I like a big breakfast. Usually, I skip breakfast altogether. I'm off by eight most mornings, and anyone who eats before that hour is a cannibal in my view."

I bit into a forkful of omelet. The eggs were properly runny inside, the onions fried enough, but not enough to lose their crunchiness. "You make a mean omelet," I offered.

"Coming from you, that's a special compliment," said Leo.

"Why?"

"You know better than most that I once wouldn't wipe an omelet pan out, let alone make an omelet."

There was no come-on in his voice. I didn't feel the need to pretend I'd missed the reference. "Leo," I said, "that was a lifetime ago."

"You always had a way with words," he said quietly, his eyes focused on the slice of toast in his hand.

I didn't understand that, not for sure; but it seemed an opening. "Leo," I began, making sure my tone confirmed my words, "I don't mean to pry. I don't want to pry. But has Margery's insomnia been going on a long time?"

Leo chewed a bite of toast, slowly, his eyes intent on mine. Then he shook his head, although his mouth was free to speak.

"If it's a recent thing, not a chronic condition, couldn't something perhaps be done about it?"

Leo didn't answer.

"Has she seen a doctor?"

He shook his head again. Then, after a moment, "It'll pass."

"There's a pattern then," I said, relieved. "It comes and goes?"

"Don't concern yourself, Jessie." A stern . . . plea.

"Okay." Rebuffed; put off, and feeling it. Feeling, at the same time, unrelieved. Why? I repeated myself. "So long as that's all it is, a sporadic insomnia, I won't worry."

"More coffee?" Leo, rising, reached for my cup.

"Thanks."

When he came back from the kitchen, he said, "We've all changed."

He had decided to tell me, after all. I waited.

"I'm growing bald and you've grown beautiful," he said.

Expectation sank. I stirred my coffee.

"And I've been writing a book for nine years," Leo said, "while you've written four in less time."

"Paces differ," I said. "I don't do anything else. Besides, I don't have to do any research. My work isn't scholarly."

"Mine won't break any academic sound barriers, I'm afraid." A rueful smile. He leaned across the table toward me. "Your books are good, Jessie. I've read two of them twice; they hold up. I'm . . . proud of you." He laughed. "What a presumptuous way to put it!"

Not all that presumptuous; but I said, instead, "On good days, I'm a little proud of myself. Of course, on days when I only manage to eke out a couple of pages in five hours, I'm not proud—and not glad to be a writer."

"Glad or not, good days and bad alike, you are one—and that's what matters." A pause. Firmly: "You've made something of your life, Jessie."

I finished the last bit of omelet before I was sure I wanted to say it. "You can take some of the credit for that."

His hurt was so quick, so strong, that I blinked. "Leo," I said, "you misunderstood. I mean it. You had the brightest mind I'd ever come across. You put me on my mettle. You see, if you picked me, if you talked to me, I had to have the beginnings of something to work with. And so . . . after . . . I began to test *myself*. The effort you put into each line of your poetry, I kept that image in my mind for years. Even now"— I paused, not wanting to layer flattery on truth—"yes, even now, I sometimes *use* my memory of the intensity with which you sought the word that would look, afterward, so natural in that place that no one, except perhaps another poet, would guess how many others you'd discarded before you found it."

What, I wondered, had happened to all the bad feelings I'd been reliving on the plane? Obviously, they had nothing to do with the man in front of me. But they also seemed to have, now, little enough to do with the boy he'd been—whom I had loved.

"Excuse me?" I said, coming back.

"I said, I haven't written a poem in ten years," said Leo. I didn't know what to say, except, "I'm sorry."

"Don't be," he said. "If there were poems in me, I'd be writing them, wouldn't I?" He looked as if a weight were off him. Having told me?

He said: "I dreaded your coming," a quivering smile relieving the sadness of his face.

"I dreaded coming," I said. My smile wasn't terribly steady either.

"Margery was so beautiful," he said, explaining needlessly.

"And shining and funny and glorious. I know," I said.

The sadness suffused his face once more. "It isn't my imagination, then?"

"How she was? No, Leo, I was also smitten with her. No one who knew Margery was entirely immune."

"Jessie," he said, bending toward me intently, "you mustn't . . . misunderstand. Margery isn't herself right now." He looked away from me.

"It's all right, Leo," I said.

Bravely, he looked at me straight; but his courage faltered, and he looked down again as he said, "Is it?"

He stood then, gathered dishes. "I didn't want you to see her . . ." He walked toward the kitchen; I followed. He placed the dishes on the sink. His back toward me, he said, "I tried to talk her out of asking you. Hell"—he turned, and for the merest second he had the carriage of the old Leo—"I didn't want you to see me."

Embarrassment overtook him. I moved closer. "Leo." He made himself look at me. "I'm glad to see you."

Face to face, then, he asked it. "Jessie, all these years. . . . When did you forgive me?"

Having come this close, there wasn't much point in holding back now. "A few minutes ago," I said.

He laughed then. "At least all that time I spent during the years wishing you knew how sorry I was—wasn't wasted, then, in the end," he said. "You do know."

116 GETTING TOGETHER

"I know," I said. "But"—briskly—"it's over now, and that's a good way to start a day. Now, I'm going for a short walk to work off that sumptuous breakfast. And then I'm going to look over my Barnard talk. It's ready, but I might want to work over parts of it again."

Leo said, "I work at home all day today. Want some company on your walk? I could use an airing myself before I settle down."

"Thanks, Leo, but I don't think so. I like to walk by myself."

He nodded. "Tell me one secret," he said. "Don't frown, you won't mind. Tell me how many years it took you to get this way?"

"I don't know what you—" I stopped myself. "Every one of them," I said.

"Thanks," said Leo.

2

Returning to the apartment an hour later, I found the door to Margery's bedroom still closed. Leo was working in his den at the very back of the apartment. I quietly closed the door to my own room and took out my speech. Shedding my shoes, I lay down on the bed and read it through. It seemed to me to read well—which meant I had to find something else to do to keep my mind off what I'd heard the previous night.

I decided to write to Alec. A letter would be evidence—circumstantial, at least—that I had not brought my typewriter along merely as an exercise in compulsive behavior. Why was I rationalizing? What was wrong with my plain wanting to write to him?

But the sheet in the typewriter stayed blank as I discarded possible subjects. There was, again, Dario: except that I would probably end up saying too little for fear of saying too much. Dario would have to be, I concluded all over again, not a story but a conversation. Leo? Yes, except that this was to be a letter, not a dissertation. Where to begin, when I had never once said *anything* about Leo to Alec? Putting him in context now seemed a formidable task. And if I went to that length, what would I say next? What could one say about Leo today that might compare in intensity with an account of Leo past? That he combed the hair on top of his head sideways to hide a bald spot? That his face was grooved with disappointments? That he was part of—party to—an apparently contorted, exhausting marriage? That he had grown a little humble, but was still hobbled by stumps of pride? Maybe, one day, one long quiet day, I would tell Alec all about Leo, but not today, not in this letter. I considered the paper; I had not got beyond "Alec, dear."

Margery. All right, Margery. Maybe writing about her would help. When I had tried to describe her to Alec a couple of times the day before I left, he had said that no one could be that gorgeous, and I had insisted that Margery was *that* gorgeous. So I began by describing how Margery looked. As for how she had otherwise changed, I said that she seemed strained, ill at ease—not so much with me, I thought, as with life in general. Margery seemed, I wrote, dissatisfied in a measure that repudiated any connection with the women's movement or the turning-forty malaise which overcomes certain beautiful women. I was, I admitted, curious to know more about the source of her obvious distress. I was also afraid of being caught up in her unhappiness somehow. Alec, knowing my susceptibility, my tendency to get *too* caught up, would understand that, and not think me unfeeling. I cut the letter short; both it and I were getting too involved at this point.

Writing the letter had clarified nothing so far as I could see. And as a letter it wasn't much, but I decided to send it off anyway. It would give Alec and me a starting point for the long, long talk I was beginning to be certain I'd feel the need to have when this visit was over.

When I came back up from mailing it, I could hear Margery in the kitchen. No point in delaying our encounter, I thought. She was leaning against the sink, drinking a cup of coffee. She held it in both hands, which struck me as an odd mannerism in someone so properly brought up.

"Hi," I said.

"Good morning." It was, in fact, a quarter past twelve—we glanced at the kitchen clock simultaneously. But she made no apology for the hour, nor offered any apologia. That helped.

"Does lunch interest you—or are you busy again today?" she asked. There was a smile tagged onto the question—and her face.

I wasn't even remotely hungry after Leo's omelet, but Margery, her thinness italicized by her thin robe, looked as if she could use some sustenance; also some company. It seemed the least I could do. "I'd love to have lunch somewhere with you, but it'll have to be a place I can get a salad made mostly of air. I had a big breakfast." There was no reason to keep it a secret—I didn't want to keep it a secret. This house had a surfeit of secrets already.

"Leo made an omelet for us," I explained.

Unmistakably, her face tightened. Her eyes bulged slightly, like muscles against restraints; but her voice bespoke control. She said, "Well, we won't go to an eggy place, then."

How tempted I was to tell her, just *tell* her, that Leo hadn't given her away. That I had asked him, but he had been loyal, had said nothing. How could I tell her I knew nothing without acknowledging that I was aware there had to be something to know? Still, pride demanded that I say—somehow—that nothing personal had transpired between Leo and me. "Perhaps Leo would like to come along," I said. Surely, I wouldn't suggest that if . . .

Margery smiled a smile overhung with tolerance, like clothes weighing down a line. "Oh, Jessie," she said, "Leo hasn't eaten lunch in fifteen years."

Had I made my point? No way of knowing. Besides, the same pride that urged me to make it once argued as firmly against making it more than once. "It'll be just us, then," I said. "When would you like to get going? Maybe you'd help me do a bit of shopping after? I'd like to pick up a present for a friend of mine, something terribly elegant he'll probably never wear."

"What fun," said Margery, refilling her coffee cup. "How about you? No need to rush right out, is there?"

"None. I think I'll join you in a cup," I said, thinking the later we lunched the better.

She poured for me, then led the way into the living room. After we'd settled down, she said, "The friend we're going shopping for, is he the one who called you here?"

I thought, Why not tell her about Alec? It seemed a safe enough subject. I wouldn't say too much; I wouldn't make him sound too wonderful. "Umm." I nodded. "His name's Alec Klady."

"Alexander," said Margery. "A handsome name, a strong name."

"Yes," I said, "I rather feel that way, too, but Alec never uses it."

"What does he do?"

"Oh, a whole batch of things, most of them well. I'm rather fond of him," I said.

"I will be sure to take that into consideration," said Margery, her eyes brightening. "Give me an admittedly prejudiced for instance."

"He plays the piano well," I said. "Not concertizing-well, but really rather marvelously. Scarlatti, much of the time, when I'm around: for me. When I was a teenager, I used to daydream that someday I'd learn to play the piano just well enough to play Scarlatti." I laughed. "It never occurred to me that that was like thinking I'd take up tennis just until I got good enough to play Wimbledon."

"He doesn't play Scarlatti for a living, I gather," said Margery.

"Hardly."

"But he does something, one of those many things he does superbly, for a living?"

"He pilots a ferryboat across Lake Champlain," I said.

"That sounds almost as romantic as playing Scarlatti," said Margery. "Is it as storybook as it sounds?"

"No, but it suits Alec."

"Is it difficult?"

"It requires attention."

"But it *is* interesting?" persisted Margery.

"Not especially," I said, "except in very bad weather. But one doesn't, I think, look forward to the rare interesting days. They can be dangerous—a captain is responsible not only for the boat but for the passengers as well. I mean, do you think an airplane pilot is turned on by turbulence?" I added mildly.

"Oh," said Margery, and looked disheartened. "Then it must be hard on him in the dead of winter."

"The northern part of the lake, where his ferry crosses, is frozen. It only runs until the end of October."

Again, Margery looked discouraged. "What on earth does he do with himself the rest of the year?" she asked sympathetically.

Remembering how reluctant I had been to accept that a grown man could fill his days for months on end without minding that he wasn't *working,* I contained my smile. "He seems to manage," I said.

"But how?" The concern in Margery's voice was genuine; I forced myself not to answer dismissively.

"He reads a lot," I said, "and he practices the piano. He works around his house, he skis—he's far from idle." I considered that a moment. "In his situation, I *would* be. When I'm not writing, my days have so little shape that I tend to turn them upside down and empty them. I'm always slightly discontent when I'm not working."

"Of course!" affirmed Margery. "Your Alec sounds—I don't think I know anyone like that."

"Nor did I," I acknowledged. "A contented man takes a bit of getting used to," I admitted.

"But you are," said Margery.

"Used to Alec? Hardly. But if he accepts my puritanical adhesiveness to my typewriter, why then I have to try to accept his comfort with a freer life, no?"

Margery was shaking her head. "No?" I repeated.

"I didn't mean no." She smiled. "I was shaking my head because what I meant, in the first place, was *your* contentment."

"Mine?" I laughed.

"Yes."

"A moment here and there, maybe," I admitted.

"You fool yourself," said Margery sternly, "if you think otherwise than that you're a very contented woman."

The intensity of her conviction would have made a lighthearted retort impossibly rude. "I'm certainly not discontented," I said seriously.

"But left-handed still," said Margery. "Tell me, is Lake Champlain far from Hamilton?"

Now I did laugh. "I may be left-handed, but you're the one who used to walk east toward the theater district," I said. "No, my dear, where it is is as far from me as New York is. It's only an hour and a half south of Montreal."

"That's perfect, isn't it!" exclaimed Margery.

"It is lovely up there, yes," I said. Leaving out the five-and-a-half-month winters.

"I didn't mean *that*. I meant your living so far apart. How ideal for romance that must be!"

I laughed. "In a way," I said. "I must admit I've never thought of it that way; and I do see him more than you might think. When he's not working, he comes to visit me about every three weeks, and stays about a week. When he is working, he stays a day and a half or two, and drives back during the night. I've been there a few times, too. It is beautiful, Margery. I'm not impervious to it, notwithstanding that I'm still a city child deep down. There's more to it than the astonishing colors of the fall leaves or the whiteness of that thick snow. Despite all the tourists, there's a serenity. As if nature is still on top of things there."

"Is it serious?" asked Margery.

"Excuse me?"

"You and Alec, is it serious?"

Now that I understood her question, I was not much closer to . . . understanding it. On the one hand, it was archaic; on the other, outrageous after all I'd said. But Margery was too fragile for the answer on the itching tip of my tongue; so I said, "Not all the time," and hoped she'd let it go at that.

Fragile or not, Margery had eyes—and read my face. "I didn't mean marriage." She smiled. "Grant me that much."

"It *doesn't* follow," I said.

"I can see that; more and more I see that. You know, in Leo's department alone, there were two divorces this past year. People don't seem to have what it takes to stick it out."

"You make it sound so grim," I said. Then, hastily, "You didn't mean to make it sound that grim."

"No, of course not," Margery said, matching my dishonesty. "Then you were as contented during your marriage as you are now?"

"Oh, no," I said. "For me, at least, contentedness seems to be a factor of growing up. And I didn't begin doing that, really, until Sam died. Mind you, I don't blame him for my retardation. You marry a father and get a father, you can't complain. But it is better this way, taking care of myself, being responsible for myself."

"What about Alec?" she asked.

"Oh, he's gravy," I said, laughing.

Margery shook her head at me. "What an awful thing to say about a man, Jessie. I think I hardly know you any more." She stood. "Of course, that only makes our getting together this weekend all the more fascinating, doesn't it? Now, if we're ever going to be served anywhere, I'd better get dressed. I'll be just a few minutes."

Twenty minutes later, Margery returned. Her face was made up, but she wasn't dressed. "I haven't a thing to wear to lunch," she declared.

"Nonsense, Margery," I said, instantly remembering the day, twenty years earlier, when she'd come back to the dorm from a shopping expedition with a dress she already owned.

"I mean it," she was saying. "Nothing fits me." She was palpably agitated; I knew at once that she was going to stay home. Why didn't I let her?

But I said, "Come, let me look. I'm a superb solver of problems just like yours."

"Look for yourself." She shrugged.

Half an hour later, after the hasty readjustment of a skirt's snaps, Margery was actually nearly dressed when Leo came into the bedroom.

"What are you two up to?" he asked.

"We're going out for a while," said Margery. "We'll be back in time for dinner."

"Where are you going?"

"We're going to find a present for Jessie's friend," said Margery, as if she'd just won a point.

"You've had lunch already?" Leo asked.

"We're doing that first. Someplace with hot popovers maybe," I said.

"I thought you weren't hungry," said Margery. "Craved only a salad with air."

"There's lot of air in a popover," I said.

"Sounds like fun to me," said Leo. "Anything else on your agenda?"

"I thought, if there's time," I said, glancing at Margery to whom I had not yet suggested this, "we might stop by the zoo in Central Park. I have an urge to see the seals."

"Sounds like just the thing," said Margery, buddying up to me again.

"Yes it does," said Leo. "How . . ." He hesitated, then plunged ahead. "How about my joining you? Would that be an intrusion?"

Margery said, "You don't eat lunch."

"I'll make an exception. What can one lunch do?" He patted his flat midsection.

"After an omelet for breakfast?" she pressed.

Leo glanced at me, then smiled at Margery. "That was hours and hours ago. Actually, if you must know, I feel an urge to play hooky."

Margery was staring at him. "Take the entire afternoon off, just like that?"

"Why not?" said Leo amiably. "It's not as if—"

"Jessie were here every day," finished Margery.

Leo's face left no question: that wasn't what he'd been about to say. But he didn't correct Margery. "That's true, she isn't." He turned to me: "If you're sure you wouldn't mind a man along?"

I didn't like Margery's being rude to Leo on my account. "You can approve my present," I said. "I'm out of practice buying a gift for a man."

Given that start, I knew even before we left the house, of course, that the chances for a successful afternoon were small; but I determined to keep up my end. Leo must have made the same resolve. For lunch, he insisted on taking us to Le Veau d'Or—no Gallic popovers, but superb mussels. During the entire time, Margery complained about the crowdedness and the noise—and the price, although she did not forbear exacerbating that by ordering a bottle of rather old Montrachet.

Still, the wine helped us all through the meal; and the first-rate food sustained me through the trek around Bloomingdale's men's department, where there was simply too much *stuff*. Leo came to the rescue, suggesting we go down to Paul Stuart, where I almost immediately spotted a dark brown leather shirt-jacket.

"You're about his size," I said to Leo. "Try it on for me, would you?"

It was simple and handsome. I decided that Alec would look marvelous in it and, even, find it useful. Still, it was a mistake, having Leo model it. In the mirror, his eyes proclaimed it: he wanted the shirt for himself.

"You'd like one, too, wouldn't you?" said Margery.

Leo checked the price. "Hardly," he said. "It's a little out of my league."

"I don't think so," said Margery, reversing her stand one hundred eighty degrees. As though, if my man could have it, so would hers?

"Really, Margery, I don't need it."

"But I want you to have it," she insisted. "My treat. Call it an advance birthday present."

"Thank you," said Leo; but he didn't look as if he'd just been given a gift.

The zoo wasn't much more fun, although the seals were in top form. Leo wanted to look at some of the other animals, but Margery became bored quickly. We made our way back to Fifth Avenue.

"I'd like to go to the Frick," said Margery. "We're so near by."

That was a little better. Margery seemed transported by the Manets. But the afternoon was coming to a close and so was the museum. Margery took that personally, and only reluctantly agreed to a walk along Madison Avenue. She didn't seem interested in the windows, although she paused when we did. Then, in front of a fancy grocer's, it was Margery who stopped.

"Do you remember?" she said to me.

I followed her eyes to the small mounds of exquisite fruit. "In May they don't seem quite that amazing, even though they are perfect," I said. "That was the beginning of February, wasn't it?"

"Intersession, yes," said Margery.

"Tell," said Leo.

"Margery?"

"You tell him," she said.

"Well," I said, "as Margery said, it was intersession. Margery and I met to go to the Frick, and after, we walked along here and we passed a store—this one or one like it—and in the window were nectarines. In February! I'd never seen anything like that. I'd never seen fruit quite so perfect, either. I suppose my eyes were popping well past decency. Margery went on in and—you can guess the rest."

"She bought a bushel," said Leo laughing, putting his arm around Margery's shoulder.

"Two perfect nectarines," I said. "One for each of us."

"And at first you refused to eat yours!" said Margery.

"It wasn't real."

"It was real enough. Those nectarines cost a small fortune," said Margery, in much better spirits now.

"That's right," I said, "they did. They cost seventy cents. For two nectarines—twenty years ago. Imagine!" I said to Leo.

"Seventy cents *each*," corrected Margery gently. "I paid the man," she added, altogether pleasantly.

She was wrong. I'd never forget how much that fruit had cost, not so long as I lived. I said nothing. What was there to say, I thought, as I moved on past the grocery window, and they did, too. That there was no reason she should remember? That having paid the man wasn't reason enough? That neither seventy cents nor a dollar forty was a significant amount of money to her? It was, I said to myself, once, twice, the idea that counted. Three times. Okay; but the idea had been . . . made less pure by Margery's insistence on the wrong price.

We walked along the avenue, the three of us, not precisely together, stopping here and again. I was following their lead now, so far as pausing went. I was remembering the petticoat and how Margery hadn't remembered accurately that time, either.

How lovely it had been. Of white tissue taffeta, printed with violets. Bonwit's had had lingerie made up patterned like their wrapping paper. Margery had a set and I had simply fallen in love with it. I'd asked, knowing it would likely be impossibly expensive, how much the petticoat cost. "Six dollars," Margery had replied promptly. It was a lot of money for a petticoat, but I had nearly four dollars saved toward a pair of warm gloves.

There are things, at eighteen, you need more than warm gloves. In a month, I had saved the remainder. I went to Bonwit's, anxious lest they had sold out. On the second floor, I approached the counter. There they were, displayed, so very beautiful. Panties, bras, petticoats. A saleswoman who looked more like a rich customer to me said, "Can I help you?" "Please," I said, "I'd like one of the petticoats, in medium." She nodded perfunctorily. I was proud and didn't mind her not knowing what a major purchase this was for me. She took a petticoat from the display case; only as she tore off part of the price ticket did I see it. "Excuse me," I said quickly, "but *how* much is it?" "Fifteen dollars," she said, her hand poised above her book as if to say, I didn't *think* you could afford it. Maybe she wasn't as hard as she seemed—she said, "The panties are only six dollars." But I was already muttering an apology and drawing away from the counter, withdrawing into my shame. I sought out the ladies' room; in a stall, I cried—and cried out against anyone's having so much money she could make such a mistake.

Of course I didn't tell Margery. Of course I lived without that petticoat. The rich and money, I thought; a bad combination. I laughed.

Margery said, "What are you laughing at?"

"Oh," I said, "just a saleswoman at Bonwit's."

"Bonwit's? There is no more Bonwit's!"

"A while back," I said.

"Well, what happened that was so funny?"

For the count of three, I was tempted. "I think you had to be there," I said.

3

Margery was in the kitchen, not wanting help. Leo had returned to his den as soon as we came home, as though to a sanctuary. I was browsing restlessly through their art books, working my way (it only occurred to me when I touched it) to the copy of our Barnard yearbook, which I had seen in Margery's hand my first evening there.

Quickly, furtively, I turned the back pages until I came to it: Margery's graduation picture. Above the photographer's makeshift V-necked décolletage, her face smiled out at me, as ebullient and confident—and lovely—as memory preserved her. Her coloring was lost in the black and white of the photograph, but not her golden quality. She was splendid; a beauty among a page full of pleasant-faced girls.

I wondered, looking hastily from one face to another, what they looked like now. Would I recognize any of them if I were to bump into them tomorrow? Would that nose, I thought, pausing momentarily over one plain Greek face, have become with age a statement rather than a blunt exclamation? And would that heart-shaped face have outgrown its insipidness? Some of the faces, I knew, would have improved.

They would have had to; to make up for Margery.

Stalling. I was stalling, and there wasn't time for it. Taking a deep breath, I turned the pages, my hands trembling slightly, like legs approaching a grave long unvisited. But, as in a visit to the grave of someone long dead, when I got there, I did not feel what I expected to. The face in the picture above my name looked . . . unfamiliar to me. The eyes were as deep-socketed as I remembered, bereft of family, bereft of home, bereft of first-loved Leo. But those orphaned eyes did not bore into mine. What was it people said about the dead? That their spirit was gone from their body, from their grave. Well, the spirit of *me* wasn't in that photograph. The photograph was empty. My spirit was in—me.

Above the bar at the end of the room, there was a mirror. Book in hand, I walked over to it and checked my reflection against the photograph to be sure.

"What *are* you doing?" Margery's voice was sharp.

Instantly, I shut the book. More slowly, I turned and faced Margery's frown. "A modest exercise in exorcism," I said. "Foolishness," I added, lying. Lying: it had not been foolish; I felt suddenly *able* to close the book on those days.

"I don't know why I didn't throw that old thing out years ago," said Margery. "I haven't looked at it since the day it arrived."

I busied myself returning the book to its place. All at once, for *her* lie, I felt terribly sorry for Margery. Turning back, I found it easy to say, "How good you were to buy me that nectarine."

"That silly fruit again," said Margery. She dismissed it with a shake of her head. "How little you wanted to make you happy."

"A nectarine in February is no small thing, old friend. More rare than a fine pink sapphire, I should think."

"Jessie, Jessie," said Margery, shaking her head again. At my ignorance about the value of pink sapphires?

"You know," she went on then, "I envied you that, wanting so little, when I wanted the world."

"Your wanting the world, Margery," I said, still trying for lightness, "was like Orson Welles wishing he had a mellifluous voice. You had everything! Didn't you know?" I laughed at the very idea.

Not Margery. Coming close to me, she said, "Didn't *you*, Jessie? Don't you yet? Don't you see, Jessie, that I felt, beside all you were, as . . . strong as chiffon?"

"Margery, I'm sorry, but I don't understand what you're talking about."

"It's a fucking way to live!"

A word not entirely absent from my own lexicon, coming from Margery it sounded the way it might from the mouth of a sweet old lady: savagely unexpected. Before I could think of what to say, or ask, Margery said, "I'm sorry, Jessie. I don't know what's got into me. I must be terminally premenstrual or something." She glanced at her watch. "But we do keep functioning around here. Dinner will be ready before too long. Have a drink in the meantime, why don't you?"

"I think, if it's all the same to you, I'll have a shower instead," I said. "I feel slightly sooty from our traipsing."

"Go on," she said. "Sounds like a fine idea. I may just do the same. And don't hurry. I don't want us coaxing Leo out of his lair *again* until we really need him." She smiled. I didn't.

"I do promise you," she added, covering, "it'll be a nice long relaxing evening." Obviously, I was to understand that she was finished now; and quite herself again.

Whoever that was.

4

When I came back to the living room, perhaps forty-five minutes later, Margery was seated on the sofa, sipping a drink; Leo, in his customary Eames chair, had his, too. Margery was wearing fresh make-up and a long skirt which had outlived its stylishness by several years. Her blouse looked two sizes too big. "Here she is," said Margery, her voice slightly louder than necessary, as though she were on stage and conscious of the need to project.

Leo turned; his face was clenched. He looked like a man who has just received bad news.

"Leo and I have been talking about adventures," said Margery. "How long is it, Leo, since you've taken a Friday afternoon off? Can you even remember, Leo?"

"Afraid not," he said dully.

"Aren't you going to offer Jessie a drink, dear?" Margery asked.

"Of course." Quickly, Leo stood and awaited my order.

"A Dubonnet will be fine, thanks," I said.

When Leo handed me the wine glass, he followed my eyes to his grip; frowning, he looked away.

Margery laughed. "All this relaxing's made Leo tense," she said. "Relax, Leo." She turned to me. "I think old friends should always be relaxed with each other, don't you?" Then, without pausing, she added, "And should keep one another up to date on their news. Have you told Leo whom he was standing in for today? Does he know all about your Alec?"

"Of course not. I'm sure he wouldn't be in the least interested," I said, embarrassed for all three of us.

"Little you know," said Margery playfully. "It's so romantic, and Leo's a romantic through and through. Aren't you, darling?"

Leo looked at Margery. I saw the face of a demolition expert poised over a bomb which might detonate in a matter of moments: that terrible, bleak calm. But when she said no more, when the danger passed, he turned to me. "Of course I'm interested, Margery's quite right. But that's no reason for you to feel you have to say anything."

"His name is Alec Klady," I said, "and he's . . . the man in my life. That about says it."

"He's a ferryboat captain," exclaimed Margery. "*I* think that's terribly romantic. Has he a beard?"

"As a matter of fact, yes. How did you guess?"

"You can't possibly pilot a ferryboat without a beard," declared Margery.

"I'll be sure to tell Alec. He's been thinking of shaving his off," I said.

"He mustn't," said Margery firmly.

"I'll inform him," I said, attempting a smile. In my peripheral vision, Leo's pale face was following our exchange closely.

As Margery turned to him, he tried to pretend he hadn't

been intent on us. Holding out her glass to Leo, she said, "I think I'll have another, darling, to celebrate." I wasn't about to ask what—lest she say.

But it was unmistakable: something further, unspoken, passed between the two of them; and Leo lost. Slowly, moving as if in some considerable pain, he got up, took Margery's glass, and poured her another drink. Vodka on the rocks. As he walked toward her with the drink, she stood and smiled at him. "On second thought, I think I won't have another. I've a few things to check in the kitchen. You two entertain each other until I get back."

Leo stood looking after Margery as she left the room. I thought, for a moment, that he was going to go after her; but, still moving slowly, he walked back to the bar and set the drink down. He came and sat again in his chair, but he wasn't there. I wished I weren't either. I considered excusing myself and going to my room, or even out; but I knew I couldn't do either one. I settled for a trip to the window. A warm afterglow of sunset suffused the sky, framing the bridge in the distance.

In a couple of minutes, perhaps three, Leo said something. I turned. "Sorry," I said. "I think I'm in love with the George Washington Bridge."

"Then the added lower level doesn't spoil it for you? It does for many people."

"I don't see it. What I see is the bridge my bedroom window looked out on."

"At home." He nodded. "Before your mother died."

"Yes." But I didn't want to wander into the past. Not if I had to stay in this room, in this time, too. "Let's not go way back," I said. "All right?"

"Of course," said Leo. "There is something I've been wanting to ask you about. It does go back a ways, but it's not very personal. At least I don't think—"

"What is it?"

"I've wanted to know, what made you stop teaching? Is that subject all right?"

How interested he was in my answer was questionable; he kept glancing toward the kitchen. Still he had raised the subject, and it served the purpose of keeping the conversation going.

"Sure," I said, "that's safe enough. I'm not all that fragile." I laughed. "It goes back further than you may think. Remember Garrett Mattingly?"

"Hunched, walked around campus with his head down. By reputation a brilliant lecturer. When he died they named a chair after him, didn't they?"

"Good old Columbia," I said. "They did little enough for him while he was alive. Anyway, you do remember.

"Well, Mattingly won the Pulitzer Prize. I was getting my Master's then. The class of his I was in was enormous, more than a hundred; and you know the way nighttime graduate students are, none of us knew each other. So there was no getting together on it, no plan. But when Mattingly came into the room, we stood, everyone did, and we applauded him. He didn't keep his head down then, and he didn't try to stop us; he stood there smiling slightly, nodding slightly, as if acknowledging our good judgment. He looked the way Kirsten Flagstad used to when she received a standing ovation: a self-satisfied Valkyrie.

"When I didn't have either the money or the enthusiasm to go on for my doctorate, I approached Mattingly, with great temerity, halfway convinced that after four courses he still wouldn't know who I was, and I asked him if he thought I could write history without a doctorate, and he said, 'I don't see why not, C. V. Wedgwood does.' Leo, I damn near floated home that evening. His praise meant that much.

"Studying history, then, with a man like that, who knew Renaissance diplomacy as thoroughly as a county chairman knows the local political scene—that was an experience.

"My students didn't want that experience. I was no Mattingly, but I knew the sixteenth century, and I loved it, and I could talk about it. My students weren't prepared to listen, though. They certainly weren't about to believe me. They didn't believe anyone was telling them the truth about the Second World War, or Korea, or Vietnam—why believe what I said about the Spanish Armada? Besides, they wanted to make history, not study it."

"Would you believe," said Leo, "that in 1968, at Columbia, I was jealous of my students? I wanted to be out there making history, too." He laughed at himself. "You're right, history today is written in pencil. So it was mainly the attitude of the students that changed you?"

"Not entirely. My drive was never really to teach, but to write. I wanted to write as brilliantly as Mattingly, as rousingly as Froude."

"The guy who wrote that long history fighting the Reformation all over again, he was so anti-Catholic?"

"Twelve *great* volumes," I said. "But, yes, he was biased. When I started writing, I found myself rewriting history, too. I kept pushing events around, making them turn out—the way they should have. Oh, I was much worse than Froude. That's not bias, that's fiction."

"So now you write fiction—how logical! How marvelous! And thank God, not historical fiction. Good books, Jessie. And you even earn a living doing it?"

"Not a smashing living, but a living, yes."

"Tell me," he said, "does it ever astonish you to realize you're doing something as utterly selfish as writing full-time and being paid for it? Or is that an outrageous formulation?" Leo's smile was, at that moment, as compelling as ever it had been.

"Not outrageous at all; quite accurate, in fact," I admitted freely. "Being able to write full-time, not needing to squeeze it in before or after a job, *is* a luxury. And to be paid for it does, occasionally, surprise me, even though I work very, very hard. But you, of course, would understand that. Your work's like that, isn't it? You teach because you love teaching, not because it happens to be what you do for a living."

For a moment, Leo looked as though I had said something nasty; then he saw I was serious, and looked away. "Oh, I don't think I love teaching any more, Jessie," he said. "Did I ever, I wonder? What I *loved,* my great time, was being the student who outshone all the rest. In the beginning teaching seemed . . . another way to shine.

"But the first time I had a student who was as bright as I'd been . . ." Leo laughed, shaking his head. "And if I soon enough found out that there were students as good as I'd been, eventually I learned, too, that I'm not the teacher everyone thought I'd be—me most of all."

He took a breath. "I worked hard, though. It takes plenty of effort, believe me, to keep up with my students. Their attitudes, their priorities change practically overnight. They change their *Weltanschauung* more often than their underwear. Sometimes, I get *tired.*

"And, Jessie?" Leo leaned toward me. "You know what? I'm afraid. I'm afraid that one day I'll find that the latest change, whatever it may be, is beyond me, no matter how hard I try. Then they won't come to me any more. Jessie, when they stop coming—will I still exist?

"You know, I'm sure there're people who think I left Columbia because CUNY offered me more money, and who think that's a lousy reason. What would they say if they knew the real reasons? That at CUNY I felt I'd . . . last longer. And that, at CUNY, there are no ghosts walking the halls—no old-timers who remember me, remember who I used to be. Awful as it may seem, it does help to be where there are fewer reminders of what . . . promise I showed.

"Sorry," he added, looking suddenly exceedingly embarrassed. He'd said far more than he'd meant to.

Still, I had to ask; he'd made me need to know. "Then your work brings you no . . . joy, Leo?"

"Joy? Jessie." He said my name as a remonstrance; as though the idea of finding joy in work was outlandish.

"No," he said now, "don't, Jessie, please don't look like that. It's all right, you see. I'm . . . content enough. After all, in this day and age being a great teacher isn't what it once was—you said so yourself. Nor, for that matter, is being a brilliant student." He smiled. "Take my word for it, the way to make your mark in a college these days is to be—"

"Charming!" interrupted Margery enthusiastically, returning. "Charming as only Leo can be." She sat down and looked from one to the other of us, doctrinaire benevolence suffusing her cheeks.

Leo and I did exchange glances, only partly, for my part, because something about Margery commanded full attention. "We were," I said to her, "talking about changes in university life. Leo was explaining what makes a professor popular these days." Why on earth did I sound defensive?

"Darling," Margery was saying, "aren't you forgetting that Jessie's Sam was also a professor? She's not exactly a novice when it comes to university life. You needn't, I'm sure, instruct her—"

"No, of course not," said Leo. Why? He hadn't been instructing me, not the way Margery made it sound. "And it could be," he rushed on, "that your husband's experience was entirely different from mine. But I must say that my students are far more interested in what they think than in what Melville thought or James, let alone what I might think. But that makes it easy, you see. Be interested in what they think and you're home—"

"And you become as popular as Leo," interjected Margery. "It was different in our day, wasn't it, Jessie? Old Cartwright didn't give one damn if we liked him or not. He probably would have considered the very idea of being liked an affront. And he never accommodated himself to our pace, fully expecting that if we had to run to catch up with him, we would. Remember, if you happened to pass him in the hallway or on Jake, he'd never recognize you with so much as a nod? His office hours were the stingiest and no more relaxed than the classroom. But goddamn if we didn't pay attention to every single word he deigned to utter to us."

Eaton Cartwright had been a member of the Religion Department in our time at Barnard. A man God himself might be inclined to defer to, I thought—still. How vividly I saw him! "I was certain that if my mind wandered for even a moment, he'd know. Not that he'd take it personally—you're right about his supreme disinterest—but it would be another small mark against my seriousness as a Barnard girl." I shook my head in wonder.

"Speaking of which, or whom—whichever," said Margery, her shrill ebullience in no way reminiscent of the way she used to be back then, "what are you going to tell the Barnard girls of today tomorrow?"

"I don't think there are any Barnard girls today," I said, striving for a light tone because suddenly Margery's unnatural bubbliness seemed to italicize the time between then and now. "I suspect the Admissions Office culls out the girls, admits only women."

I glanced at Leo, intent upon bringing him into the conversation if I could; but his attention was plainly not on what I was saying, and I turned away quickly. He seemed riveted on Margery. I talked on, feeling foolish and frustrated and more than a little angry. I hadn't asked to be here.

"It's not the students I'm talking to, anyway, but alumnae, remember," I heard my voice saying. "The theme of reunion is 'Changing Course.' I didn't write *The Mourning Cake* until I was thirty-four; that's what I'm going to be talking about."

Margery's eyes were focused on my mouth, which increased

my sense of disassociation with the words coming out of it, more or less of their own volition.

She said, "It sounds positively fascinating."

I said, "Maybe you'll come, after all?"

At once, regretted; Margery shifted, then stood. "Maybe I will," she said. "It certainly sounds like fun." And she headed back to the kitchen.

It certainly sounds like *fun*?

My back was tensing, the muscles practicing sailor's knots up and down its length. I stood and moved about the room, trying to undo the knots before they got too tight. I ended up at the window again. Outside, a purplish-grey peace; how I wanted to introduce a shade of peace to the room.

"Hearing you talk about CUNY before," I said, turning to Leo and waiting until I had his attention, "I realized that I still think of you as integral to Columbia. I can't seem to think of it without you or you without it. Is that sheer sentiment? I mean, do you, living here, so close by, do *you* feel any connection still?"

"Can't think of one of us without the other," he repeated, as if echoing the words to a foolish old song. "Afraid not. The first couple of years, I occasionally saw members of my department for a drink; once or twice, just by chance, on the subway. But even the chance encounters don't happen anymore, don't ask me why. Maybe you have to keep an eye out, I don't know. Anyway, Jess, *ten years*."

"Yes, of course," I said. I had not softened the grim mood of the room by my question. I stumbled on. "I asked Margery if she'd ever gone to a reunion, living so close by."

"Margery doesn't go in much for going places," Leo said with, it seemed, exaggerated lack of emphasis. I thought, I've said enough that doesn't work; let *him* try. I stood there, facing him, until, finally, he did.

"Is this your first time back?"

"Yes. I wonder what it'll feel like."

"Coming back in triumph?" Leo tried it out, softly.

I lied to him. "I wasn't even thinking in terms of being *asked* back, simply of going back."

He wouldn't expect me to lie; he believed me, and said, "Not a negligible difference."

It wasn't fair to lie to him, not after what he'd been telling me. "You're right, of course," I said. "I never went back before I *was* asked.

"Maybe it's a by-product of never having fitted in: of having felt the quintessential outsider. Eventually, there was this sense of being accepted—in spite of myself, somehow, not because of what I was. What I was, was confusing—to me, even. I knew I put people off because I communicated a certain confidence, even arrogance—but I didn't feel confident, and I don't think I had any arrogance in me. Mostly, I was scared of everyone at Barnard: everyone was either smarter than me or prettier or more adept socially—and certainly richer. I suppose I might have been jealous of them for one quality or another they had that I lacked—yes, I did think of having money as an attribute—but I was too busy being awestruck. God, maybe that was what made me seem so damned self-assured. I was *watching* people constantly, and they must have thought I was being judgmental while I was only—only mesmerized. I guess people who are uncomfortable make others uncomfortable; and I certainly never felt sufficiently *part* of Barnard to relax. You know, I was never surprised when someone I met didn't like me; I rather expected that reaction. Of course, I didn't like myself much in those days, and that never helps." I heard myself clearly going on and on; but I wasn't embarrassed.

"I know what you mean," said Leo.

An idle kindness.

"No," he said, reading my reaction, "you're wrong; but I suppose you wouldn't have known. It's the truth, Jessie. I didn't either—like myself much back then."

"Leo," I said, "really."

He looked aggrieved. "Do you think you're the only one who ever hid how you felt? Did you think it was easy being on stage my last two years, everyone watching me, waiting for me either to do something earthshaking three times a week or to botch up in some grandiose, final way? Keeping up with an image is a strain on the heart muscles," he said, and I would have felt more sympathetic except it sounded so smooth, that phrase, I felt sure he'd said it before. Maybe it was a line left over from a poem he'd never finished.

But then he got me. Leaning forward, almost in a whisper, he said, "Don't you think that I had doubts about the way I treated people?"

I *would* not look away. "No one but you can know that, Leo," I said, chalking a hem.

"Let's not do that, Jessie. You know."

"Come on, Leo, let's not do *this*. Let it go. If there's ever a time for such a conversation, and I'm not sure there is, this definitely isn't it."

"You *can* sound confident," he said; then, "I'm sorry. But I do have something I want to ask. Will you let me?"

I shrugged; the lowest form of assent.

"Have you ever thought," he said, "that what's happened to you these past few years, what you've accomplished, is a kind of compensation . . . for all you lost back then?"

Was his life, then, a retribution? "That's not the way it works; I don't think so."

"Do you know then *how it works*?" The sarcasm in his voice was shot with bitterness.

I retreated. "No, of course not."

"How what works? What don't *you* know—of all people, Jessie?" said Margery, as she crossed the threshold of the room, tripped over the edge of the rug, and fell, scattering hors d'oeuvre before her.

In a second, Leo was at her side, helping her up, getting

her seated in a chair. By then my paralysis had abated and I took care of gathering the hors d'oeuvre on the plate, which I placed on the coffee table; better than standing there holding it as a reminder. But neither of them was paying any attention. Leo was trying to determine if Margery had hurt her knee, and she was dismissing his solicitude.

She smiled at me, not a twinge of embarrassment visible to the naked eye. "We women know how to take these teeny tiny domestic accidents in stride, don't we, Jessie?" She winked. There was not even a sliver of doubt: Margery was drunk. I found it hard to believe—on a practical level, to begin with. How had she managed it? She'd had only one drink before taking off for the kitchen; back for a while, she hadn't had another.

The kitchen. She was drinking in the kitchen. She was spending so much time in the kitchen *in order to drink?*

But I was sure that the night I arrived, she'd had only a minimal amount of liquor, no more than I, who have the barest credentials as a social drinker. And last night, when I'd come in, she had seemed tense and remote, but not drunk.

Too much to take in. Besides, she was looking at me as though I'd forgotten my manners. "Of course it doesn't matter," I managed. Just. I had to do better than that.

"Let's eat them." I reached for one of the hors d'oeuvre and bit into it. "It's delicious, Margery," I said. It had no taste at all.

"The rug's a Kashan that belonged to Mother," said Margery. "I don't get all the credit." She took one of the hors d'oeuvre and ate it daintily. Then she said, "Leo is too meticulous to eat these itinerant tidbits." She giggled at her joke.

Automatically, Leo took one and ate it. "It's good," he said tonelessly.

"You really like it?" said Margery. She was taunting him.

"I really do."

"Then why don't you have another?"

Leo ate two more.

"If you like Kashan," she said to me, dismissing Leo. "Now we can dump the rest."

"That's not necessary," I said, meaning nothing in particular.

"Don't ridicule me, Jessie!" Margery commanded.

In the silence, I looked at no one, so I can't be sure, but I had the feeling that none of us was looking at anyone else. Finally, after what may have been no more than half a minute, Margery said, "Forget it. You were only joking, I know."

I hadn't been joking, I hadn't been *anything* except maybe trying to toss balloons into the void. But I said, "Yes, I was. I'm sorry if that was unclear." I glanced at Leo; the relief in his face stung me as sharply as Margery's accusation had.

Margery got up, not quite as unsteadily as I would have expected, and came over. She kissed the air beside my cheek. "Think no more of it," she said graciously. "I should be used by now to the banter of those nearest and dearest to me. Excuse me." She bowed, first to me and then, cursorily, to Leo. "I think I need to turn down the flame under our food."

I watched her walk out of the room, exaggeratedly erect, taking mincing steps, walking a straighter line than a sober person would think to adhere to. I turned to Leo; he was looking into his drink. "Leo? Is it anything to do with my being here? Am I to blame?"

He looked up; the polite smile formed by his lips seemed to pale them drastically: he looked ill. "No, Jessie," he said, his voice devoid of texture, "you're not to blame. Believe this, since you arrived, she's been trying. . . ." He shook his head, as if berating himself for an indiscretion. "Let's talk about something else."

"Of course." But there didn't seem to be any other subject. Still, one could keep quiet; I did.

In a moment or two, Leo shrugged ruefully. "My mind's a

blank," he apologized. "Would you mind if I went to her?"

"Leo, what kind of question is that?"

He shrugged again. "The foolish kind I tend to ask these days," he said, and left the room.

I sought refuge at the window. The view, especially my childhood's bridge, began to soothe me: whatever this night held, it would not likely be balm; and I sucked in the light-spattered blandness outside as though it were fresh air. But, too quickly, Leo was back.

"She doesn't want me in there," he said; which wasn't surprising if my surmise that she was drinking in the kitchen was accurate. Sinking into his chair, he said, "Whatever made me think she might?"

I could not deal with so much pity: what I felt for her and for him; what he felt for her—and for himself. Better not even go near what she felt for herself.

"Your son," I said, "Margery's terribly proud of Jon. Are you close to him, too? I imagine, with your reputed way with the young . . ." I smiled, I hoped encouragingly.

Leo looked at me like a doubting, ill-tempered piano tuner. In the end, however, he seemed to find my tone acceptable. "Neither one of us is particularly close to Jon right now. We used to be. But he doesn't come around much."

"All young people—"

"No!" said Leo sharply. "The truth is hard enough to live with without needing to accept it over and over because other people keep saying it isn't true. Jon stays away because—he thinks it's a good idea."

"That sounds . . . thoughtless," I said. "Margery said he was kind."

"She wasn't lying. Jon is kind; Jon seldom comes home." He sighed. "No, I don't understand it, either. Margery thinks it kind if he comes home twice a year. She expects nothing from him. Don't look like that, Jess. Don't you see, it's the obverse of how she used . . ."

Quickly, I nodded. Wanting urgently to go on, to get past that awkward, painful place, I said, "He's a brilliant student, Margery says. She says, even more perhaps than you were."

An unpained smile; this didn't hurt him. "Perhaps not more brilliant—but better, I think. More inclined to think than to bellow the results of each and every thought, as I was. Jon will make his mark."

"Oh, yes," said Margery, returning. "Oh yes! Jon's our pride and joy, isn't he, darling?" She came and sat on the arm of Leo's chair. He put his arm around her waist; he was holding her steady.

"Did I tell you, Jessie, he really wanted to meet you?" said Margery.

"Yes, and I wish I could meet him."

"But you will, you will. Soon. I'll arrange it," said Margery—and lost her balance. But Leo's arm was there and she was all right. She ignored it all. "You must be on your mettle, though, when I do get it set up."

"I consider myself warned."

"I nearly forgot, we can eat now," said Margery, getting up. Her face was flushed. Leo caressed her cheek, as though its high color were from the heat of the stove. He held her hand; she let him. I followed behind. Leo held her chair for her, then mine. On Wednesday night, he hadn't held either.

Margery looked coquettish. "Leo always serves dinner," she said. "It's one of his liberated mannerisms." Leo's face showed no response; he went off to get our food. I knew better than to offer to help.

Reaching for the open bottle of wine on the table, Margery said, "We don't absolutely have to wait for Leo, he won't mind." She poured for me and for herself; when a little spilled over onto the flat base of her glass, she wiped it with her finger, which she then licked.

She raised her glass. "What shall we drink to?" she said;

then, without pausing for a reply, "To everything, to one and all, and their cousins and their aunts, here and overseas, on ship and on shore." She put the glass to her lips and drank the entire contents without pause. Setting down the glass, she meticulously patted her lips with her napkin.

Leo entered with a platter. On it were some lamb chops, dried out to curliness, a pile of limp grey-green spinach, a mound of mushy rice. Without either word or glance to signify that this meal was in any respect different from our meal two nights earlier, Leo carried the platter around to my side and I served myself. I took some of everything, thinking I'd figure out how not to eat it after. When he held the tray for Margery, she waved it away. "I'm not very hungry," she said. "All those hors d'oeuvre."

As Leo served himself, and he and I began to make eating motions, Margery refilled her glass and drank it, slowly this time, although again she didn't set it down until it was empty.

Leo—someplace else to look—was doing a better job of eating as little as possible than I was, it seemed to me. He chewed the way I imagine a long-term prisoner sorts laundry. I tried to emulate him.

"Lamb chops are Jessie's favorite," Margery said to Leo. "That's why we're having them." Then, explaining the universe to a child, "Wednesday night we had coq au vin because it was your favorite. Tonight is Jessie's turn."

No one said anything. It was hard enough to eat; she was watching us. After a few minutes of turgid silence, Margery queried, "That's fair, isn't it?"

"Excuse me?" I said.

"Yes," said Leo, "of course it's fair." To me, swiftly, "Alternating our favorites."

"Very fair," I said, feeling suddenly as though I'd gotten into a locked ward by mistake. What sort of conversation *was* this?

Margery said, "Tomorrow night, you know what would be

the fairest thing?" Waiting for our answer, she refilled her glass.

"To have shrimp," said Leo.

"Exactly!" Margery exclaimed. To me, with apparent excitement, "You know why, don't you?" Happily, she drank.

"Because shrimp are your favorite?" I felt that, in another moment, I might cry out. Or cry. Do *something* loud enough to override this insane conversation.

"Jessie, our genius, strikes again," said Margery, refilling her glass a third time. She held her drinking arm with her other hand to steady it.

Leo took the bottle and held it over my glass, but I hadn't touched what Margery had poured in there when we first sat down. "Don't be a party pooper," said Margery, "drink up. There's plenty more."

I looked at Leo, nodded; drank a little. He poured in an equivalent amount.

"Leo, don't be so stingy," chided Margery. "Give the girl some wine."

"The glass is full," I said.

"Then it's your fault, not Leo's. Drink your wine, Jessie, like a good girl." She turned to Leo and shrugged artfully. "I won't turn you down, darling."

Stolidly, Leo went to her, and poured. "Don't you be stingy with me, my love," she said playfully, but there was the hardness of a diamond under the sparkle. His hand tremulous, Leo kept pouring.

"My mother," said Margery, never taking her eyes off the glass as Leo compliantly filled it to the brim, "used to insist you never fill a wine glass more than a scant half full—but I noticed that the only rules of etiquette Mother took seriously were the mean ones." She picked up the glass and, incredibly, raised it to her lips without spilling a drop; she drank it down, and smiled at us with enormous self-satisfaction.

"Have you had enough to eat?" Leo asked me, as though he were as out of touch as Margery.

Carefully, because Margery seemed to be noticing some things minutely, I said, "Remember, I had a big breakfast and a big lunch."

"Exactly!" said Margery, who had not eaten any breakfast or much of her lunch. "Which is why I'm not ravenous either. It's all right, dear, you don't have to finish everything on your plate." She was perfectly serious; perfectly drunk.

Leo removed the plates. While he was in the kitchen, Margery poured herself another glass of wine from a fresh bottle on the sideboard, which she reached by tilting back her chair as far as it would go, a precarious act she seemed to find amusing. She didn't offer me any more but drank hers with loving attentiveness. When Leo brought in coffee and cake, she was humming. She waved away both.

Leo and I drank our coffee in a distended silence. Margery drained another glass of wine, placed the empty glass ceremoniously in the center of her clean dinner plate, lifted them both with delicate care, and put them down a foot forward. Everything in its place, Margery silently, slowly—gracefully—lowered her head onto her folded arms on the table. In a few minutes, her breathing, although heavy, was regular.

Even then, Leo and I didn't speak, not right away. Encased in our private thoughts, we sat there at the table beside the sleeping Margery—as though that were, if not commonplace, possible.

Finally, for me, it wasn't. I got up. Without looking at Leo, I said in a low voice, although the obvious depth of Margery's sleep precluded disturbance, "Can I help you with her, or the dishes, before I go to bed?"

"Thank you, no," said Leo, a reserve in his tone, a formality, which invited no questions. What he couldn't know was that I didn't have any, not tonight. More accurately, I had too many to begin to know which to ask—even truer, they were so many that, I thought, there might be too many to ask *any*.

I started toward the foyer. "Jessie." I turned. Leo said:

"I generally go to my office half a day Saturdays, so I'll be gone when you get up. If Margery doesn't turn up for your talk, don't be put out. I know she wants to come, but she may . . . forget."

I generally go to my office half a day Saturdays: life goes on, even in face of this. This was not the first time, then: no question about that.

I nodded. "Good night," I said.

"Good night," echoed Leo. "And Jess? I'm sorry."

I shook my head. I didn't know what to say. Of course he was sorry. A night like tonight had room for a hundred regrets. Finally, I said, "I'm sorry, too."

"I know," he answered. For the first time since Margery laid her head down on the table, I looked directly at Leo.

"I know," I said. In the joylessness of the moment, we shared that much. Margery began to snore, a rough not soft snoring. It didn't startle her awake. I turned again and went to my room.

Some minutes later, more comfortable in the dark, I lay in bed and thought, At least we had the grace not to keep talking away at each other in front of her, as though she were dead.

Not dead; and, yet, there was something . . . dying about Margery.

The dark was no longer comforting enough. Alec—I wanted Alec there, beside me; to hold me within the grasp of his normalcy, his aliveness, his gift for joy. Those were what I needed to bring me back.

With my mind, I went for him. And, as always, found him in my corner. *With* me. The soothing force of the extraordinary mutuality which had grown up between Alec and me. The way he, as no other man I'd known, not only let me be me, but insisted on it. The delight of knowing that despite that—because of it?—when I needed him, he would be beside me. Here. Felt. A love that wanted to be beside, not over, not instead. Beside me, Alec. I felt him now, like a calm spirit, a whispering wind, embrace me; softly, caressingly, like sleep.

It was the weight of a package I felt. Light. The paper plain, the ribbon knotted without grace. I glanced at Alec, who nodded. I opened the box.

Inside, I saw nothing. I bent my head, lower, into the box. And felt . . . warmth. I glanced at Alec, who nodded. I set the box aside.

And, at once, felt another. I lifted this one. Also light; again, its wrappings unimpressive. At Alec's nod, I opened it. Empty, too. I bent into it. Nothing. Then, as weightless as a butterfly's wing, I felt it brush my lips: the box contained a single kiss. But could a box contain a kiss? I looked to Alec, who nodded.

I lay back, not exactly content, but not discontent, either, and waited. Sure enough, I felt the weight of another box. If you could call something that light a weight. Rapidly, I undid the unimposing wrappings and looked inside. Empty. Not disappointed, I bent my head. Still deeper into the box. Nothing. No warmth, no kiss. I turned to Alec.

He was smiling. "What did you expect," he said, "the world?"

Trembling, I dared not answer. I had been given an empty world before; I certainly didn't want that again. Instead, I said, "Is it really empty, the box? There's nothing in it?"

"Not yet," said Alec.

But his voice was so kind, so loving, that I didn't believe him; I kept poking my head into the box. Nothing. Quite frantic finally, I said, "Not yet! What does not yet mean! Will you put something in it later? When?"

Alec shook his head. "No, I won't be putting anything in it."

"But why would you give me a box with nothing inside!" I cried.

And crying, woke, all comfort gone. I huddled, listening to the silence, almost wishing to hear the angry voices of Margery and Leo, but hearing only silence outside my room. And inside me.

Alec seemed very far away. All I had was me. I could not bear it without some comfort. My hand was already there, in place before the thought. I had to work hard; it took a long time and when, finally, I did come it was feeble, it almost went by me.

The theologians were wrong, I thought, about that, too. There is something wrong with masturbation; you can't hug yourself.

I slept, because one sleeps; but only after a long, long time.

SATURDAY

1

It was inconceivable. They'd let me past the gate, instructing me to hurry, and I'd run. The plane was there, the door at the top of the steps open; a stewardess standing in the doorway waved me on up. I rushed across the short space of airfield, ran up the stairs—a few steps only to the top. I glanced up at her, happy to have made the plane, grateful even. Her smile contorted into a fierce, disapproving glare; she shut the plane door in my face. I stood there, hearing the engines rev up; quickly, too quickly, the plane seemed to be starting, moving. It wasn't! The stairs beneath me were moving! Ground crew were removing the stairs—

Falling.

It wasn't that far; I only scraped my knees. I picked myself up and ran for the train. Ran quickly, ignoring the stinging of my knees. I got to the station: there it was, steam puffing out of it, the platform empty except for a few people waving goodbye to passengers already aboard. Several cars up ahead, a conductor motioned to me, waved me on, smiling encouragement indulgently, a man who had seen several generations of latecomers make the train at the very last minute. The wheels began to turn, the train to move; slowly, but moving. I ran faster, my heart beginning to pound now. I was almost able to reach a handrail and pull myself aboard—when the train suddenly speeded up. I kept running, but there was no way, now, to get on. I watched it—and the conductor, the modest smile still between his teeth, like an habitual cigar. The smile shrank; he was getting smaller. I was left behind again, my heart pounding in my throat.

The bus was my last hope. The pain was like stucco in my throat, rubbing it raw as I ran. I saw it, finally, coming my way, a block off, stopped for the light. I ran for the bus stop; this time I ran only because I was used to moving that way—I had plenty of time. The light changed, but I was nearly there. The bus approached, slowed; I lifted my hand to signal the driver—an effort, but I didn't want to leave even the slightest margin for error. The bus slowed further, the doors swung open, the driver looked down at me—and the doors swung shut. The bus drove on past me.

Spastic movement; tears thick and uneven as freshwater pearls heaved up by my contorted innards: I couldn't *stand* missing my last chance to get there: I could *not* stand. My body folded under me like a Jacob's ladder. Passersby ignored me. I lay piled on the sidewalk, a bundle that cried.

The dampness of the pillow woke me. It didn't feel soothing, comforting, comfortable like the wet bed of my childhood. Awake, crying still. The dream clung to me. I tried to remember where I'd been trying to get in my dream. Its name wasn't in my head, or its face. Only its unreachability. Somehow, not knowing what it was, where it was, why I needed to get there, made its inaccessibility even worse.

For a time, I lay very still, my head on the dry side of the pillow, waiting for the dream to wear off, like an injection.

Eventually, it did, leaving a soreness: the ache of a drunken Margery asleep at the dining room table.

I made myself get up, wash my face diligently with soap and water, washing the sleep out of me. My face felt dry. I hadn't used soap on my face in decades: adults know when a dream is over. And when their friends are in trouble, they keep a clear head. I looked out the window; a grey day. The clock reported half past seven. Too early to eat. I'd take a walk. Good for clearing the head.

Dressed in jeans, I let myself out of the apartment.

The benches along the Drive were finely misted still, but I didn't feel like sitting anyway. I walked along, trying to keep a pace that would stir the blood a bit. I passed a number of early walkers who made me feel inadequately attired without a dog. I wanted to be among people who were out here at this hour for themselves, not as accompanist to an animal. Down below, in the park, there would, I felt sure, be joggers. I didn't have to be at Barnard until ten thirty; there was plenty of time. I walked down.

There was no one in sight. Maybe the joggers were all in their showers by now. I didn't mind having the park all to myself. It was a shame, I thought: at night, most people avoided the park, these days; now, when there was no need for concern, most people were rushing off to work. The old people who sat on the benches along the Drive later on probably never walked this far; the neighborhood kids were apparently all sleeping late.

I breathed in the solitude: a portion and seconds of peace wasn't more than I could use at the moment. For quite a while, I walked contentedly, savoring the silence, my quiet pleasure intensified by knowing that the morning-busy city was right up there over the wall.

But I didn't have all morning; and after a time I turned

back. Guided by landmarks along the Drive, I knew I had quite a long walk: I was just south of Riverside Church when I headed downtown again, and I was almost back home when I finally passed some kids up and out despite its being Saturday. Girls, evidently sisters, both small and thin; the older could be as old as twelve, the younger as young as nine. They were playing leapfrog, taking turns jumping over one another.

"Hey, miss."

I paused, half-turned. "You in a hurry?" It was the older of the two girls. The slightly younger one was sitting on the grass, holding her ankle. They were pretty, with taupe skin— Indian, or Pakistani. Politically, I knew the difference; visually not.

"What is it?" I was still half-turned away, ready to be on my way. I had to dress, get going.

"Go on, she'll be okay," said the older one. The other girl nodded, her face scrunched in contradiction.

"You twist your ankle?" I asked her.

"Lady, I said it was all right. We'll manage," the older girl said, and tried to help her sister up. She wasn't that much bigger, and was unsuccessful.

"I'll help," I said, hurrying over. It would only take a couple of minutes. "Here, lean on me."

Between us, we helped the younger girl upright; walking slowly, with her between us, we achieved the path. "Which way are you going?" I asked.

"Up there," the older said, pointing to the stairs leading up to 103d Street, which I'd been heading for myself.

"Good, that's my way, too."

We started upward, the injured girl leaning against me, surprisingly heavy, her sister supporting her on the other side. We had to negotiate each step individually, the child's weight hampering me. But I was in a hurry, so when they didn't suggest stopping to rest, I didn't either. Hard as it was on me, it must have been harder on the girl whose ankle was hurt; and midway up the stairs, she stopped, her weight against me. I was trying to straighten her somewhat, to take a small portion of her weight off me, when the older girl began to run up the stairs—her little sister behind her, undeterred by any injured ankle, my shoulder bag in her hand.

"Hey!" I yelled after them, "Hey!" But that was all I did. I stood there, my breath coming hard, paralyzed by my astonishment at the guile of them, at how easily I'd been conned. By the time I started moving up the stairs after them, it was hopeless. The dead weight of the younger girl had tired me; besides, I wasn't nine or ten or twelve, and I was no runner. When I reached the top of the stairs, they were out of sight.

I stood there, thinking, Dreams, the worst dreams, are easier: you wake up and your handbag is on the dresser. Mine was gone. Not much else, I realized, as I began to collect myself. I'm in the habit of emptying out my bag at night and I'd only grabbed some loose change, a package of tissues, and the keys—the keys! Suddenly, I was very angry: at the girls, but at Margery, too. God only knew if she had awakened yet from her drugged sleep. Or, if she hadn't, whether my ringing the doorbell would rouse her. I had to dress: even today, I didn't think jeans would do for a reunion speaker. Besides, my prepared remarks were in the apartment. I didn't even have carfare to get to Barnard! The temptation to cry was gaining on me. I *would* not cry. I jammed my hands into my jeans pockets to overcome the second temptation: a sudden regressive urge to bite my nails, an activity having more to do, in my past, with craving succor than with nervousness—and found the keys.

Angrier still. At me: for forgetting that I'd slipped them into my pocket instead of the bag. At me: for taking the damn bag with me. I'd simply reached for it out of habit. I hadn't had any intention of going near a store; and if I'd had an overwhelming need to wipe my nose, my hand would have served. Tastelessness seemed for the moment a more acceptable attribute than dumbness. Dumb to take a bag I didn't need! Dumb to fall for the girls' sting! So angry was I that I kept at it, at myself, until I was inside the apartment.

Then, it dawned on me that now I didn't have to wake Margery, a contingency underscored by the silence of the apartment. Nor did I have to tell her later what had happened. The prospect of neither concern nor chiding appealed to me. No one knew except me—and *them;* and they wouldn't be telling anyone I knew.

For the first time in my life, I thought, standing under the stinging spray of the shower, I understood the silence of the rape victim: it was dumb to walk alone on the street on which you were attacked; it was dumb to wear tight pants; it was dumb . . . to be female?

I did not, in my bleakest moments, think that. I'd better clear my head out before Barnard—as thoroughly as I habitually emptied my handbag of the day's accumulation of stubs and used Kleenex and junk mail. Because of that two-minute nightly ritual, performed as unthinkingly as brushing my teeth, my wallet lay on Jon's bureau, my traveler's checks beside it; my make-up case, pad and pencil, and a paperback thriller that didn't—no loss at all, if lost—were all there. The handbag itself was a good one, but past middle age. I'd been meaning to replace it for more than a year. I hadn't, I thought, done all that well by the girls.

I smiled, revolving under the spray, rinsing off the energetic lather I'd worked up, thinking it was almost as if I'd conned *them.*

And, observing my reflection in the mirror backing the door as I toweled down, it occurred to me—ridiculously, for the first time—that I had gotten away unscathed physically. They hadn't bruised anything but my ego. And that was making a rapid recovery.

2

I was on my way out when Margery emerged from the bedroom. She looked terrible. Every day she looked worse. Or was I only able each day to see a little more clearly how she looked? Margery seemed worn out; as though she had lived a life without antimacassars. Her face looked blighted: her eyes leaked at the corners; tiny red lines mapped the thin skin of her puffy cheeks. She must have seen in my face a little of what I saw: she wiped the corners of her eyes, pushed at her hair. A thin smile interrupted the bleakness of her face as she said, "What you must think of a hostess who keeps oversleeping. Where are you off to, looking as if you've been hours at Elizabeth Arden?"

I ordered myself to smile; I eked it out, out of sympathy and embarrassment. Slim pickings for a smile. All you can do is . . . all you can do. "Thanks," I said. "I can use a small boost right about now. I'm off up the street to old alma mater—who always had a critical eye."

"Your speech!" Margery's dismay was genuine. "I was planning to come!" She clutched at her robe, pushed her hand through her hair again, overwhelmed by the extent of her unreadiness.

"I promise, I'll tell you all about it as soon as I get back," I said. "I've got to run." Despite which, I moved toward her and gave her a clumsy embrace. She smelled bad, I noticed; sour. Ashamed of minding, I hugged her again and hurried out.

I walked quickly up the hill, holding tight to my good black handbag and the manila envelope containing my remarks, my eye out for children at play. On the far side of Broadway, I caught a taxi uptown. The cab was decrepit; the cabbie hated people, animals, and other cars, but we made it to the corner of 116th Street without incident.

As I waited for the light, a notice on one of the pillars of Columbia's front gate caught my eye. WELCOME TO GAY COLUMBIA was the headline. I would have read further, but I had the light now and it was getting late.

Crossing Broadway, I thought the place looked different from what I remembered, but the people looked the same. The subway station was new to me; most of the stores along the west side of Broadway between 115th and 116th streets were also. But the teachers looked like teachers, the undergraduates looked like undergraduates, and the graduate students looked put upon, as always.

As I entered the Barnard campus, I noticed, first, how much less of it there was than there used to be—where limited areas of grass had been there were now buildings. I couldn't for the life of me imagine why they didn't look more squeezed in: there hadn't ever been that much grass. It was only then, glancing around, that I noticed that the green gate was gone. It had probably been gone a long time, but standing there, for fully five seconds, I missed it. Sure, it had been protective in the pejorative sense, but it had been sheltering in another sense, too. I walked quickly up the steps of Barnard Hall. On the top step, I gave myself another momentary free trip into the past: just there, behind the column directly to the left of the door, one summer's night, Leo and I, for the fun of it, had made love standing up—with brief, boisterous success. I went on in.

On "Jake," the dedicatory emblem on the floor, coinciding with the central meeting area of the college, a long registration table was set up, manned by students. If "manned" was unacceptable, what *did* they say? I wondered. The student registrars were still doing business with alumnae arriving too late for the first events of the morning. Arriving in time to hear me? I approached a woman standing behind one of the tables; a bureaucratic overseer, obviously. When I gave her my name, she introduced herself and promptly escorted me to the gym, the entrance to which was perhaps twenty feet away. Her cool businesslike treatment of me—dear God! what had I expected?—had a salutary effect.

As I stood inside the entrance to the huge room, enough to the side to be out of the way of those entering, I felt . . . steady. Not oversize, not undersize. Certainly, nothing less would be expected from Barnard plus nineteen, I thought, not afraid to smile.

For the time being, the room was filled mainly with straight-backed chairs. Row upon row of them, so many to fill. Would they be filled? Of course, I decided at once. The Barnard person in charge of determining how many chairs to have set up doubtless was expert at estimating such matters accurately. And, slowly, they were coming in now, program-laden alumnae seeking and greeting familiar faces, checking name badges to confirm memory. Aside from reunion addicts, few alumnae return more frequently than every five years, if that: so some recognitions took a bit of second-glancing.

The age range of the women was broad, yet they weren't any of them dressed radically differently from one another. Certainly, they didn't look sufficiently different, stylistically speaking, to account for six decades—seven even!

As the women took seats, I looked at some of them more closely. On the side aisle, right up front, sat two alumnae in their sixties. The ease of their talk bespoke many reunion encounters over the years. Nearby, two women in their early thirties were engaged in a conversation that looked more exclamatory. Perhaps they hadn't seen each other since graduation. This must be their tenth reunion, the first big one. I looked around for people my age: there, *they* might be. But it was hard to tell these days; they might also be several years older. No, I decided, this was their twentieth, as next year would be mine. If I came. Even if I didn't, I thought, and smiled again. I recognized neither of the women whose twentieth reunion I had designated this; but I should recognize one of them . . . a little? Not a familiar face. Nowhere in the room. But only a quarter, at most, of the chairs were filled. There was time.

Not finding familiar faces, I searched the faces of strangers. Noticing one woman's pearls, unsuccessfully incognito on her plain jersey dress, I thought: What was it like for you here? And another, exquisite in her mid-fifties: What was it like for you? Did it matter to you that Barnard was . . . the way it was? Or was your world so fine that anywhere would have done?

Not for me. When I was here, there were altogether perhaps only twice as many students as there were presently chairs in this room. I wanted to go over to the two older women in the front row—ask them, Did you like it that Barnard was small in your day? They would understand.

Jessie. How would they understand what Barnard's smallness had meant to you?

For me, it had made all the difference, that summer be-

166 GETTING TOGETHER

tween my sophomore and junior years. I had, before now, thought of it—more than once: how, if I had been attending a city college—which would have been the logical thing given our financial circumstances—when my mother died that summer, three months before my nineteenth birthday, I would have had to quit going to school days in order to earn enough to pay rent someplace and feed and clothe myself and go, instead, nights. And with my academic flaccidness, I don't think I would have stuck out night school. I think I would have dropped out of school altogether. But when Mama died, instead of being at a city college, I was halfway through Barnard, and they assumed responsibility for seeing me the rest of the way. Out of twelve hundred students, there weren't an awful lot of orphans.

It was the last week of July that my mother died. A week later, at the end of the official deep mourning period, I telephoned and asked if there was any officer of the college on campus. I was told that Dean Pearsall was available, and I was put through to his secretary who, after a minimum of questions, made an appointment for me to see him the following day.

I arrived, a deep-eyed robot in a black piqué dress greyed by a week of daily ironing, and was ushered into the dean's office by his solicitous secretary, who seemed to be trying not to stare. I wondered if she'd never seen a nearly grown-up orphan before.

There he sat, behind an important-looking desk, a large man I didn't recall even having passed in a corridor. I suppose, under other circumstances, he and the setting might have intimidated me. But a week and a half after your mother has died with flagrant suddenness, and you find yourself out a mother, out parents, out a home, important persons and important rooms recede in impact. I was calm.

Dean Pearsall had a folder in front of him. He tapped it. "Your record," he informed me, once I'd seated myself and he'd offered his condolences and I'd accepted them. "I've been reading it."

I nodded without enthusiasm. My record was nothing to bowl over a dean. I had the previous year, bored with requirements, taken courses mostly in my major and, therefore, done relatively well. All right, well. But freshman year there had been the shock of competing, in rough first-year required courses, with students many of whom had arrived at Barnard from the quality-conscious scholastic factories of Brooklyn with 98.6 per cent averages and the like as the norm among them. I personally considered 98.6 normal only for temperature. My own high school average was not quite 83 per cent—which made my acceptance, let alone my survival for two years, novel. I had, sophomore year, done particularly well in the classes of two notoriously hard teachers: those two A's were, to me, worth anyone's straight B+ average. What worth Dean Pearsall might attribute to them remained to be seen.

He didn't mention them, or my muddy freshman grades. He said, "You won the Gildersleeve Prize."

"Yes," I said. I'd won it for two reasons: first, I'd found out, through a fluke, that I had the lowest entering average of any freshman in my class and the Libra in me thought something to balance that off might be nice. The second reason I set out to win the Gildersleeve Prize, the main reason, was that it would be a gift for Freddie, my winning.

After Christmas break freshman year, she had not come back; she would, we were told, be out the entire spring semester. She had a history of tuberculosis, they said. I heard later that that was not the sort of sanitarium she was in; but that wasn't until much later, and it wouldn't have mattered anyway. What did was that she wasn't allowed visitors, or even mail, except from family and her very closest friends. I knew that if I won, her best friend, another member of the English Department, would take the news to Freddie; and that Freddie would know it had been—my trying, working truly hard for the very first time in my academic life—a get-well gift for her. I'd been right. After I won, her friend returned from a visit to Freddie with a message: Freddie was proud of me, and happy.

I didn't think Dean Pearsall needed to know that much about me and the Gildersleeve Prize. Still, he seemed to be waiting for me to say something. "It was for a paper that was only ten and a half pages long," I said. "The paper that was runner-up was seventy-two pages."

"I cannot tell," said the dean, "if you are ridiculously modest or outrageously vain. At the moment, I'm not sure it matters. You did win the only prize open to freshmen, indeed the only prize you compete for until senior year, and that must be taken into consideration."

"Thank you," I said.

"Miss Littman—may I call you Jessica?—"

I nodded. No one called me Jessica except my mother, but I bit my tongue and let him. It was just a name.

"I see that your financial situation wasn't . . . entirely adequate even before your mother's death," he said.

"My tuition was always paid on time," I countered; thinking, What he really means is that it was presumptuous of us to think we could make it through here on our income. If he only knew. . . . But even I had only found out for sure during the past few days, going through her papers, coming on a copy of last year's tax forms, literally how little Mama had managed on. I wasn't shocked; I think I had known all along, I think it was part of the way Mama and I managed, that I pretended not to know exactly how bad things were— or else how could I have allowed it to go on? No matter how much she wanted it. How much she wanted it!—could this man—would anyone—ever know? What would he say if I told him that I was pretty sure mine was the only scholarship application that exaggerated family income in order to be considered?

Dean Pearsall was looking at me patiently. He must have said something. "I'm sorry," I said. "My mind seems to keep wandering."

"Of course. I said, I meant only that it must have been difficult financially, your coming here." There was sympathy in his voice, not condescension.

I still felt resentful. Difficult? It had been damn near impossible. But we didn't need sympathy. Sympathy was one thing my mother never needed, never wanted. Barnard had been *her* choice for me. The sacrifices she made were voluntary—willful, even. And private. He was waiting for me to say something again. I had, I reminded myself sharply, come to him because I needed something. I said, "It was very important to my mother that I come to Barnard."

He nodded. "Wanting you to have something she hadn't had, yes, of course," he said. Knowing Jewish parents, he supposed.

"No." Why did I insist on his getting it straight? The man was being kind, he kept *trying;* and I kept correcting him, not only in my head. But he was alive, and she was dead, and the least she deserved was that the record be straight.

"Dean Pearsall, my mother was a graduate of the University of Kiev. What she wanted for me was what she did have, a first-rate education. I had to go to a school as good as this one, she insisted on it." I swallowed and told him the truth. "She would have given her life for it." And, maybe, had. But I didn't say that to him; I didn't have that much head about me.

If I wasn't shrewd enough, he *was* kind enough. He said, "Well, then, we shall simply have to see to it that you finish, won't we?"

And they had. A few days later, a substantial midsummer contribution to the college was credited to my account. With that, and the jobs the placement office helped me get, I managed.

Ancient history, I thought, looking at a small cluster of

alumnae who couldn't have graduated more than a year ago. When they'd helped me, when I'd managed, Barnard cost—everything: room, board, tuition—fifteen hundred dollars a year. Certainly, to me, then, a fortune; but nothing compared to today.

Why was I edging away from the point? They had seen me through.

Not only financially. In the weeks after school began, three teachers saw me through. Saw through me? No, I think they were more kind than perceptive. They thought I might kill myself; in fact, I didn't feel enough to do that. I spent most of my time wandering, literally and figuratively. I was unable to focus on anything, and that disorientation was what they saw as pain. I did not, in those weeks, feel pain over the death of my mother. The pain I had to feel would keep for six years, until a time I could afford to cry, when I could afford to wish I were dead because there was enough resurgent life in me by then so that I would be giving up something.

If they did not understand that I was not up to grieving, they helped me nonetheless. They took turns, the three of them, summoning me to their office on one pretext or another; I presume to make me feel that my presence in the world was noticed, mattered. I managed to feel the first; the second eluded me longer than mourning.

If I lacked the emotional energy to grieve, if I didn't have sufficient interest in me to kill myself, I did, little by little, summon the will to do more than wander through my academic life. To flunk out would have been to spit in my mother's dead face: to me, that image was real—and horrifying. By November, I was studying some; concentrating seemed a feat of Olympian stature. Eventually, the semester was lost. The high C's I got were not worth straining for. Still, those three teachers persisted in caring; and I did much better in the spring.

The room was more than half full now. All these women coming to hear me . . . so I would not have to stand up alone in this room. . . .

At first, when Mama died, I had wanted nothing. I didn't even want her still to be alive. The doctor had said that, had she lived through the stroke, she would have been an invalid. *Mama?* It would have . . . killed her. So what was there for me to wish for? Then, after those first few weeks, I—really—remembered: how much she had wanted me to have a Barnard education. At first feebly and sporadically—but, after a year, fiercely—I wanted that. For her.

With secondhand passion, I raised my grades the second semester of my junior year to a B. The scholarship committee did not begrudge me money for my last year; it would have been out of character. Senior year, despite losing Leo, despite that second unexpected death in my life in little over a year, I made good grades. And, despite the registrar's conviction that no one ever made honors in her major who was not at least *cum laude,* the head of my department went down in person to her office and insisted, and my marks in my major were averaged. I had earned honors.

They were to be handed out, separate from the Columbia graduation ceremony or the Barnard diploma ritual, here, in this room, on the morning of graduation day. The gym would be filled that day, of course.

That day everyone but me looked forward to. For me, the day held mortification. I had no one to come.

Everyone wanted more graduation tickets than the allotted four, except me. I gave away three of mine; but I could not bear to give away the fourth—to say out loud, by that act, that there was not a single human being in the world who should be there. To see me graduate; to see me win honors. To *see* that I had seen Mama's wish through.

Two weeks before graduation, I wrote a letter to my uncle in Detroit, a man I had met only twice, when my father died and when my mother died. He was my father's older brother and he had, when I was nine and Papa died, bought me ten comic books of my choosing and a dozen packages of bubble gum.

I barely knew him; he was practically a stranger.

I wrote anyway. But I didn't want to make him come by saying how humiliated I would be to be all alone that day. I lie: I didn't think he'd understand, because I knew that his children had not gone to college. In my mind, I showered limitations on him; what other protection did I have? The note I sent was reserved and very short: I told him I was graduating and the date and the place, and that I would be happy if he could come.

He didn't answer my letter. My only comfort was that I had not revealed to him how much his coming would mean to me; he would, I decided, not have come anyway. Detroit was far. He was old. His wife was chronically ill.

I hated him for not coming.

Only shame made me hang on to that last ticket.

At seven fifteen on the morning of graduation, the night watchman called up to say there was an old man downstairs who said he was my uncle.

How I ran down the stairs! And there he stood, an old, poorly shaven Jew in a baggy suit and a shiny tie: he was so *beautiful*. It occurs to me only now, for the first time, why the night watchman sounded suspicious: he must not have thought that Barnard girls had uncles who looked like that. I did. *I did!*

My uncle held out his arms to me; his rough cheek felt like balm to mine. We neither of us, I think, said a single word for the first minute or two. Later, over a cup of tea in Riker's, he told me that his daughter, who lived in Chicago, had arranged to take the day off from work to stay with his wife in Detroit. She had arrived late last night and he had taken the first plane out this morning. He would, he told me apologetically, have to leave early enough for his daughter to fly back to Chicago that evening. I kept nodding. All I could think was: He came! He came! He came!

This day I wouldn't have to get through alone.

Later that morning, at the honors assembly, when my name was called, he leaned over and patted my hand with his thick-veined calloused one. I was too filled with gratitude to have room left to feel guilty because I had underrated him: whatever my uncle understood or didn't understand about college or honors or my mother's dreams, he understood about being there.

At the end of the day, after both graduation ceremonies, when he left, without time even (he apologized again) to take me to dinner, he gave me, out of his jacket pocket, a brown bag containing six pairs of nylon stockings. The size, I discovered days later, was wrong. But if I had not known him well enough to know that he would, if asked, come, how should he have known my stocking size? Ten comic books and a dozen packages of bubble gum. I was twenty, not nine: I kept those stockings for years. And to the day he died, I loved my uncle because on the one day of my life I needed him to be my uncle, he was.

"Jessica Littman?" The woman was out of breath.

"Yes."

"Thank God. We have to begin and I couldn't find you. I'm Deirdre Kennan, English. I'll be introducing you. I have your bio, of course, but is there anything special you'd like me to say?"

"No," I said, following her up on the platform. I took a seat while she went to the podium.

The gym was filled. That was flattering. If they hadn't come . . .

But I knew, now, that it wouldn't be hard to get through *this*.

There are some things, some days, no one can help anyone get through. People—just people—won't do. The days I mean are those you aren't *supposed* to be alone; if you are, you are, on such days, most alone.

Rosh Hashanah. I sat on the steps of Brooks Hall, chilly in my Bermuda shorts, unwilling to go in to dinner, to eat off a tray; not tonight, not my first holiday alone. I waited out dinner, then I went in. I ate a candy bar, then another. Six. Nine. I vomited until my throat hurt. That made it easier, pinpointing the hurt. I didn't cry for six years.

The other bad day, capitalized among the lower-case bad days, was my birthday that year. Mama died on the last day but one of July; in mid-October I turned nineteen. How little that tells you, if you don't know what birthdays were like in my home.

Birthdays were your day, the one day of the year singled out for celebrating you. It was for my birthday, not Christmas or Easter (or Chanukah or Pesach), that I would get a new dress. However poor we were that year, I got a new dress. Always a present, too: something Mama knew you really wanted—guessed, because in my family you didn't often ask for things. The main thing you got on your birthday was attention: you woke to being sung "Happy Birthday" to; and were wished it, again and again, until you went to sleep that night.

On this, my first birthday without a family, I wandered through my morning classes like a stateless person: without a passport, you have no identity; without a family, you have no birthday. I wanted someone, anyone, to wish me a happy birthday. Never mind that it wasn't happy, never mind that it couldn't be. Without the acknowledging words, it wasn't my birthday. Without a birthday, do you exist?

At twenty minutes of twelve, I met a friend who knew and said it: Happy birthday, Jessie. It wasn't her fault it didn't ring true. Mama, Mama. . . .

Never again will I feel this alone.

I could arrange it. If you didn't love someone as much as I loved Mama, then when they left, you didn't miss them this much.

I made myself a promise: it was my gift to me on my nineteenth birthday.

Dear God, *I did.* I made that vow.

And kept it? How much had I loved Leo? I had loved Sam, but not *that* much. Alec? Alec? Sweating: I didn't know.

Silence. Eyes. On me. Deirdre Whatever-her-name-was was moving away from the lectern now. The introduction was over. I was thirty-nine, not twenty; and I was on.

I went to the lectern. I straightened my notes. I looked out at the audience, women who had gone to Barnard—like me? Suddenly, I wanted to tell them what it had been like for me here. I wanted to tell them about what I had felt in this room, the morning of the honors assembly. What I had lived through. But these women hadn't come to hear about my life at Barnard; it was my professional life they'd come to hear about. That was why I'd been asked. But not, of course, why I'd come.

"I wasn't asleep," I said, "I was remembering. That's why we come back, isn't it, because we remember something?

"I was remembering—mainly—how different I felt when I was here. Different from the other women in my class. I don't feel . . . very different any more.

"What I did five years ago, what I'm doing, choosing to work at a new profession, is not so different from what hundreds of thousands of women are doing across this country. I didn't like the way my life felt . . .'' I was reading now from my prepared remarks and felt secure enough to look around the room.

It was then I saw Margery, midway back, on the far aisle. She had apparently arrived at some point when I was oblivious to the audience, or surely I would have spotted her. Or would I have? With her washed-out blond hair, in the beige tweed suit she'd worn to lunch yesterday, she didn't stand out— except that she was crying. Why had I made her feel she had to come? Obviously, being here was painful for her. Did my being up here make it worse? Point up how far we each had come since our Barnard days? I wanted to go to her, to comfort her. As soon as my talk was over, I would. If only I could tell her that—but there was no way. Tears continued to dribble down her face. I had to look away or *I* would cry.

The page was blurry; I willed it to clear. "I didn't like the way my life felt," I read again, "so I did something about it."

I told them how I'd lost interest in teaching history; how I'd then tried to concentrate on writing history, but found myself making things up about the people I was writing about. Finally, I told them how I'd decided to take a chance on making people up altogether. This was what they wanted; and I gave it all to them. I didn't stop with the first book but told them about the second, how that was harder to write; about the third, brave one; and even a little about what it felt like to have turned in the fourth book. Only then did I feel entitled to say something personal.

"There are a few closing remarks here; but I've changed my mind about what I want to say in these last few minutes." I took a breath.

"None of what I've told you of how I came to write novels, none of the books I've written or will write, is entirely unconnected from what happened to me in this place. That in my mid-thirties I decided finally to find out if I had a novel in me seems far less daring to me than that I decided, with a lot of help from a few people here, fifteen years before that, to choose living over mere survival. Each student is different. Perhaps my case was a little more different than one might wish. I must admit, I would wish for no student here the particular experience I had; but of course no one ever repeats anyone else's exact experience, good or bad. I do wish for all Barnard students, today and tomorrow, *my* Barnard.

"To me, Barnard was more than a place to study, more than a place to learn, more than a place to live. It was the place I learned again, as someone severely injured must learn again to walk, that those things—studying, learning, and yes, living—were worth doing.

"This school has someone like me in it: someone who won't make it through here, let alone through life, without a few people prepared to pay special attention. That person needs my Barnard. For her sake, that Barnard must still exist."

Their faces were quiet; their hands still. I sat down, because there wasn't anything else to do or say. I looked down, thinking, Maybe I overstepped the bounds. The women sitting out there were, some of them, ladies of the old school: they might have found my remarks emotional and therefore unfastidious. And the much younger women, my juniors by ten or fifteen years, might they not have found what I said at the end intellectually sloppy? How did I know that the Barnard I owed so much to did still exist—because I wanted it to? Jessie. Ending on a wish? And then I heard it begin, low, a beat, a rhythmic sound; it persisted, not getting louder, but neither weakening, until I looked up. And they were standing there, almost all of them were standing, applauding quietly.

Hear that, Freddie? Hear that? Those ladies, even the oldest among them, are ladies of *this* old school. They want Barnard to be as good for the young woman in difficulty here today as it was to me. They were, I knew—dear God, how few moments in life are you given to *know*—praising, acknowledging, not me, certainly not me or my talk, but *our* school. My wish was theirs. Of course. Barnard had, in however less traumatic circumstances, been there for them, too. That's why they were here: for the same reason I was. I stood then and joined in the applause, a contained but sustained tribute to the fact that no institution is bigger, or smaller, than its people.

And I had not invented Barnard.

Directly afterward, people clustered around the platform. To my astonishment, I immediately recognized as Ellin Guerin a sleekly handsome woman, the first to reach me. Ellin had been a class ahead of me, and was, therefore, attending her twentieth reunion. She looked little beyond thirty.

"You look completely different. You look wonderful!" she exclaimed. Her hand went to her mouth. "Jessie, excuse me."

"Don't apologize," I said. "We do look better, both of us."

At school, Ellin had been hugely overweight and if that interesting, slightly mysterious face had been there all the time, wedged within layers of fat, I certainly hadn't seen it. I recognized her by her hair: as thick and black and shining as a Chinese beauty's, she wore it, still, cut with straight bangs and clipped just below her ears.

"I wanted to tell you," she said, reaching for my hand, "that when you were talking I kept seeing Freddie, as if she were actually here—only not scowling the way she used to. Grinning. Standing there, grinning at you, for being here, the way you are, and for saying what you said."

I put my hand over hers and squeezed, because my throat felt as rough as a saint's knees at her words; for a second, no word of mine could edge by.

"You didn't think of her?" said Ellin.

"I did," I said.

"For me," said Ellin, "she was the best of this place." She lifted her hand and moved off.

Seven or eight women were waiting to speak with me. When I had worked my way down to three, I looked past them briefly for Margery, to signal her that I was almost through; but she wasn't in her seat, or standing nearby. I rushed the remaining women some, anxious to find her; but the last was not about to leave without her say.

"This is my thirtieth reunion," she told me. "I never came before. I've never kept in touch with any of my classmates. I only came today because . . . my life has emptied out, and it was something to do, not because I felt anything about Barnard. But now I think I'll spend some serious time thinking through what Barnard may have given me that I might have overlooked." She smiled a dazzling smile. "For a start, I met my first husband in Brooks' living room. He was waiting for another girl." She—winked; and walked away.

I went to find Margery. There was hardly anyone left in the gym, and she was nowhere in sight. Had she left before my talk was over? Had she waited for me afterward, but given up, because there were too many women wanting to speak to me? I felt torn. I was due in McIntosh Center for lunch. I'd said weeks ago that I'd stay. I was expected. There is in me a thick streak of puritanism which insists that if you've said you'll do something, you do it, regardless of what comes up, short of death or flood. Margery didn't qualify as that dire an emergency, did she?

Didn't she?

I stood poised outside the gymnasium, undecided, when a hand took my elbow and a voice said, "Hard to get away, wasn't it? Madge Dunne." She offered me her hand; her grip was strong. "Good to meet you in person at last."

At least I wasn't supposed to recognize her. Hearty woman, plain of face and dress. A gym teacher? Biology, perhaps?— bigot! Admissions! Madge Dunne was head of the Admissions

Office. They'd requested copies of my books a couple of years back—they were starting some sort of library of alumnae books—and she, Madge Dunne, had sent me the nicest letter afterward. It was so sweet, I answered it. "Same here," I said.

"We're late," she said. "Let's walk over together."

Of course I had to go. Madge Dunne set a brisk pace and we reached the Center in a couple of minutes. "You know," said Madge, "the part of these things I enjoy most is the meals. The food is awful, of course, and that's wonderful. I mean, to know that some things never really do change is a comfort, isn't it, in this world where everything changes as relentlessly as a clock? But the bad food's only half the fun. The best part is talking with the students. They're so *intelligent*. I listen to them and I think, if we were half as smart as they are, we weren't dumb. And, would you believe it, that cheers me up as much as a double martini?"

3

Nervousness rose in me like nausea during the bus ride down Broadway. I had gotten away after lunch as fast as I decently could, but there wasn't a cab in sight, so I had to settle for the bus. What if Margery weren't there, I thought.

What if she were?

She was sitting in the living room, still wearing her suit, a glass in her hand. She raised it high. "Hail, O orator!" She drank. "I'm celebrating," she said. "You, I'm celebrating your celebrity. And your devotion. And your gratitude. I certainly never knew you owed *everything* to Barnard."

"They saw me through a rough time," I said mildly.

"Your friends might have helped—if they'd known," said Margery.

"You knew a lot—and you helped a lot," I said. "Margery, you know that."

"I *know* that you were . . . less than honest about how

hard that time was for you," said Margery. "You had your secrets, Jessie, didn't you?"

"I wouldn't put it that way."

"I would. I want to put it that way. I was your friend and I didn't know the half of it. You kept secrets from me, Jessie, terrible secrets."

For a moment, I thought I was going crazy. Not only had Margery been reading my mind before I got up to speak this morning, she'd been reading my mind since I'd arrived.

"You said—you told them all today—that you wanted to *die*," she cried.

I hadn't, of course, said *that*. Still . . .

"You never told me! You didn't talk to me about it. Why couldn't you trust me, Jessie?"

In that accusation there was an uncomfortable proportion of truth. I hadn't told Margery about a lot of things. "Margery, I did what I had to do to get through that time. Not talking about it was one of the ways I managed. There's no reason to take it personally. Besides," I added, "it was twenty years ago."

"Oh, is there a time limit on secrets?" she said. "I didn't know. Now, Jessie, don't frown like that, it's aging. I forgive you. I do. If you keep what's going on inside you secret from a good friend—what's a friend for, if not to forgive you? Don't you agree? Anyway, here's to you." She raised her glass again. "Join me."

"It's a little early for me," I said.

"Better early than never," said Margery. Raising herself jerkily from her seat, she went to the bar, poured a hefty dose of vodka on some rocks, and brought it to me. I set the glass down on a coaster.

"That's a bit strong for me," I said. Grasping for some easing of the tension I felt in the room: "I'm not a vodka person."

"Well, you ought to be!" said Margery, returning to her seat and her own drink, which she held up for my inspection. "It's Russian, you're Russian," she said, explaining the two-times table to a slow child. "You should get along marvelously."

She whirled the glass in her hand admiringly. "Isn't it wonderful? It has no color until it gets in your mouth. Then it's orange tipped with bright red—gorgeous. *We're* good friends, aren't we?" she said to the glass.

She looked up at me. "Aren't *we?*"

"You know we are," I said.

"How *should* I know?" said Margery. "All these years, you hardly kept in touch."

"*We* hardly kept in touch," I said gently.

"Umm," muttered Margery, noncommital about my correction. Finishing what was in her glass, she renegotiated the way to the bar and got herself a refill. Carrying it gingerly, respectfully, as if it were a Sung vase, she came and stood in front of me. She looked at me intently for a long moment, then went and resumed her seat.

"You're right," she said. "I'm so tired."

"Why not go in and lie down, then?" I suggested.

"I'm tired because it's heavy—and lying down doesn't make it any lighter," she said; and then, intensely, "I want to get rid of it!"

"I'm afraid I don't understand," I said.

"No," said Margery, "you wouldn't. Because you wouldn't be like that, you wouldn't need to be." She took a drink, keeping the liquor in her mouth before she swallowed it. "It's so good," she said. "Aren't you going to have some before it turns to water?"

I picked up the drink she had made me and took a sip.

Margery giggled. "You should see your face," she said. Then, reassuringly, "The first sip every day is the only one that tastes like that. After that, it's better and better." To emphasize which, she took another swallow of her own drink. Then another, a quick one.

"I felt too guilty," she said.

Drunk as she was, she could read the confusion in my face. "*I* did not keep in touch with *you* because I felt guilty," she said, very, very slowly, so I would be sure to understand. "I didn't deserve to continue the friendship." Lesson two; clearly, slowly.

The possibility that she knew about Leo and me flashed on in my head like a warning light on a computer. But it didn't check out and I turned it off.

Steadily, methodically, Margery was emptying her glass again. As soon as it was empty, she heaved herself—the second time successfully—out of her chair and wended her way to the bar.

"Margery, do you really have to do that?"

She turned, looked at me, at her glass, making no pretense of not understanding what I meant. With the quietness of a direct-hit bomb, she said, "Yes."

Returning to her chair, she bumped into a small side table, knocking over a Wedgwood ashtray. Automatically I rose to help. "Leave it!" she commanded. I obeyed. She was right: it was empty and unbroken. In the face of what was happening in the room, it couldn't matter anyway.

Margery, having achieved her chair again, said, in the most reasonable voice you could imagine, "It's not my fault, you know."

"It didn't break," I said, stupidly.

"It's not my fault that I drink," said Margery, talking English, loudly and clearly, to a Yugoslav peasant. She waited.

"I see," I said, seeing nothing except that she required a response.

"The hell you do!" Thrusting herself out of her chair once more, spilling part of her drink, not noticing, she stalked to

SATURDAY *185*

the sofa where I sat and stood glaring down at me. Then, like a cotton doll, she folded onto the sofa beside me. She smelled bad. I was surprised; I thought the thing about vodka was that it didn't smell. Then I realized: the smell wasn't from her mouth. It seemed to be coming from all of her, a sour odor, almost as though she were vomiting from her pores. She moved closer to me; I forced myself not to move away.

"If not for Leo . . ." She was resting her drink on my thigh, her face was flushed. Suddenly, she smiled conspiratorially: girls at school.

"Leo married me on Saturday morning, remember?"

I nodded.

"He promised on Saturday, right? He was unfaithful the first time on Thursday," she said. "How about that?"

It wasn't possible. I remembered that Saturday, and how she had looked—and how Leo had looked at her: a man heart over head in love. It was not possible.

"She didn't last. Actually, very few of them lasted more than a few times. Leo wears women out quickly," she added girlishly. I shivered under her glance.

"But not all of them,"—she patted my arm—"as quickly as some. Pru lasted only a week, Helene barely two, Sara only the one time. Sara was Tuesday—yes, I'm quite sure, Tuesday."

And the first time Thursday. Not the Thursday after their wedding, but some Thursday, possibly years afterward.

"Never in the world, Jessie, you mustn't for a minute think it, would I have begun to drink more than—*you* do, if Leo hadn't had those women. Women! I call them women. Many of them were girls, especially in the last years. The older Leo got, the younger the girls got."

The idea that Leo—any man—might choose to be unfaithful to the woman sitting beside me was unfortunately not difficult to comprehend; but that Leo had been unfaithful to Margery for a long time, that he had been unfaithful to anyone anything like the Margery he had married—who had been stunning, lovely not only on the outside but inside, too, vibrant as a fireworks display, everything a man could want—no, I could not conceive of it.

Margery was giggling. "They'd be veritable nymphets by now if he hadn't stopped finally," she said. "No, he doesn't do it any more. He stopped on Wednesday."

"What happened Wednesday?" I asked. Was I taking advantage of Margery's drunkenness, or was this the only way to talk with her when she was like this?

"Did you know," asked Margery portentously, "that I was born on Wednesday?"

"No."

"Wednesday's child is full of woe," she said. "When were you born?"

"Friday, I think."

"Of course you were," said Margery.

"Of course?"

"Of course, 'Friday's child is loving and giving,' isn't she?" she said.

"It's only a nursery rhyme, Margery," I said.

"That's easy enough to say if you were born on Friday," she answered fiercely.

This was no territory to explore further, I decided. I backed up one topic, impelled as much, I must admit, by curiosity as by a desire to deflect Margery from me. "Margery, what happened Wednesday?"

"I told you, I was born."

"With Leo—that Wednesday."

"Oh, *that* Wednesday. I killed myself."

So much for smoother territory.

"He never came home when he said, he was always late. That day of all days, he came early," she complained. "But in the hospital, I made it clear to him—I'd do it again. He couldn't watch me enough to stop me. Oh, Jessie, you should have seen him. He was as pale as if *he'd* had his stomach pumped. And he looked . . . he hadn't looked at me that way in years, as if I were his own true love. And he cried, he cried a *lot*," she said, as if he'd fulfilled a quota, "and he asked me, he begged me, to tell him what he could do that would make me promise not to try again."

She sighed. "It was such a sincere offer. I had to think for quite a while—he thought I was deciding, but I was just trying to think if it would really make me feel better. You know, I wasn't sure it would really make that much difference to me. Still, it would be . . . right. So I told him, if he would never ever sleep with any of them—or anyone else—again, why I wouldn't do it again. I said, 'You be true to me from this day forward and I will not kill myself.'"

An effigy of a smile was on her face. "I didn't lie," she said, "but I fooled him." She lifted her glass from my thigh and took a decorous sip, replaced it.

"Or don't you know that liquor can kill you? It works slowly, deliciously slowly—but in its own good time, it does the job."

She sat up straight, and said, "Leo will be sorry." Not threateningly, assuring me that it was so. "He'd do anything to get me to stop. He'd do anything to help me now."

"That's true, Margery, I know it is," I promised her.

"*I* know," she said. "But if I stopped, how would he remember he was to blame?"

She looked at me as though that were a totally reasonable question.

"You drink to keep reminding him?" I said dully; thinking, That isn't possible. It isn't even possible that she thinks that's what she's doing.

"It works, doesn't it?" she asked matter-of-factly. "Of course, one could argue," she added, "that Leo isn't the *first* cause." The ingenuity of the thought pleased her. As if to reward herself, she got up from the sofa and made her way to the bar. Refilling her glass, she turned to me and lifted it in a toast.

"After all," she said, "if not for you, Jessie, none of it would have happened." She drank.

I felt as though she'd aimed the liquor at my face instead of down her throat. The feeling was so strong I wiped my cheek.

Maybe it was the look on my face that made her decide to keep her distance; maybe she just couldn't face the hike back to the sofa. She sat down in the chair closest to the bar. Most of the length of the room was between us. Her voice soft, cajoling rather than accusing, she said, "Don't you see, Jessie, that if Leo had married someone like you, he wouldn't have done all those terrible things. And then I wouldn't have had to drink."

Drunk or not: "No, I don't see that, Margery," I said firmly.

She would persuade me. "With someone like you, he wouldn't have felt the need to have all those other women." She began crying, softly. "He wouldn't have done it to you."

A woman like me; me. If Leo had married *me*. Leo had never come close to marrying me. Even I, who had desperately wanted what I had with Leo to continue, who thought what we had *had* to go on, had not ever thought in terms of marriage. There hadn't been time before it ended for me to get to that place. Before he ended it. Stay away from that, Jessie; not now.

"Don't you know," Margery said, "that Leo's always been sorry he didn't marry you instead of me?"

It wasn't true: it was simply not possible. But in that ridiculous distortion of what had happened to us—to me and Leo and Margery—that might be one tiny hard malignant nodule of truth. *Did Margery know?*

I said, "Margery, I don't think you know what you're saying."

That didn't stop her; suddenly I knew that nothing would.

"I don't blame him for that. How could I?" she said. "If Leo preferred you to me, I of all people could understand that."

She got up; holding on to things, she got herself back to the sofa. She reached out and caressed my cheek. "You look as though I'm telling you something strange, Jessie. Don't look like that. It's about us, the three of us. How can it be strange?"

She looked at her wedding band. "That's the only reason I married him, you know," she said.

"Margery, if you think I understand a word of this—"

"Of course you do. It's not complicated. I'm not nearly as intelligent as you, and it's very clear to me. I got to marry Leo, not you, right?"

Like an idiot, I nodded.

"Good," said Margery, affirming my comprehension. "Well, by marrying him—with your man—I'd be more like you. You see, I'd have Leo. It was sort of like having your quickness. You know?"

Of course I didn't—and given the way she was talking, maybe she *didn't* know about Leo and me. Maybe this was just a fantasy, a crazy drunken made-up—I had to know. "Margery," I said, "whatever gave you the idea that Leo thought I was so special?"

"Oh, Jessie, just because I wasn't as smart as you, you mustn't underestimate me that much." Then, kindly, "You're thinking about *me,* about how much I loved Leo."

I saw her: waiting for his calls those early October afternoons. And, later, after a call, when she'd come back to our room, her pleasure like a laugh she couldn't hold back. And, still later, when she'd been out with him, the flush in her cheeks. Even now, the way she had loved him made my heart close in on itself like an arthritic hand.

"As you said, you loved him a great deal. You loved each other very much. I never doubted that." Does one doubt that the sun and the moon have a working relationship?

"I'm sorry, Jessie, truly I am, for needing to fool you about that. Yes, I was happy—I was high. We didn't have that word—but what I was *was* high. High because it was working, because I was taking Leo away from you, managing to do it—and then because I had done it. I'd pulled it off. I had Leo, and you didn't. I had him! That was what I felt!"

I shook my head. "Margery, I can still see your face."

"Why won't you believe that what you saw was joy, not love—what you saw was triumph!"

I shook my head again, but I said nothing to contradict her. There was nothing to do but hear out Margery's revisionist history.

"Jessie, get me a drink," she said.

"There's still some in your glass."

She drank the last few drops and smiled. "Now there isn't." She held out the glass to me.

I suppose she knew she couldn't negotiate another trip to the bar and back. Good. I didn't reach for her glass.

"Get it, Jessie, or I won't tell you the rest."

What made her think I wanted to hear any more? I didn't move. Amazingly, her hand, holding the empty glass out to me, also didn't. It was perfectly steady. I knew I was staring. I was doing, saying, all sorts of things I never thought—I got up, took her glass, and refilled it.

"Thank you," she said, sipping it this time as though it were China tea. "You see, I never loved Leo, I never wanted Leo, not for himself. Only because of you, to be more like you. I tried to do my part, really I did. I gave myself to him willing—" She paused, reconsidered. "All right, not willingly—willfully is closer to the truth. And we're telling the truth today, aren't we, Jessie?"

I was far from sure, but I nodded.

"The whole truth, then," she said. "I was . . . diligent in giving myself to Leo. In the beginning, I never said no. But I think he knew, almost from the start, after he got over the sheer excitement of its being me he was in bed with, that I didn't want it. At first, he thought I was shy, innocent. I wasn't either, I just didn't want *him.* Leo was smart; it didn't take him long to figure that out." She sighed, sipped her drink.

"I did try to love him. I knew I should. But I just couldn't, Jessie. He was so . . . hairy."

I couldn't tell she was Jewish, said Cynthia Martell's grandmother.

"I really did try to make it work," Margery was saying, "you have to believe that."

Why did I have to believe it? Why, for that matter, did she have to make it work? Why didn't she just leave him? "Because of your mother," I said, instantaneously seeing this one part clearly.

"See, Jessie, how perceptive you can be when you're not fighting me? Yes, it was partly because of Mother. If she hated him . . . well, I couldn't very well let her know *I* hated him to touch me. Sure, I know, I wouldn't have had to admit that to her; but she would have guessed, Jessie, she'd have known."

Margery's mother wasn't a senile old lady like Cynthia Martell's grandmother. She would have been harder to fool. And you, Margery, and you? When people are drunk, they say things they don't mean. When people are drunk, they say things they really mean. Which was it? I couldn't remember. Let it not be true, I prayed. No; I decided. We were—after all —*friends.*

"Believe me," Margery was saying, "I tried and tried and tried." She paused, drank, looked at me closely. "He didn't help at all."

"Margery, he loved you so." Despite all she had said, no matter how much of it was true, that *was* true.

"Not enough to do what he should have done." Adamantly.

"*What,* Margery?"

"He should have made me love him!" The cry came from a place so deep within her that it had never felt the sun.

"And you!" She stood, barely able to, holding her arms out for balance. "What did you do to help? You were my friend. You pretended to love me. But as soon as Leo and I were married, you disappeared from our lives. You should have been around to help me, to show me how to make Leo love me more, to . . ." She was weeping now, tears plummeting down her face. *"So I could copy you."*

I stared at her. Margery's drunkenness seemed to make whatever she said at once believable and unbelievable. She bent toward me; part of her drink spilled on my skirt, she didn't even notice. She lost her balance—I put out my hands, eased her down. She was sitting practically on top of me now, hanging on to my hand. As she spoke, she dripped on our hands: from her glass, from her eyes, from her nose. To my surprise, I wasn't disgusted; it was too terrible for disgust.

"Jessie, I'm sorry. I'm so sorry. Say you forgive me." She sounded like a child; and my strongest impulse was to gather her to me, to reassure her, comfort her—but part of me held back. One thing; I had to know one thing.

I was ready to know.

"For what, Margery? You must tell me for what," I said.

"Oh, darling Jessie," she said, "for the pain you were in, for the pain I put you in." She caught her breath, searched my face, something like suspicion mixed with her sorrow.

"Even though you seem to have gotten over it easily enough," she said.

I stared again.

"Well, yesterday—since you came—seeing Leo doesn't seem to bother you at all."

There was . . . disappointment in her voice.

"But *then,* back then, it did hurt you? *I* did—as much as I thought?" Margery's voice seemed to hold both eagerness and grief.

"Yes," I said, my own voice barely audible to me, "yes, it hurt . . . enough."

Margery spoke quickly now that she was reassured, her words coming at me headlong. "Not that I wanted you to hurt, seeing him again—I didn't look forward to that, God forbid, Jessie. But when I saw that you . . . didn't *mind* seeing him—that you . . . enjoyed being with him yesterday—well, I wondered. You can understand that, can't you, Jessie?"

How much was I *expected* to understand?

I said, "You knew all the time?"

"Not all the time, Jessie. . . . Soon." Her face was a plea with features.

"I thought I had done a better job than that of hiding my feelings." Tired out; tired with years-old effort. Wasted effort.

"We were *friends*," said Margery.

"Yes," I said. We were; still.

"At first, I only guessed, but I made Leo tell me," Margery whispered, as though there were a mesh-wire partition between us.

"When?" I asked. Now, twenty years later, I needed to know exactly when.

"When? I'm not sure exactly." Another sin, not being sure? her eyes asked me.

"Try," I said.

"Before your birthday! I remember that, because I forced myself not to buy you an extravagant birthday present. I didn't allow myself to try to make it up to you that way." There was pride, unmistakably, in her voice.

I could understand that. What I could not understand still: "Margery, you took him from me . . . on purpose?"

"I had to, don't you see?"

"No."

She whispered: "Marrying Leo was the closest I was ever going to get to . . . being you."

"How long has Leo known?" My voice sounded as though it were coming from a long way away. Maybe twenty years?

"Jessie? *Leo* doesn't know. How could I tell him? Tell him I *never loved him*?"

I had, of course, been thinking about *me*, what she had done to me, not what she had done to Leo.

Or to herself.

A crying that was more movement than sound. I reached for her, let her come into my arms, because that way one of us would be comforted.

Her crying was so muted that I could not be sure when she stopped finally. I was worn out clear through and wanted to lie down; certainly, her need was as great. I half-walked, half-dragged her to her bedroom, and laid her on the bed. I took off her shoes, removed her jacket, opened the top buttons of her blouse. There, at her throat, she caught my hands.

"Don't leave, Jessie."

"I'm not leaving," I said, assuming she meant that I would, in anger, be going away. "I'm only going to my room. Sleep awhile, you'll feel better."

"I'll never feel better," she said, "unless you forgive me."

I hadn't yet, had I? Exhausted, I sat down on the side of the bed. I let her hold onto my hands and tried to think what to say to her.

"How do I go about forgiving you for what I never knew you did?" I said finally. "What you did, taking Leo, seemed to me at the time . . . only natural. You were so beautiful, Margery, so very, very beautiful, and bright, and light, and . . . so beautiful. I wasn't surprised that once he met you, Leo began to stop loving me. Of course it hurt me. I loved Leo." Time to face the truth: "But not with all of me—maybe all I had at the time, yes, all of that. But for a long time after my mother died, there were . . . limits to how much I loved anyone. I guess there was too much space between me and anyone else—space in me, space another person couldn't fill. *I had to fill it.*" I paused again, the newness of the insight dizzying. "It took a very long time for me to do that."

Had I done it?

"Jessie, stop talking. Hold me. Please?"

I was so tired, it was easy to stop trying to figure everything out. I lay down beside Margery on the bed. We were both facing the same way, and I held her lightly at the shoulder.

After a while, I realized that she was crying again. I tried to comfort her. "Anyone would have loved you, Margery, the way you were, anyone. You didn't have to go after Leo, he would have loved you anyway, don't you see?"

She made a choking sound; her shoulders began to shake. I tightened my hand on her shoulder. She covered it with one of hers and wept. I moved closer; I whispered, "Margery, it was a thousand years ago. What I didn't know—that didn't hurt me *more* then." I took a breath, testing. "It doesn't hurt now."

As she turned, burrowing into me, I thought, It *doesn't* hurt. I'm all right. Margery was whispering something. I bent my head to hers. "The bathrobe . . . I didn't know. . . . How *could* I know? . . . Oh, Jessie, Jessie, how could I *know*? I'm so sorry. I'm so *sorry.*" She was sobbing again.

"Margery, that was a sweet and good and kind thing you did. I'll never forget it."

She was shaking her head vigorously from side to side, heaving tears.

"Margery, what *is* it?"

She said something.

"I can't hear you," I said.

"I *didn't* realize—I only bought it on a whim!" she cried. Uncontrollably now, she wept.

"It's all right," I said. "It's all right, Margery."

"But do you forgive me?" she cried out through her crying.

"But do you forgive me?" Like a litany. "But do you forgive me?"

I pulled her tight to me. "Yes, Margery, of course."

"*Say* it."

"I forgive you."

Instead of quelling her tears, that seemed to start them afresh. She grabbed my hands, held onto them. I tried to free one, to pat her head. Instead, she placed it on her heart. I thought, for a second, she was going to make me swear that way. But she began to rub my hand across there—not her heart, actually, but her breast, I realized now. It was as though she were rubbing *herself*, the way I occasionally do, when I want comforting, only she was using my hand instead of hers. I didn't pull it away; I didn't mind. I *wanted* to comfort her if I could. I moved my hand on her breast; her hand on top of mine eased its pressure but stayed atop mine as I soothed her, stroked her. My hand passed over her nipple and it grew hard; surprised, I moved my hand away. But Margery's hand was still on top of mine and moved mine back.

"Forgive me," she said. "Prove you've forgiven me?"

So I left my hand there, her nipple erect beneath my stroking fingers, the skin puckered. She raised her head, her face riven by tears. I bent and kissed her eyes shut; my lips came away wet. But she moaned with such animal gratitude that I kissed her forehead, and her damp cheeks, softly, over and over; and she moved slightly, ever so slightly, so it was her lips I was kissing, softly, gently, comfortingly. If she had responded—but the only response she showed was that the wracking of her body slowly abated. I was holding her close, kissing her brow, when she stirred, readjusting her body to mine. I accommodated her, without paying attention. I was thinking how temporary was the comfort I was offering her, wondering what I might do to help her beyond the present moment when, suddenly, the moment was more present than I was prepared for. Margery was sucking at my nipple. For a moment, I thought of an infant seeking comfort, and that kept me quiescent. I was wondering how I hadn't felt her opening my blouse, drawing out my breast, when I realized that Margery's sucking was intensifying, and getting results of an unexpected kind: the skin around my nipples was tightening, the nipples reacting to her lips by becoming larger, hard. But then, for all I know, I thought, this happens to nursing mothers. Because it was automatic, all of it; I felt something plainly physical, but not sexual. Still, I knew I should stop her now. But I could no more push Margery away at that moment . . .

After a while, she took my hand and guided it down to where her skirt had ridden up around her thighs and she ran my palm up against the insides of her thighs to where, at the top, I could feel the wetness of her through her pantyhose. She held my hand there, and said, "Please, Jessie, please?" And so I bent over her and pulled off her pantyhose. I paused then, unsure—of whether to . . . of what to . . .

"Nan used to kiss it," whispered Margery.

I put my hand over her mouth, and she was quiet. I couldn't do . . . that. But, gingerly, because I had never done it to a woman's body except my own, I put my hand on her and then along in there, where it was wet, and I moved my fingers up and down. "Higher!" Margery cried out impatiently. I went higher, and I found it, and then I moved it around and around in a steady rhythm as she lay there, her eyes shut tight, her face tightening too, frowning with concentration. And I kept moving my finger in that triangular pattern and thought about Nan Saltonstall, Margery's roommate before me, who'd transferred to Radcliffe to be near her Harvard fiancé, a girl almost as lovely as Margery, with chestnut hair in a soft page-boy and a lithe figure. I tried to imagine her doing what I was doing to Margery, I tried to imagine her kissing Margery where I was touching her. But I couldn't. I could only conjure them up in their impeccable Brooks Brothers' shirts,

Margery's invariably blue, Nan's usually pink, looking as if they never went to the toilet, let alone to bed with each other. Margery's breathing was getting thicker. I had to move slightly, my arm was falling asleep; it would only take a second. She cried out: "Don't stop now! You always stop!" I found the place again, and knowing that she no longer knew it was I doing it to her made it somehow easier to keep doing it—confirmed my feeling that this wasn't like making love at all. It was almost as though I *were* patting her head instead of her clit. And, finally, her face grew rigid, her back arched, and she let go: she was comforted. Almost at once, her breathing grew even and she slept. I nearly laughed at the impersonalness of it: I wasn't there for her any more; she was through with me. Hooray for cuddling men, I thought. But I wasn't kidding myself. There was nothing truly brittle about how I felt; or funny.

I stayed there, at the foot of the bed, not moving, thinking how—odd—it was that I had done it, that I had . . . done it to a woman; and odder still that I hadn't felt as though I were making love at all but, rather, that I was . . . doing what a friend had to do. Margery's breathing was deep now, even. I edged off the bed, straightened my pants, buttoned my blouse, moved away from the bed. I didn't leave the room, though. I went and sat in a chair by the window, looked out at the lowering sun, and tried to sort it out.

But it was too complicated, too tight, for me to untangle, like a chain that's been left long in a box with other small pieces of jewelry. My mind, faced with interminable-looking knots, rejected the task of untangling altogether. I thought of Freddie.

I had supposed, although I had never admitted it to anyone, exactly as others had supposed, that Freddie had wanted to make love to me. To do to me what I had done to Margery —and more. But if that were so, why had she never made a move to do it? She could, I knew now for the first time, have seduced me if she had wanted to. Not because I was . . . like that; but because, I had just learned, where there is feeling, where there is the impulse to please . . . or comfort . . . there are no border guards between the country you've always lived in and another. Freddie had never been my lover because she hadn't wanted to be. She wanted to be what she was, my teacher. It was she, not I, who had chosen.

Why couldn't I have managed as well this afternoon? Why had I let Margery make me make love to her? Why couldn't I have said no, in all kindness, but no?

I knew. I'd found out this afternoon that my losing Leo had cost Margery more in the long run than it had me. That was her hold over me. I looked at her, lying asleep on her bed, pity in my heart. And fear. I shook my head, trying to dispel a dybbuk, and quietly left the room.

4

Lying down proved an exercise in exacerbation: I could neither rest nor relax; and the effort made me even more tense. Giving in, getting up, I wandered, restless as a rainy-day child, from room to room. There seemed to be no getting away from it: these people, out of my life for twenty years, were in it again, squatters in my brain and belly. Part of me wanted, in the absence of anyone save Margery, who was absent in her own particular way, to pack my things and get out of there: escape. Was I not, in the twenty years' war in this house, an innocent bystander? Unfortunately, I had long since decided, during a different war, that there's no such thing as an innocent bystander.

There was no way I could leave yet and go in peace.

In which case, I had better find something to do to recharge the battery of my sanity.

Cook something with many ingredients—take two aspirin, drink lots of liquids, and rest. As often as not, it worked.

In the refrigerator, I found a package of chuck. I had thought there might be shrimp, but ground meat suited my purpose better. I was pleased Margery had forgotten about the shrimp she was going to get for *her* favorite meal; it confirmed her general forgetfulness when she was drinking. That meant there was a chance she wouldn't remember what had happened between us in her bedroom, or the archaeological uncoverings preceding it. I felt relieved, and then not. I didn't want to be the only one to know. As dreadful as was the idea to me of Margery's and my sharing the secret of that afternoon, it was even more dreadful to contemplate being the only one who knew. A squirt of loneliness seemed to invade my system, as harsh and foreign as a liver injection.

I focused on the chopped chuck. A meat loaf was what the occasion required: a meat loaf with everything. I foraged: to the meat, in a large mixing bowl, I added an egg yolk, a handful of chopped parsley, several tablespoons of butter, about one and a half tablespoons of bread crumbs, a big glob of white horseradish—and then another, a small can of tomato sauce, a large chopped-up onion, a teaspoon of lemon juice, another of oregano, and all that remained in a container of grated Parmesan cheese. In a cup of water, I melted a beef bouillon cube and half a stick of butter. While this was happening, I mixed and folded and squished and pummeled the other ingredients into a tidy little loaf in a buttered pan. Pouring the bouillon-butter mixture over it, I placed the meat loaf in the oven set for 350°.

The world was beginning to feel manageable again. I made a salad dressing, washed some romaine and a bit of chicory I found, dried the greens, and tore them into a bowl. With some thin slices of red onion, that would do nicely. A meat loaf and a salad: enough, I decided.

Enough for whom? *I* wasn't hungry.

Standing there, leaning against the refrigerator in Margery's kitchen, I remembered a time when I had been.

* * *

I'd been invited to dinner at Cynthia Martell's house. It was the middle of my freshman year, the first time I'd ever been asked to dinner on Park Avenue. When I got home, my mother said, "Did you have a wonderful time? Tell me all about it."

"Give me something to eat, and I'll tell you." I was *hungry*. That evening was my first exposure to how the rich stay thin.

All that silverware and so little food. There were chops, tiny baby lamb chops, one for each of us; and there were creamed onions, too slippery to take on; and peas—eighteen on my plate alone. Yes, I counted them; it was easy, there was plenty of room on the plate for them to spread out.

Mrs. Martell did ask if anyone wanted seconds of anything. I was dying for another one—or even two—of those chops; eighteen more peas would have been nice, too. But no one else said yes, and I was not going to be the only one.

Mama made me a second batch of French toast, and we sat together at the kitchen table, me eating, Mama drinking her tea through a piece of sugar, and the two of us laughing at what she had already named "My princess and the peas."

Culinary class distinctions.

The day John Kennedy was assassinated, I went over to the apartment of another friend, who happened to be richer than Cynthia Martell's grandmother's father—and probably his cousins and his aunts. I was upset, as was she. When she'd asked me to come by, I was glad. I wasn't devoted to John Kennedy, but he wasn't supposed to be *dead*. We sat in her vast living room and talked, for perhaps an hour and a half. Then I left. She had offered me neither a drink nor tea. My second shock that day.

Doesn't food mean anything to these people? I remember thinking that as I tried to summon the courage to ask for seconds of dessert at Margery's bridal luncheon. I was nervous: I was hungry; and there was this strawberry thing that tasted luscious and comforting and—I wanted more. There'd been only three strawberries in my portion; in everyone's, I had to admit, because I checked around the table. How did three strawberries, however large, constitute a portion?

I didn't ask my question, or for more berries. I was, truth to tell, much too nervous. For one thing, I had never heard of this ritual before: less than two hours before the ceremony, the bridal party and assorted relatives were meagerly fed and lavishly wined at the home of the bride's brother's girl friend's mother, who wore a plaid cotton shirtwaist and a diamond the size of a chunk of rock candy too big to eat without breaking.

Among the things I was nervous about was that I might drink too much—or too little. There were many toasts. I gathered one should not discriminate, so I drank each one; a sip. Even so, as I walked down the aisle a little later, I had difficulty keeping to the slow beat of the organ. I was in a hurry to get it over with; I hated the jaundiced way I looked in the buttercup yellow bridesmaid's dress Margery had insisted it was customary that she pay for. The dress was of broderie anglaise, with a slim skirt and a wide sash—and I looked awful in it.

But I did not delude myself that it mattered very much how I looked that day. All eyes, including mine, were on Margery, who outshone herself and made conventional bridal radiance seem ersatz, as she made her way to the altar on the arm of her father.

It was the only time I ever saw him, and even then it was a brief appearance. After the ceremony, he disappeared. Less than a year later, I noticed in *The New York Times,* he died in the South of France. But that day he was as handsome and fair as she was, the daughter he had come across the ocean to give away. I thought for one moment, at the foot of the aisle, that he might not relinquish her to Leo. They embraced; it went on longer than a symbolic embrace need have done. Her face, as she drew away from him, seemed to draw him back to her; but the impression lasted only a moment, and the ceremony proceeded exactly the way it was supposed to.

Unlike the marriage, it would seem. I had the sense of huge mounds of unhappiness, rancid without being stale. I shivered: the things people do to each other, and call marriage.

I sighed, put the salad in the fridge to keep crisp, and returned to Margery's room. I opened the door stealthily, but she was sleeping deeply. There was little doubt in my mind that she wouldn't be up for meat loaf. I would, in fact, be surprised if she were up before morning. It would be a blessing if she slept through the night.

Yes, of course, for her; but for me, too. I moved closer to the bed and looked at her, searching in that face, as in "Hide and Seek" at the Museum of Modern Art, for the myriad faces I knew must be there. I was especially looking, I admit, for any face of the Margery I used to know. But they were not to be seen, the faces, happy or sad, in the leveled face on the bed. I bent closer still—then pulled back. This was no painting I was staring at. Even in a drunken sleep, Margery deserved privacy. God knew, she'd kept little enough for herself.

I left her and was looking out the living room window at Riverside Park, thinking about the two young girls who had snatched my bag that morning and how difficult it seemed to fit everything that had happened in this day into a single day of my life, when Leo came home.

"Hi," he said, inhaling. "Margery in the kitchen?"

"In the bedroom. She's asleep."

Leo took off his jacket, tossed it on a chair. "You're the cook?"

It *was* a bit presumptuous, taking over someone's kitchen uninvited. "It was something to do," I apologized.

Leo nodded. "Smells good," he said.

"You hungry?"

"Sure," he said. Then, "I'm sure I will be a little later."

"Sure," I echoed. "It won't be ready for an hour, anyway."

Leo sat in the Eames chair, I sat on the sofa: two people in position to have a conversation.

After a minute, Leo had a go at it. "Tell me about your talk. Was it a success?"

"I think so. It was . . . funny, being back there."

"Memories?" asked Leo.

"Yes."

"I would imagine," he said. "We were so much younger and stronger then."

"That wasn't the kind of memory that came to me today," I said.

"Oh?" said Leo, but it wasn't a question; he looked uncomfortable. "I think that's why Margery's never gone to a reunion, too many memories. She's never set foot in the place since graduation."

"She came today."

"She did?" Surprised, wary, his eyes reconnoitered my face quickly, as if looking for obvious damage.

"Yes, I was surprised too," I said. "I looked up in the middle of my talk and there she was." I did not say, crying.

That sounded all right; Leo looked relieved. "I guess she must have felt better when she got up this morning. It could have been one of those twenty-four-hour bugs," he said, not looking at me.

"She left before I could get away," I said, to say something.

"She probably wasn't feeling all *that* well," he replied, using my idle remark to confirm his story.

He got up, went to the bar. "Care for anything?"

"No. Thanks."

He poured himself a short Scotch and came back; slowly, he sipped it. He looked far more at ease than when he'd come in a few minutes earlier. I couldn't let the whole subject die there, as though Margery really had a bug.

"Leo?"

"Umm," he said. "Sorry, I'll perk up in a little while, I promise. I always need to recoup a bit when I get home."

Another story? How many, I wondered, were there? Arabian nights? "Leo, when I got home, Margery and I talked for a long time."

His face didn't change expression. "Catching up on old times," he said, more evenly than if it were a question.

"You could put it that way."

My voice caught him on its edge. He didn't say anything; all the questions were in his eyes. "Yes," I said, "we talked a long time. A lot came out."

There was no edge to my voice this time; but I don't think that's why Leo didn't flinch. "That's all right," he said. "I figured she'd tell you, sooner or later. Luckily, you didn't have to do much revising of your image of me."

"Leo, don't do that, okay?"

He shrugged. "Sorry," he said. To oblige me, I decided. Why not? I saw how unimportant after all, in Leo's eyes, was what I might think; how unimportant he was. Margery was what mattered. Margery, and what he thought he had done to her.

"Actually, it's an impressive record, looked at objectively," said Leo. "I didn't make it as a teacher, or a poet, or a husband. A well-rounded failure. My father's son, all the way."

Leo made a sound; a laugh? He passed his hand over his carefully combed hair. "You know, the only good thing about my father was his hair. He had this thick wavy leonine hair. In every other respect, he was an under-achiever.

"Now my mother, she was an achiever. She always held a job, she ran the house like a shop, and she ran my father. Unfortunately, baldness ran in her family. When I was still a kid, ten, maybe twelve, I swore I'd marry a woman with soft hands, who brushed her hair a hundred strokes a night, who laughed a lot, and who never ran anything except a bubble bath."

And ended up with someone who's controlled you, in her way, for years.

"Margery had soft hands, soft skin, soft hair," said Leo. "She was beautiful. She was beautiful, that's all. What I did to that beautiful girl was criminal. Being married to a woman like that, and going after other women. It never did make any sense—but that didn't stop me. Oh no! And not only did I do it, I didn't have the decency to keep it a secret."

"You stopped," I said.

Now he stopped. There was a cavernous silence while he looked at me.

"I think we've said enough," he said then. "I'm sure you got enough of the picture from Margery without my filling in any ugly details." He got up, poured himself another finger of Scotch. "Sure you don't want a Dubonnet? Anything?"

It was his life; he was entitled to end the conversation if he wanted to. I stood. "As a matter of fact, I'd like to take a walk. I'm feeling kind of edgy; a walk always helps."

Reflexively, Leo glanced in the direction of the bedroom. "I meant by myself," I said.

"You can't," he said. "It's not safe."

Good Christ! Of course it wasn't. I sat down again. "You're right; it'll pass."

"No," said Leo, "let's go."

"What about Margery?"

"Let me go check."

He came back in a minute. "She's sound asleep. She won't wake up for a while, I'm certain. She *needs* sleep."

"All right, if you're sure. But only a short one, just enough to clear my head."

"Whatever you say," said Leo.

I didn't want to walk along Broadway, where Leo and I might bump into mutual memories. We walked along the Drive. "I love this time of year," I said, "because it's not dark yet."

"It's still not safe. It's not even safe in broad daylight these days, according to some of the neighbors."

"No," I said. "I don't imagine so." The running girls ran through my mind; I pushed them on and out.

We walked, mostly in silence, at a fair pace. Once, a car came careering along the Drive parallel to us. Protectively, Leo took my elbow, then let it go. "I guess I'm a little edgy, too, tonight," he said.

A little later: "It's good walking like this, with someone. With a friend," he amended.

"Yes," I agreed.

"Do you walk much at home?"

"Yes. But for a long time, I couldn't take walks there." I laughed, "You see, there aren't any sidewalks by my house, and I seemed to need sidewalks—blocks—and cross streets. To keep track of my progress, I guess. I got over that, finally. The same way it took me years to learn how to eat at a picnic. I used to need a plate or I wouldn't know how much to eat."

Leo laughed. "You can take the girl out of the city . . ." he said. A block later, he asked, "Do you still love the movies?"

"I don't get to see as many as I'd like, but I still love them.

There's only one movie theater. It seems to play Walt Disney and X-rated stuff on alternate weeks, mostly. I watch on television, sometimes in the middle of the night. I set the alarm to get up for Irene Dunne and Cary Grant."

Again, Leo laughed. "Are you never lonely, living alone?" he asked.

"Never? Sometimes—not often. I like living alone."

"I hate being alone," said Leo. "At school, during office hours, it's usually very busy. Once in a great while, though, no one shows up. I can never seem to read then, or even do paperwork. I just sit there, waiting, and feeling desperately lonely. Ridiculous, isn't it?"

I touched his arm, said nothing. We walked on.

"It's funny," Leo said after a bit, "being able to talk to you like this. Not exactly like old times."

"No," I said, "not exactly."

He was quiet again for a time; I guessed we were both thinking back to our time together.

But then Leo said, "Margery tried to kill herself." He wasn't with me, then or now.

"She told me," I said quietly.

I didn't think he'd heard me. "She came so close," he said, not to me exactly. "I promised her then—it's funny, you know, during the wedding service you make that promise: to be . . . true; but I didn't make it seriously then, because that day I could not conceive of being with any other woman, of wanting any other woman, only Margery. Walking down the aisle toward me, she was the most beautiful girl in the church, the most beautiful girl in the world—walking toward *me,* solemn, about to give herself to me forever." Despairingly, Leo shook his head. "Only a few months later, what did I do to her—out of the clear blue sky—"

"No, Leo!" He *had* to see it the way it had really been. Getting a crucial sequence of events right and then running and rerunning that correct sequence past my mind's eye until I knew it by heart was the only way *I'd* ever found to be able to cancel that kind of memory-show in my own life.

"Not now, Jessie! We have to go back," Leo said. "I have to get back!" He took my arm, turned me around, and began walking quickly homeward. It was as though Margery might, at this very moment, be trying to kill herself again. He had to get back in time to stop her!

Leo hurried directly to the bedroom, leaving me to close the door. I stood helplessly in the foyer for a moment; then I went into the kitchen, alerted by the smell. The meat loaf was done—and a bit more. I removed it from the oven and left it covered with foil on the stove. Leo came in.

"She's still asleep," he said somewhat sheepishly, but there was real relief under that. "Sorry I rushed you back here."

"That's all right," I said. "My head's clearer. We can eat now, or wait a bit."

"What do you want to do?" he said.

"Let's wait. I'll have a Dubonnet," I said.

"Good idea," said Leo, relieved, too, to resume his role as host.

After he brought me my wine and poured himself another finger of Scotch, he set his glass on the table beside his chair and filled a pipe.

"This is the first time I've seen you smoke," I remarked.

"I don't, except this, and only once in a while. Do you mind?"

"I love the smell. I only gave up smoking a few years ago."

"Five for me," said Leo. He lit the pipe.

"That's when I stopped," I said.

We laughed, as if it mattered, as if we were discovering we both loved Haydn.

Leo puffed on the pipe. "You used to smoke Camels," he said.

"You were worse. Gauloises," I said.

"That wasn't a brand preference, it was an affectation. I

switched to Pall Malls when they started making Gauloises in America. Eventually, I switched to Kents. Toward the end, I kept switching; I must have tried fifteen brands. Each time one lower in tar came out, I tried it.''

"I always assumed they wouldn't taste like anything," I said.

"They didn't," he said. "I tapered off on tastelessness. Sounds like a slogan, doesn't it? I bet you never switched—smoked Camels until the end?"

I laughed. "You win that bet. I was luckier than a lot of people, though; once I decided to stop, I was able to do it. The only place it was really hard was at the typewriter. For a couple of weeks, I had to chew gum constantly while I wrote. But I *was* lucky; that passed, too."

"Margery's lucky," said Leo. "She never started."

Even if she'd never smoked, Margery didn't seem to me to be a lucky woman, but I let it go.

It was Leo who, after a minute, said, "She didn't have much luck otherwise in her life, did she?"

For someone who'd said it twice, I wasn't sure I believed in luck. I mean, it's an expression, not an explanation. Not an excuse.

"I loved her so much, Jessie, and I was so cruel to her. Explain it," he said to me.

That I couldn't let go. "Leo, before, you said you hurt Margery, you started womanizing, shortly after your marriage, for no reason."

He looked at me. "Do you remember what Margery looked like? What she was like? Did I have a reason?"

Christ, Leo. I said it quietly. "Yes."

He looked at me as though I had thrown a rock through the window. Had I gone crazy? his face asked.

"Margery rejected you first; that's a reason."

"Where on earth did you ever get an idea like that?"

"Margery told me."

"She never said that to you," protested Leo.

"I told you, she said a lot of things today."

"But that? I didn't . . . think she knew."

"Didn't know she'd rejected you?"

"That I'd felt that. Jessie, Margery didn't reject me. She was . . . she couldn't help it. She tried."

Hadn't it ever occurred to him that it was strange that Margery, the liveliest person we knew in those days, wasn't interested in making love with her husband? "Yes," I said, "that's true. She did try."

But she couldn't pull it off; she didn't want you. And you . . . went after other women in a pathetic attempt to make sense out of something that made no sense. If Margery rejected Leo, then her marrying him was . . . canceled out, wasn't it? He had not won her. He had never won her, had he? Poor, poor Leo.

But Leo didn't need my pity; he had enough of his own. "If you knew how many nights, when we were first married, after we'd gone to bed and . . . again . . . nothing or almost nothing. I'd come out and sit and think—search for why she'd married me."

I didn't say anything. It didn't matter; he wasn't really talking to me. When he was ready, he went on. "She could have had anyone. Someone who would have made her happy, been right for her."

He had it all wrong. "Leo, no—"

"Yes, Jessie! Do you understand, can you understand, what it did to me, knowing that?"

I had to get through to him. "Leo."

I waited until I had his attention. "I know why Margery did it."

"Did it? She didn't do anything. Margery couldn't help the way she felt, Jessie. Don't you see?"

It was Leo who had to see. What could I say?

He was saying, "If only you knew how often I see—plainly as I see you right now—what I did to her by marrying her."

I went to him then. I sat on the edge of the hassock and

leaned toward him. I waited until he looked at him and then I said it. "Margery *planned* to marry you."

"Sweet Jessie." Leo patted my cheek absently. "You don't know what you're saying, dear. You of all people should remember how badly I wanted her, how I went after her—what I did to you!" His eyes showed the strain of unaccustomed honesty. "I would have done anything to get her," he said.

It was, even now, hard to hear without blinking. The truth, as I remembered it. But not the whole truth, as I knew it now, as Margery had filled in memory with fine shards of reality.

"Yes, I know that. I know, Leo. Only, you see, it wasn't necessary for you to do much at all. Margery wanted *you*. Margery picked *you*."

"That is without doubt the most ridiculous notion anyone ever dreamt up, Jessie."

"She told me," I said.

"Margery said those things?"

"Yes."

"What had she had to drink? She'd been drinking, hadn't she?"

"Yes, she'd been drinking."

"Well!" He threw up his hands. "Don't blame yourself, Jessie, for misunderstanding. Sometimes, Margery drinks a little too much. And sometimes, then, she says things. You don't want to believe what someone says who's been drinking, Jessie, don't you know that?"

You don't want to believe it. What would you do with all your guilt, all the years of guilt, if it turned out to be true? Still, you'd be free to decide, Leo. Anyone deserved that.

"Leo, you're right, Margery was drinking—quite a bit—and she wasn't making perfect sense. But I believe the essence of what she was saying. It *rang true*."

"Just forget it, Jessie, would you?" said Leo.

Just forget it. I got up, went to the window, and looked out at the night. There seemed a lot of it. In the distance, the lights of the George Washington Bridge festooned the indigo sky like diamond chains around the neck of some blue-black African princess. Once, years ago, my mother had called me a princess—her "princess and the peas." But Margery had really been a princess—to us all. To Leo, still. Reflected in the window, I could see him. The princess's consort. He looked old and shrunken.

I went back to him. "Forgive me," I said, "but I have to tell you what she said. Will you listen?"

Leo shrugged. "If it will make you feel better."

His face was blank now; he wouldn't listen. I said it anyway; maybe some of it would get through to him. "Margery told me that she knew about us, about you and me, almost as soon as she got back to school. My face told her that first day back that something . . . wonderful had happened to me over the summer."

The face before me was that boy's face. No; gone. All my pain had been over *him?* I took a breath.

"Then, right after, we met you on the street, and she knew that it was you. She guessed . . . how much you meant to me." Another breath. "She decided to take you away from me."

"Jessie, this is ridiculous! I went after her!"

"Yes, you did. She didn't have to work hard either," I said, a layer of silt rising to the surface of my voice. I cleared my throat. "It doesn't matter. The point is that she wanted you as much as you wanted her."

"Jessie, if Margery told you that, she was . . . inventing it. Sometimes, she . . . daydreams . . . makes up stories. That's not the way it was."

"Did Margery ever tell you she couldn't see you if you were seeing someone else?" I was guessing now.

"I don't know. Maybe. So? Margery could afford to be choosy, to set certain terms."

"She didn't tell you she knew who it was," I said.

"I didn't want her to know," insisted Leo.

"But she did. Think back. Didn't she, finally, ask you about me?"

"And when I admitted it, she was terribly upset! I can still see her face. She felt awful. I—God forgive me, I tried to play down our relationship, so she wouldn't feel that bad—or think less of me."

"Oh, if only you'd realized you had it made, that you didn't have to worry. Leo, Margery was pressuring you by putting you off—by acting concerned about me—to choose: to make the break clean." I sighed. "She should really have known you'd choose her eventually; it was only a matter of time."

"Jessie, listen to me," said Leo. "Don't you remember her at *all*? She would never have done anything devious. She couldn't have. Margery was the most open, the most giving—"

"She didn't give herself to you, though, did she?" I said coldly. He had to hear.

"No, but that was my fault. Maybe if I'd been less crazy about her, if I'd been more patient. . . . Don't you see? It's not possible that she . . . wanted me, the way you say—and then changed so quickly."

"It wasn't exactly that way," I said. "There's more."

"If you really feel you want to . . ." Leo, obviously, didn't.

Want to? *Want* to break a confidence? Margery had said, "Tell him I *never loved him*?" It was her secret. But, finally, now, weighing it all, I did have to tell him.

"Leo, I don't know how to say this except to say it, because I can hardly believe it myself. But Margery says she went after you because of me."

"What sense does that make!"

"She says, getting you was the closest she was ever going to get to . . . being me." The words scratched my throat as they came out, like a dislodged chicken bone.

"What could that possibly mean except some drunken attempt at—I don't know. But it's *crazy*," said Leo.

"Yes," I said mildly.

"Jessie, no one knows better than I how terrific you were, that's not what I meant, but Margery—"

"Was a golden girl. She had everything." I nodded. "Yes, I thought so too. She didn't think so."

"She thought you had something she didn't?"

"Yes. Don't ask me what," I said.

"Jess, there's no need to belittle yourself—"

"Leo, I'm not," I said truthfully. "But there's no reason—at least no rational reason—why Margery should have envied me."

Leo looked at me as though I were a puzzle with a single piece missing. Then, very slowly, almost expressionlessly, he said, "Her mother always told Margery that she was . . . like her father. That she not only looked like him, she *was* like him. That she had no spine, no resiliency—that, like him, she was weak." Leo stopped. He was looking past me now. I waited; he came back.

"You were strong. That year after your mother died—Margery often talked about the way you'd handled everything. How you didn't drop out; the way you worked thirty hours a week. How you *held up*. I remember her saying it, her voice filled with awe. 'She's a survivor.' "

"A small bonus that comes with the blood," I said curtly. But then, seeing it more and more, "And *you* were Jewish. Maybe they went, in her mind—strength, surviving—with being Jewish. Hadn't her mother made clear enough that Jews were different? Dear God, no wonder she wanted Jon to be Jewish."

We looked at each other: the things people envy.

At a Barnard tea, my junior year, my only tea: a Columbia man, a boy from Philadelphia with yellow hair and Roman numerals after his name, said to me, "May I ask you something personal?" And I nodded, my hopes up. "Why," he asked, "now that they let all the Jews into Columbia who want to go, do they still get A's?" I told him I didn't know, and lost him to a red-haired girl passing cookies. My few lies never did pay off. I should have told him a giraffe has a long neck even when you've removed it from its natural habitat.

I said to Leo, "Whatever her reasons, that isn't what matters. What it did to her does. She always felt guilty because of what she'd done—to me and to you. And angry—because while she'd done it to herself too, she thought—she expected—that you'd make her love you."

"*Make* her love me?" echoed Leo incredulously.

"Leo, think back to when you first started seeking out other women. What did you tell yourself about why you did it?"

"I know why I did it. When Margery didn't want me, it was as though the prize which had been given with one hand was being taken away with the other. I suppose it was a way of blustering it out . . . of denying the hurt . . . of hurting her because there was too much hurt to keep it all to myself."

"*Back*, Leo, you wanted to hurt her back."

He looked at me, controlling anger. "Jessie, I've no doubt your intentions are good, but I don't know what you think you're doing. There is no way you can turn that part around. *I* was unfaithful, not Margery. Margery was faithful to me, always."

He was too besotted with guilt to hear me—to hear himself, even. He'd admitted he'd been hurt; now he was denying that she'd done anything to him. Could I get through to him?

I had to. "Margery began her relationship with you under false pretenses. She felt guilty. Yes, she was faithful. She gave you very little and every other man none. Is that what faithfulness amounts to?"

"You make it sound like an ugly little virtue," said Leo.

"A virtue? Doesn't a virtue have to *affirm* something? Margery's fidelity to you was just another negation."

How angry he looked. And who could blame him? Whatever I said seemed to make it worse. I could shut up. Or I could keep trying to get him to see the truth. Either way, I wasn't about to win any prize for popularity—or trust, I reminded myself. I stood; moved away. I went back to my refuge, the window. I thought again of the girls who'd taken my purse: a small dose of reality *I* disliked enough to keep it a secret. These people weren't characters in a book I was writing. They were real people who had a right to their secrets. I turned back to Leo, resolved to leave him where he seemed to have to stay. But he looked so thoroughly beaten that I knew, grotesque as it may seem, that I couldn't make things worse now—even if there was only a small chance I could make them better.

I sat down on the sofa. For a moment, I talked to God. Then I said, "Leo, Margery told me she drinks in order to remind you of the womanizing you did years ago."

"I accept the blame for that!"

For the women? For the drinking?

"She also drinks to pay you back for not making her love you."

"That's crazy!" said Leo. "That's sick!"

Me? Or her? No, I didn't matter: it was her. Thank God, her. I let the words swirl through the air; they came to rest slowly. Finally, I said, "Yes, it is sick. Margery's a sick woman, isn't she?"

A blank face met mine; then anger slowly filtered through the mask. "Jessie," warned Leo, "you go too far."

"I've no doubt about that," I said. But she had brought me here, got me here, for some reason. Maybe, just maybe, to help her. And if I am to help her, it has to begin with honesty.

"Leo, we have to—"

"No we don't! Who in hell do you think you are anyway, coming in here like this and dissecting our lives under your dirty little novelist's microscope!"

I hadn't done *that*. And I'd been invited. I said it twice to myself. But to go this far? "You're right," I retreated. "I'm sorry. I've no business. Let's let the whole thing go, Leo. I won't say another word, I promise."

"*No.*"

How can a whisper be a shout? How can one word effectively contradict dozens?

"No, Jessie," he was saying, "don't stop. Talk to me about it. Maybe it's time. I never have, never. Jon tried to talk to me a couple of times—but I couldn't. She's his mother! And Jess, she's been a good mother. Honest to God. Until four or five years ago, it wasn't like this. We used to do things together, the three of us—it was when she and I were closest, then. Over him. How *could* I talk to him about her?"

She'd been this way four or five years. That cleared up one mystery: why Leo had backed out of a bar mitzvah for Jon. The fear of exposing her—them. . . .

"But you," Leo was saying, "you're her friend, and mine. Maybe that makes it all right. . . . Do you know, Jessie, what it's like to live with a person who hardly ever remembers in the morning what she said the night before? Or what you said? What threats she made—or you? What promises? And I, I seem to compensate by remembering everything twice as clearly—twice as terribly."

I remembered the wetness between Margery's thighs. There are some things you can never tell; but they can help you understand. "It's as though what happened between you didn't happen for her," I said.

"Yes, that's it," said Leo, "and sometimes I'm grateful for that. It's bad enough sometimes that *I* know what goes on between us."

"Leo, I'm confused. The way you're talking, I get the feeling Margery's drinking is . . . regular. Yet the first night I was here, she didn't drink, not to speak of. A glass or two of wine, like me. And Thursday night, when I came in late, she was drinking coffee—she was sober, I'm sure she was. How do you account for that?"

"Will power. Every ounce she had." He sighed. "It was a test. Margery devised it. It was why she asked you. She thought of it when she first got a notice about the reunion speech, but it took her weeks to decide that was the way."

"The way to what?" One tardy invitation explained, now that it was way past mattering.

"To prove she's . . . all right—to prove everything's all right. To prove"—Leo was pushing himself to some limit—"that if only I'd stop hounding her everything would be all right."

"But why me? Why wouldn't having just anyone around do?"

"You hadn't seen us in twenty years. You knew nothing of what had happened. Whom could she have had? We don't have . . . friends. People . . . drop away. Besides, you were Jessie, and if you couldn't tell—but it's clearer even than that, isn't it? You told me Margery said you were everything she wanted to be. Why, then, if the paragon couldn't tell . . ."

"But she drank." It was coming back to me. "Last night, when I came into the living room, she was drinking vodka. You looked very upset."

"Margery was angry."

"About what? At whom?" But maybe I knew.

"At me," Leo was saying. "Because I went downtown with the two of you. She felt, several times during the afternoon, that you and I were saying things—making references—that went back a long way."

"You know we didn't do that. And if that's what she told you," I added quietly, "she was lying."

"Jessie! Don't you see how it may have seemed to her?"

"No, Leo. Margery told me this afternoon that she was surprised because seeing you didn't seem to . . . hurt me. She said she hadn't wanted it to hurt me, but when it didn't—well, she was . . . disappointed. And, I think, angry. I think Margery felt she was entitled to that much."

"It's my fault," said Leo. "I should have refused to let her invite you—to put herself to such an impossible test. Don't blame Margery. It's all my fault."

And the drinking, that was his fault, too. Leo was hunched over with his burden of guilt. "Damn me! I really had to invite myself along yesterday, didn't I? She'd been making such an effort. If only you could understand how hard she tried, what it took for her to go two days with hardly anything to drink—only a couple of glasses of white wine. And she performed! The night you came she made a real meal. A delicious meal. She got up, made up—all that. She even got herself to your talk! God, Jessie, how she tried.''

She cooked. She made up. She *got* up. Dear Lord, how did they live?

He came to me. ''Don't look like that, Jess. It'll be all right —if you help her. Now that we know for sure how much she looks up to you. Those first two days, it was your being here that kept her from drinking. I know she'll get better if you're willing to help. Please, Jess?'' His hands worked mine.

Part of me was thinking, What can I do? I think Margery's an alcoholic—but I don't *know*. I don't know anything about alcoholism. How can I help her stop drinking? All right, she got up, made up—for me. Cooked—because I was here. For two days, she didn't get drunk; because of me. What was I doing up to my eyeballs in someone else's life? In Margery and Leo's marriage? There was no way I could disentangle the knots they had used to tie themselves to each other all these years. You can't help someone work out his life in a few days. Good Lord, it had taken me nearly twenty years to work out the major knots in my own life. *No*.

But there was another part of me, two thousand years old, that knew it wasn't easy to fade into the background again once you'd been spotted as a potential contributor. I *was* here. She *had* tried on account of me. I had . . . made love to her. I was in this.

I had to help.

My hands returned the pressure of Leo's. I didn't say anything. The plea in his face seemed to me to preclude not only a refusal, but even words of acceptance. It had to be. I had to find a way to help Margery.

I would compose *Carmen,* discover relativity, invent psychoanalysis, play second fiddle to no violinist in the world: I would find a way to help Margery stop drinking and put her life together again. In the day that was left of my visit.

But now, this moment, I had to release some of the tensions in the room—do something ordinary.

"Let's eat," I said, "and then we can talk some more. There's a meat loaf. I never basted it, but I think it survived."

"From a Jewish meat loaf," said Leo, relief suffusing his face, "I wouldn't expect less." He even managed a smile to accompany his joke.

We ate in exhausted silence. The meat was dry on top, but edible. The salad had, however, turned icy crisp. I didn't apologize for the food. I assumed it mattered to Leo as little as it did to me. We neither of us ate very much, but it gave us time to breathe plain air in and out, instead of gusts of truth.

Leo went to make coffee for us and I sat, thinking how we were like people waiting for someone to die, and how Margery had said she was killing herself, that that was what the drink would do in time; and I didn't know if it was true, but I thought she sounded as if she knew it was. I knew for sure only that I wouldn't be able to tell Leo that part.

Any more than I would tell him that I had held Margery and . . . touched her. I looked at my hand. It was . . . almost impossible to believe.

Margery's voice, crying out from the bedroom. Sheer sound, no words. Leo came runing past me from the kitchen: to her.

I went and poured the coffee, which was ready, and took it into the dining room.

I waited.

In a few minutes, Leo came back, moving with obvious effort; walking through water.

"How is she?" I said.

He looked as if he hadn't understood the question.

"Leo . . . ?"

Cries, again, from Margery's room. Leo turned toward the sound but this time his legs didn't move. "She wants you," he said to me.

"Leo, you didn't suggest—"

"Of course not! I don't suggest *anything* when she's like this. She said you're whom she wants. She didn't want me. She *said* it."

He sat down, his head dropped into his hands. I sat still. His sense of rejection thickened the air. He wanted me to help, but *he* wanted to ask for it, not to have Margery ask. He wanted to be her major help; what did he have left but that, to be the one who went to her when she cried out? I stirred my coffee.

Again cries. More impatient now. A howl. Leo raised his head. "How can you sit there? What kind of friend are you? For God's sake, go to her!"

When I entered the dark bedroom, I found silence and a strong, unpleasant odor, not altogether unfamiliar. Margery seemed to be asleep in the room of a baby. It was urine I smelled. As my eyes accustomed themselves to the dimness, I saw that Margery's eyes were open, although she lay very still. And through the bathroom door I spotted a pile of bedclothes. She must have wet the bed; and Leo had, of course, changed the sheets, and her.

I put all that somewhere; it wouldn't help me now. I approached the bed.

"Jessie?"

"Yes," I said. The other smell, of Margery herself, rose up to greet me. I would not, I told myself sternly, mind it as much in a few minutes.

Margery reached out a hand for mine. I hesitated. I didn't want to touch her. Not because of the smell; because of before. Whatever she remembered or didn't, *I* remembered; and I knew that nothing even remotely like it must happen again.

"I dreamt," said Margery, "that we were very, very close, the two of us."

Before electric shock they sedate you, I thought, as the charge coursed through me, *hurting:* she would realize, in a minute she would realize, that it hadn't been a dream.

"As close as we were at school," Margery was saying. "Jessie?"

Safe. I took her hand. "I'm here," I said.

She sighed, content. "It took a long time."

She closed her eyes, her breathing became more regular. But then, her eyes still shut, she said, "In my dream, I did something really awful to you." She giggled. "Really awful." Again, a giggle. "I can't remember what it was, but, believe me, it was just terrible." With her free hand, she patted my hand which lay in hers. "But you forgave me."

"Of course I did," I said, listening to the ordinariness of my voice.

"That's what friends are for," said Margery, "right?"

"Right," I said.

"Now that you're here," she said, "you're not in any hurry to go, are you? I mean, you'll stay. . . ."

"I'm here," I said, watching my words. If she didn't remember, I did. I reminded myself: Make no promises you won't be keeping.

"You're here," repeated Margery. "And you'll stay," she said, soothing herself, "until I fall asleep, no matter how long it takes me."

"Of course," I said, thinking how easily I'd been let off.

For now.

It took a long time for Margery to fall asleep, and longer until I could be absolutely sure. When I came out, finally, Leo was sitting in his chair, smoking his pipe. The Schubert Octet was playing on the stereo. He turned at my step.

"She's sleeping," I said.

"I did the dishes," said Leo. "The coffee got cold. How about some fresh?" He obviously had had time to get himself in hand.

"Don't bother," I said. "It keeps me awake, anyway."

I sat on the sofa, pulled my legs up under me. By unspoken agreement, we listened to the music in silence. As the record revolved on the turntable, the scene in the bedroom turned in my mind.

When Margery had asked me to stay, she had meant only until she slept; but I felt something . . . beneath that. As if she'd wanted more but had backed down. It was just possible that if she had asked me for more at that moment, emotionally depleted as I was, I would have been unable to stand my ground. But if I had fought her, if I did fight any attempt to make me prolong my visit—my involvement—what would Margery do?

I thought I knew. She would say that I had to stay, that I owed it to her. It was not inconsistent with the things she'd said during the afternoon. She might say that if it were not for me, her life wouldn't have turned out this way; if I hadn't led her to think that if only she had Leo, her life would be better, more like mine. She could—Margery could—accuse me of leading her to think that I had everything. Hadn't she said that I should have been around, during the early years of their marriage, to teach her how to . . . make Leo make her love him? It was like being caught in quicksand; you get pulled in deeper and deeper.

No.

I had to help Margery without getting sucked in further. I reached out, for help, to her misconception of me, her image of me as someone who had everything that mattered: the strength to survive. To Margery, because I survived when my mother died, I was invincible. I survived because the alternative was to die. I would tell her that, explain that to her, show her how wrong she was about me.

But if I did show her she was wrong, there was the danger I'd only be proving to her once again that her entire life had been meaningless. All her life she'd wanted to be strong like me; now I was going to tell her the choice I'd made was *instinctive*? Where did that leave Margery, who was sure my survival had taken Brobdingnagian effort? Maybe it would be better to let her go on thinking it had taken every atom of effort I had, that I believed surviving was worth that kind of effort.

I did. However reflexively I had done it, I had chosen to live—and that was no small thing. Margery had the same—real—choice to make.

But people had helped me! How could Margery do it alone? No; there was a flaw in that: no one had helped me choose to live. That decision I had made alone. Once it was made, people helped me do what I had to in order to survive. But they didn't make the choice for me. Only I could do that; only Margery could make her choice. If she chose life, I felt sure there would be people to help, people who knew how to help an alcoholic. But she had to take that first step by herself, worn out as she was. I prayed that somewhere inside that woman in the bedroom there still lived the girl I once knew who loved life . . . and wanted more of it than she had.

If she didn't choose life? If she couldn't? Then she'd die; she'd said so herself. I couldn't let that happen.

Jessie. Even God lets terrible things happen.

Good for God; maybe that's why so few people want to have a relationship with him.

Could I help Margery? That was the first question.

I wasn't God; but I could try.

And if I could help her—I spun around to the beginning of the circle again—should I? Had I any business here?

Even God lets terrible things happen.

I was so tired.

"Leo," I said, "I'm really very tired. Do you mind?"

"Of course not, Jessie. Go to bed. I'll see you in the morning."

I started out of the room. "Jessie?"

I turned.

"Thank you."

"Leo, I haven't promised you anything."

"Jessie, with a friend like you one doesn't require a notary." He smiled. Leo had taken to making old-man Jewish jokes.

"Good night, Leo."

In bed, too tired to sleep, it came to me: Shelley, in bed, fifteen, maybe sixteen years ago. A rundown hotel in the Village, a set from a Tennessee Williams play someone had forgotten to strike. A Sunday, midafternoon, a warm sunny day. I walked into the dilapidated lobby, took one skeptical look at the elevator, and walked upstairs to the room number she had given me. No one stopped me, no one questioned me: it was obviously not a place where someone asks the first question. I knocked at the designated door; nothing. Again; nothing. I checked the slip of paper in my hand, and tried the door. It was open. Inside, on that warm sunny day, it was dark, the cracked green shades pulled down to the sills. A dank smell. And in the bed—when my eyes had adjusted to the dimness—Shelley. Lying still: on her side; huddled under bedclothes. The arm that showed wore a sweater.

She had called me, forty-five minutes earlier, to say she was there and couldn't get up.

It took me two hours to get her out of that bed. I didn't know what I was doing, so I did it all: I coaxed, and soothed, and bullied, and threatened, and pleaded. God knows which one worked.

"She would probably have gotten up anyway, eventually," my psychiatrist said, the next day.

Where were you when I needed you? I thought. Where were you when she needed me? "That would have been nice to know yesterday," I said.

"I cannot always be available," he said, and waited.

"You mean, I can't always be available for Shelley," I said. He waited. It was his best thing.

"But she's my best friend," I said.

"Yes," he said, and waited.

"Even so?" I asked.

He waited. He wasn't going to tell me. He liked me to tell him.

"If I hadn't gone, she would have gotten up on her own?"

"Probably. I don't know," he said.

"And now *I* never will?"

"You will," he said, "because you won't always be available." He had the smallest smile I ever saw. I hoarded his smiles; in three years and three months, they didn't add up to a single broad grin.

Now, miles and years away, I could smell the room Shelley had been in, and the real leather in my psychiatrist's office. Maybe I should send him a post card: "Remember that Monday you told me I wouldn't always be available to help Shelley out of one of her depressions? You were right. Incidentally, I saw her only the day before yesterday, and she's fine—in her fashion. And that's fine with me. That's two you owe me. Sincerely yours."

I have, before, thought of sending him post cards. Once, a few months after I moved to Hamilton, I bought one in the bigger drugstore, a pastoral scene of the town in midwinter, and wrote on it: "Wish you were here. Sincerely." But I never mailed it. I wasn't sure he'd get the joke.

Okay, I wasn't sure it was a joke.

Another time, I was tempted to send him one saying: "Guess what? I remember my dreams now. Sincerely." It had been a difficulty, when I was in therapy. Now I sometimes even remember a dream weeks later.

Last night—the night before? The travel dream. Such a funny, terrible dream . . .

About Margery. It was about me and Margery. In the dream, I'd been trying to reach Margery, to get to her, to help her . . . by normal, ordinary means. But no matter how hard I tried, normal means did not avail me. I couldn't get to her to help her.

I can't get to her. I don't have the means to reach Margery and help her. It is—beyond me.

As the realization seeped into me I felt, first, dismay; then relief. If I couldn't do it, I didn't have to try.

I started to compose another post card to my psychiatrist: "Guess what? I can even figure a dream out once in a while." I let it go. He didn't have to know. I did.

I *did*.

I let go, and slept.

Every one of us had on a long white gown. Some of the gowns were stunning; many of them were beaded or had sequined embroidery which caught the light of the huge chandeliers overhead. But no gown was like Margery's. All the others were full-skirted; hers was slim. The others were of soft, young fabrics; hers was of heavy satin. Radiating upward from her slim waist were rows of bugle beads, curving over her strapless bodice, which ended in a narrow band of ermine. Her golden hair piled high on her head, held in front by a dainty diamond tiara, Margery looked like a princess everyone knew would one day inherit the entire kingdom.

Everyone wanted to dance with her, all the slim, blond, handsome young men, and not only because she was the princess, not only because the party was in her honor. She was the most beautiful girl in the room, the most desirable, I thought, as I was waltzed around the floor by one of the slim, blond, handsome young men awaiting his turn with Margery.

It was such a splendid room that it would be easy to imagine it was the grand ballroom of a grand hotel, instead of the living room of Margery's aunt's penthouse. Viewed from the balcony, all the lights of Manhattan saluted Margery. Overhead, the stars took over.

The waltz medley ended and my partner thanked me—and left me. I didn't know many of the people; most of the girls were Margery's friends from childhood and Miss Porter's. I decided to find a bathroom. We had, when we arrived, been shown to a room that was to be used during the evening should we "need to freshen up." The only trouble was, I couldn't remember which door of the huge living room we had originally entered—there were three doors—and the "powder room" was directly down a short corridor from that one.

I decided to be logical and try the closest door first. When I got there, Margery's aunt, standing just to the left of it, shook her head, pointing delicately down the room. I headed for the middle door. There, Margery's brother stopped me, directing me to the last door, at the end of the room farthest from the orchestra. Relieved that I was finally headed for the right one, I moved quickly. As I neared the last door, I had to pass Margery's mother, whom I'd finally met for the first time that night. She seemed to remember me. She smiled and waved me on, and I went through the door, smiling back at her, and—I fell . . . falling . . . screaming . . . falling . . . screaming . . . falling—

I was sitting upright in bed, in Jon's bed, my face damp with sweat, my heart still pounding with fear.

It took some time to come all the way back. From Margery's twenty-first birthday ball?

I hadn't been there.

I had not been invited.

I made myself lie back on the pillow, *to be here.* To remember that it wasn't then, but now. It never had to be then again.

When I was quite sure I believed that, I allowed myself to remember.

The night of Margery's birthday ball, after the limousine came to pick up what Margery called the "dorm contingent," and drove off, leaving me behind, I had told myself it didn't matter. I didn't have a long white dress, nor the money to buy one. I didn't dance very well. And the three Barnard girls who *were* asked weren't friends of mine, so I wouldn't have known anyone there except Margery—that much of the dream was true.

But the girls from the dorm who went weren't friends of Margery's either, not really good friends. Two were daughters of good friends of Margery's mother; one was a girl who'd gone to dancing school with Margery when they were children. That hurt; that they weren't good friends and were asked, while I wasn't.

What hurt more was that Margery never said a word. What words might have made it better? Yes, I wanted her to *say,* My mother won't let me have a Jew to my party. Because I knew, and she knew I knew; but without the words it wasn't honest between us.

Oh, yes, I did know for certain. It wasn't a simple case of paranoia. I knew because Leo wasn't going. Margery had said that much, between clenched teeth, thinking, I suppose, that that was saying enough—if he wasn't invited . . .

I was sitting in my room, Margery's and my room, thinking about how *silly* it was for a party to be . . . restricted, and crying, when there was a phone call for me. I dried my eyes and went to answer it.

"Come on down," said Leo. "I'm in the lobby. We'll take

a walk on the Drive and then we'll sit down somewhere . . . probably by the waters of Babylon.'' I put down the receiver without a word. I didn't have one clever, or cruel, enough. If he thought this was a bond between us, that neither of us was invited, if he thought this was something to *share* . . .

Not being at Margery's ball.

Margery's ball. How vivid it had been in my dream: no more vivid, though, than in my daydreams years ago. They were the source. In them, and in tonight's dream, I'd made up Margery's ball. All those details. Every one. For Margery, I suppose out of delicacy, had never described the ball to me. Not the room, not the lighting, not anyone's dress. I had never seen the dress Margery wore, not even a picture of it. I had made it up, out of whole cloth, all of it.

If I had invented some part of Margery's life—and had not my dream been proof of that?—why was I so surprised that Margery had done the same with mine? Had I not imbued that party with more magic than it could possibly have had? And she had imbued me with more magic than I had. I had thought she had everything; she thought I had everything that mattered. Which of us was the more mistaken?

And if I had more, even then, than Margery, what about now? Suddenly, there, in Jon's bed, in the middle of the night, I felt the need to count my blessings.

Not like a child.

I began with my work, the most consistent good in my life. I had it to do; and I did it well; and I even earned my living at it. Whatever benisons the new book might—or might not—bring, I had, the past couple of years, been earning my living writing exactly what I wanted to write.

And because I was in a house where there was sickness, I counted my health. For someone who *sat*—to write, to think, to rewrite, to read, to revise again—I was quite fit really.

Especially lately, since I had, upon Alec's mild urging, taken to taking walks. Real walks. Long walks. Walks that counted. I ate both sensibly and sparingly. And I hardly ever missed smoking any more.

My head was in pretty good health, too. There had, for some years, been a small problem there: I kept wondering why the world—the men, women, and children in my life—didn't seem to be getting around to offering me some sort of compensation for being an orphan. Reparations. (When I said "some years," I hedged; it was sixteen.) But the night I finished my first novel and, right then, knowing it was *all right,* wrote a precise, loving dedication to my parents—it was over. I was thirty-four years old: I had at last done something of which my parents would be proud: I sent them away.

I wasn't an orphan any more.

I was . . . okay. I had good work, good health—and good loving. Alec. I hadn't forgotten, I was saving him for last: the icing on the cake. Alec, who, despite his being so different from me about work, never tried to put himself where my work should be. He always seemed to feel there was room enough for him.

There was, I decided, plenty of room for him; and hugging that happy thought to me as though it were Alec himself, I slept again.

SUNDAY

1

I awoke sure. Or as sure as you can ever be about anything more important than which purse goes with which shoes.

I called the airport and, yes, there was space on the noon flight to Syracuse. I canceled my reservation for the evening flight and made one on the noon plane. Then I started to dial the operator, to call Alec: the urge to talk to him was strong this morning; but I put down the phone. I decided to wait. I'd call him as soon as I got home; then we could talk as long as we wanted. Now, I still had things to do.

I dressed, made my bed, and packed. I opened my typewriter and wrote a note to Margery. If she was up before I left, I'd have to tell her face to face that I was leaving, of course; but I didn't think there was great chance of that.

That didn't comfort me much, the likelihood that I wouldn't have to face her. I wasn't confident about my note; I felt that, in black and white, I had to sound more sure. And of course I wasn't absolutely sure I couldn't help Margery. I was only as sure as I had any chance of being. I had all I would get to go on.

I went to find Leo. To tell him I was leaving; to leave the note with him. I didn't expect it to be easy.

He was in the living room, bent over the *New York Times Magazine* and drinking a cup of coffee.

"Good morning," he said.

"You've been out already," I said.

"It gets delivered," said Leo. "Let me get you some coffee."

I let him get the coffee and bring it to me; but when I held the mug in my hand, I couldn't bring myself to drink it. I was accepting his hospitality under false pretenses. Was I going to drink his coffee, maybe help him with a word in the crossword puzzle? If not, I had better get on with what I *was* going to do.

I said, "I'm leaving, Leo."

The needle didn't break the skin. "I know," he said, "the time's gone so fast. But we still have this afternoon together. Margery will get up. The three of us can talk—or, if you think it's better, just the two of you. I want you to know I don't mind, Jessie, if that's what's best for her."

"No," I said.

Leo misread me; hope spurted up into his face, displaced as a single blade of grass growing out of a concrete walk. "Well, then," he said, "if you're really sure that I won't—"

"Leo, I'm not leaving tonight, I'm leaving now. I'm catching a noon plane."

"You check your ticket," he said, the indulgent, reasonable professor. "You'll be here all day."

I shook my head.

"But you have to be," he said, and blinked, as the needle finally did pierce his skin.

"I have to *not* be here."

"I don't know what you're talking about," he said because he was beginning to.

"I know. I'm sorry."

"But you can't just leave! You have to be here today! You have to wait—at least until Margery wakes up. What will she think, your leaving so suddenly?"

I started to hand Leo my note, to give to her; but something . . . It wasn't a very good note. I wanted someone to verify for me that what I said in it would, if it did no good, at least do no harm. But Leo couldn't tell me; he wouldn't know. I held back.

"Tell Margery for me—" I started.

"No! Don't you use me this way! Anything you have to tell Margery, you tell her yourself. You stay and tell her!"

"I only want you to tell her . . . I'll see her at our twentieth reunion, next year."

"You dare to say that and leave? You're guaranteeing she won't be there!"

"I don't think so," I said, wishing I could be sure, knowing I couldn't. "It's up to her, of course. I'll be there. Just tell her that."

"No!"

"Then don't." The note would have to do. I'd leave it. *No.* I wouldn't—it wouldn't do. It said too much—and not enough, probably. Was I trying to make my leaving easier for Margery—or for me? No message, no note. I had to leave cold turkey.

"Leo, I know you don't understand what I'm doing, and I am sorry, but I do have to leave now."

"Ssh." He rose quickly, turned toward the doorway. Now I heard them, shuffling sounds, a thud (a body bumping against a wall?), more shuffling. Margery, disheveled, in her nightgown, walked past the living room door into the dining room, toward the kitchen. Leo seemed frozen—then he moved. Slowly, as though he didn't want to startle her, he went after her. But before he got to the kitchen door, Margery came back through it, not looking up, moving right past him, her entire concentration on a medium-sized mixing bowl she was carrying, hugging it to her. Every few steps, despite her care, a few drops spilled over the edge; but she did her best, persevering, as she made her way back through the dining room and into the foyer. Obviously, if she didn't acknowledge our presence, we couldn't see *her*. Passing the living room doorway, she paused, smiling at her progress—and bending her head to the bowl, slurped some of the liquid it held. Then she proceeded to her bedroom. A door closed.

Leo stood where she had passed him. He was turned away from me, and he stayed that way. I counted to thirty, which was as long as I could stand it, and then I went to my room and got my things.

When I brought my suitcase and typewriter to the door, Leo was sitting hunched on the hassock, a man in mourning. I knew he couldn't come to me; I went to him. I handed him the doorkeys.

"I thought," he said, "that you meant it when you said you'd forgiven me. You've picked a harsh way to get even with me, doing this to Margery."

There was nothing to say. I had to leave; he had to say what he said. Maybe that egregious thought was his hold on the rest of the day; maybe that alone would sustain him until Margery called for him.

"Good-bye, Leo."

His face rode down in the elevator with me. It was gutted by disappointment and anger and self-pity and pain. And then I saw his face as it had looked, in the center of his group at the West End: emblazoned with intelligence and strength and promise and power. I had once looked to that face for everything.

2

For a moment after I got into the taxi, I was tempted to tell the driver to go past the West End; it was only a few blocks out of the way. But the cabbie was already disgruntled, begrudging me the trip to the airport. Besides, this wasn't a funeral cortege. I was just going home.

It began to sink in. I had been so intent on deciding the right thing to do; so focused, then, on leaving. I had not thought of what it would feel like to have left—to be on my way home.

It felt . . . sane. I would concentrate on that.

But I couldn't. It wasn't right. I had left so much pain behind me. Sure enough, right on cue, the guilt hit: sharp as indigestion.

No. It isn't like that. You're not leaving because you're refusing to help someone. You're leaving because you can't. Sometimes you *can't* help. They can pull you down, you can't pull them up. Another mental post card to my former psychiatrist? "Dear doctor, I'm learning. I'm *learning.* Very truly yours."

Only Margery could help Margery. It was sad; it was awful. It was true.

Like a good-sized swallow of psychological Maalox, the insight began to work. The guilt receded.

There was something else pushing at the borders of my mind. Something about my life. About my . . . responsibility for my life. That was it? But I had assumed responsibility for my life. Everything was all right in my life now. I was okay.

No. Yes, you're okay. You've done all right with the past; you have your parents in their place, even Margery is in place now. But getting the past right is only what you have to do first. What about the future? Are you up to doing that right?

As if the future were up to me.

If not you, whom?

Part of me was certainly coming on strong. I didn't see why. I mean, was that tone called for?

You decide, Jessie. By the time you were thirty-four, you'd managed to figure out that your parents hadn't died on purpose and that no one really owed you reparations because you'd lost your home at, yes, a very awkward age. It only took you those sixteen years after your mother died to decide you were whole.

All right, that was a long time. It was, still, *in* time, wasn't it?

In time for what?

What?

But I remembered now: my promise to myself on my nineteenth birthday. To set limits on hurt, I had set limits on love.

Alec was the icing on my cake. I'd said that to myself only last night. And even Margery, I recalled, had balked at a similarly depreciating description of Alec. All right: Alec was part of my life. *All right*—at the core.

Was he? Was I ready to let him in that close? Me: an unorphaned whole person?

Me?
Yes: now: me.
Go on.
Whom no one can make less than whole; whom no one can make unhappy.
Whom no one can make happy.
Except me.
And why not?

It seemed in no time we had arrived at Allegheny. I paid off the cabbie, throwing in an extravagant tip he didn't acknowledge, and carried my bag and typewriter inside to the ticket counter.

"My name's Littman, Jessica Littman," I said. "I have a reservation on the noon flight to Syracuse."

The clerk began tapping the keys of her computer. "Wait," I said, "I haven't finished."

"What is it?" She had one brown eye and one blue one; and held every Allegheny passenger accountable.

"What time is the next flight to Burlington?"

She made a pretense of looking it up; but she knew. "In a little more than an hour."

"Is there space?"

"It's not anywhere near where you're going," she said.

"Yes it is."

She didn't return even part of my smile, but she talked to her computer and it answered. "There's space. You want to go to Burlington?" she asked, as though, in two minutes, I might want to go in another direction still, maybe to Cleveland.

"Please," I said. I wished I could keep from smiling at her.

I paid, and pocketed my ticket. There's a long way in LaGuardia between the Allegheny ticket counter and the Allegheny gates, but I didn't check my typewriter through. It was safer with me.

I had to pause, several times, and set it down. Once, I stopped right near a bank of phones. I should call Alec, I thought. Then: it would be nice to surprise him. No, I should call. And then I remembered. Alec was working the morning shift: he was on the lake. No way to reach him except by ship-to-shore radio, and this was no emergency.

What I had to tell him would keep until I got there.

When the plane came down in Burlington, it was half past one. I waited for my suitcase, surprised that I wasn't more impatient, and took a taxi to the ferry landing.

At the ticket booth, I asked when the *Champlain* was due in. "Three-quarters of an hour," the girl said.

"I'm looking for Alec Klady," I said.

"You a friend of his?"

"Yes."

"Okay, go on through. Just tell that to the guy collecting tickets. But you've got a *wait*."

She couldn't have been more than eighteen; it didn't seem like such a long wait to me.

Not then, and not while I drank a cup of coffee in the shop on the dock. It occurred to me that, if not for Margery, I wouldn't be there. And I realized, not without a certain sadness, that Margery had given me more during my visit than I'd been able to give her.

Through the window, I spotted the ferry on the horizon. I went outside and stood on the dock. I could make out the pilot-house now; but I couldn't see Alec.

He was there.

I watched him bring the boat in, fitting it into the slip neatly on the first try. It looked easy; but it wasn't, not to do it that smoothly.

As I waited for the cars and pedestrians to come off, I looked at the sky. It was an unexpectedly bright blue, like

Alec's eyes. The water was grey-blue. Around the dock, here and there, I could see sparse patches of green. There would be a lot of green around Alec's house. Soon, there would be the greenest green you ever saw around that house. He had said once, "Almost as soon as the snow melts, the grass seems full grown, as though it's just been waiting for the chance."

Yes, it would be lovely around here now. It wasn't always winter.

People were boarding. I picked up my suitcase and the typewriter and approached the ticket taker. "I'm looking for Alec Klady," I said.

"He expecting you?"

"Not exactly. But I'm a friend."

He let me by. On the way to the pilothouse, I stopped for a moment at the rail and looked at the water. It was quiet, moving ever so slightly beneath the boat. And I remembered how unmoving the lake was in midwinter, when you could drive a car out on it. I shivered, remembering, when I was here for a visit over last New Year's, the bite of the air. As cold as—home.

At the steps to the pilothouse, I set down my cases. They'd be all right; I wanted to have my arms free.

I climbed the narrow steps carefully. Three steps from the top, you open the door. The next step. When you come right down to it, I thought, you make your own weather.

Toby Stein won the Virginia Gildersleeve Prize in Writing while a freshman at Barnard. In her mid-thirties, she abandoned a successful career in advertising to write, read, think, listen to music, and talk with her friends. She lives in Montclair, New Jersey. Getting Together *is her second novel.*